MW00634040

# Glory To God

# THE KINGDOM OF LOVE

## Book 1 of 4

# Michael J. Rigby

Stop The Madness Publications

In coordination with Get Right inc.
Bruda Heru B

In association with B.A.N.G. Ent.
JonBoii Era

Copyright © Michael J. Rigby, 2022
All rights reserved

Trade Paperback: ISBN: 9781735902838

Cover Design by: Bombshell Graphics Inc.
Jennifer Rivera

Without limiting the rights under copyright reserved above, no part of this publication may be reproduced, stored in or introduced into a retrieval system, or transmitted in any form, or by any means (electronic, mechanical, photocopying, recording, or otherwise), without the prior written permission of both the copyright owner and the publisher of the book.

PUBLISHERS NOTE

This is a work of fiction. Names, characters, places, incidents, events, and all quotations, including but not limited to, Bible Verse Quotations and Qur'an quotations, are the product of the authors imagination, or are used fictitiously, and any resemblance to actual Scripture quotations, Qur'an quotations, Bible verses, actual persons, living or dead, places, incidents, events, businesses, establishments, locales, cities, states, and countries, is entirely coincidental.

The scanning, uploading, and distributing of this book via the Internet or via any other means without the permission of the publisher is illegal and punishable by law. Please purchase only authorized electronic editions, and do not participate in or encourage electronic piracy of copyrighted materials. Your support of the author's rights is appreciated.

In Memory of
*Everel E. Lewis*
*&*
*Regina C. Ralph*
My Grannies

To know wisdom and instruction.
To comprehend words that give understanding.
To receive the instruction of wisdom, justice, judgement,
and equity.
To give prudence to the simple.
To the young man knowledge and discretion.
A wise man will hear and will increase learning.
A man who understands will attain wise counsel.
To understand a proverb and an enigma,
The words of the wise and their riddles.
The fear of The Lord is the beginning of knowledge,
but fools despise wisdom and instruction.

_ Solomon, The Son of David, The King of Israel

# THE KINGDOM OF LOVE
# BOOK 1 OF 4

# 1

"Whoa! What the? Whoa! Whoa! Hey! Reboot! Reboot the system immediately!"

The Senior Meteorologist startled his subordinates with his highly unusual request suggesting the most state of the art equipment in the field of meteorology, was for the first time ever, malfunctioning.

Everyone quickly scrambled to the screens of various devices, and began punching commands into keypads at the speed of their racing heartbeats.

No one knew why they were doing what they were doing, but everyone knew it was not a test.

"My God!"

As the Senior Meteorologist stared at the screen in horror, he shouted,

"Relay the information to the G.P. Supercomputer Centre in Lugano for confirmation immediately!

"No one is permitted to contact anyone outside the facility, or to accept any form of communication from anyone, anywhere, regardless to the seriousness of the situation! The government will be here very soon to ensure that no one has leaked any information, so do not leak any information!"

A woman's voice, hesitantly said,

"But... We don't even know..."

The Senior Meteorologist harshly cut the woman off, screaming,

"Look at the screens! Can't you see? This is an extinction level event!"

## Swiss National Supercomputing Centre
## Lugano, Switzerland
## 30 Seconds Later

"Ha! Look at what the stargazers down at The W.M.O. just sent to receive, listen to this:

*"Verification of the possibility of the physics of a recent event."*

"Are you serious?"

"Am I? This is definitely one of those moments where I really wish I was joking, but, this is the world we live in!

"These highly educated astronomers are asking us to verify if something that "just happened", can actually happen, and they need the answer to this difficult question, not now, but right now, like right now.

"I should just respond, "Duuuuh! It already happened!"

The female busted out laughing, and asked,

"So, what are they saying happened?"

The young man's entire demeanor completely shifted, and he quickly sat up in his chair to reread the description, as the female nervously asked,

"What? What are they saying Josh?"

Without taking his eyes off of the screen, Josh hesitantly said,

"They... They said... Are we live?"

"Of course we're live! We're always being broadcasted to anyone who tunes in to the e-channel..."

"Go off air!"

"What?"

"Take us off air like right now! Seriously!"

"Josh, you're scaring me."

Josh gave the woman a silent furious stare, which made her realize he was serious.

She pursed her lips and started disconnecting the recording equipment, as an ocean of concern poured into her stomach.

As soon as their every move was no longer being broadcasted to the world, Josh typed in the coordinates of the Hubble Space Telescopes' observations of some strange activity around the planet Mars.

The room was silent, as Josh received the results, shook his head, and initiated a recalculation, saying,

"The W.M.O. actually asked a very good question."

# 2

After a few more moments of silence, the woman finally said,

"What's happening?"

While typing, Josh briefly glanced over at the woman, shook his head to the negative, and initiated a second recalculation, saying,

"This is like the worst thing the worst imagination can imagine, all-of-a-sudden coming out of that wicked mind, to literally destroy us all. That's the equivalent to what this thing is saying."

The woman looked sick, as she asked,

"What do you mean?"

Josh bit his bottom lip, and started sending the results back to W.M.O., as he said,

"Karen, do you remember when I told you how I really feel about you, and that the only reason I don't get into relationships is because I'm just too focused on my career?"

Karen could hardly respond, as she struggled to say,

"Josh... I..."

Josh finished sending the results back to W.M.O., and for the first time in it's decade of operating, he initiated the destructive process of corrupting and crashing one of the world's fastest supercomputers.

Karen shot out of her chair looking like she'd seen a ghost, as she witnessed Josh commit a crime that was punishable by up to 5 years of imprisonment.

Karen shouted in a whisper,

"What are you doing? You're going to get us both in serious trouble!"

A red light started flashing, followed by a loud blaring sound, as Josh finished punching in the final commands, turned to karen, and shouted over all the noise,

"The whole world is in trouble Karen! Billions of people are going to die!"

Karen covered her mouth with both her hands, while Josh suddenly got down on one knee, grabbed Karens' hand, and shouted,

"We got no choice but to get married now! We don't have one second left to waste!"

Tears poured out of Karen's' eye's, as she said,

"I'm scared Josh, why did you crash the system?"

Josh looked directly into Karen's' eye's, and screamed at the top of his lungs,

"Will you marry me?"

"Yes! Yes! You know I love you Josh! But what's going on?"

Josh quickly rose to his feet, while screaming,

"Hurry up! Hurry! We gotta hurry!"

Josh grabbed Karen's hand and rushed her out into the hallway, straight towards the elevator.

As Karen ran behind Josh, she frantically shouted, "Where are we going?"

Terrified, Josh looked back at Karen, and then straight ahead at the steal elevator doors that were quickly approaching, while shouting,

"Before my dad died, he built a bunker in Zurich, deep underground! He filled it with 2 decades worth of food and supplies for 8 people! That's where we're going, someplace where we're going to be safe!"

As they stopped at the entrance to the elevator, Josh had succeeded in making Karen feel even more nervous and sick than she was already feeling.

In that moment, Karen concluded that the situation was indeed very serious, as she realized Josh had proposed to her so that, as his wife-to-be, she would have a claim of ownership to the bunker.

As soon as the elevator doors opened, Karen said, "But, why did you shut the system down?"

# 3

When they were finally inside the elevator, descending ito ground level, Josh let out a strong sigh, looked over at Karen, and said,

"Look. Something happened just off the orbit of Mars that, up until a few minutes ago, should've literally been impossible, but somehow and someway it happened, and real soon, it's going to be crashing into this planet pouring itself all over the surface like furious streams of molten lava pouring out of an enormous volcano.

"We gotta worry about ourselves right now. We can't just wait for the government to come put guns to our heads and tell us where we can and can't go and what we can and can't do, because if we wait around, that's exactly what will happen, and they'll either just kill us both, or they'll have us stuck here on observation duty until just hours before the day of destruction, and then, they'll stuff us in some cheap government bunker with a crowd of coughing, farting, imbeciles, while a bunch of undeserving crooks break into my father's bunker and greedily scarf up 2 decades worth of goods in just 2 weeks! No! That's not how things are going to happen!"

Josh looked at his watch, and said,

"It's 3 o'clock in the morning, so the day shift won't be here for another 4 hours. Me, you, and W.M.O., are the only people on the planet who know of the danger right now, who aren't part of any national government.

"So, before all the chaos and confusion and traffic and foolishness that will occur when the rest of the world starts trying to prepare for it's doom, we're going to secretly disappear unnoticed, and we'll leave everyone else to figure things out in the morning when they fix the system and learn of the danger. Trust me, we're doing the right thing, we're giving ourselves a much needed headstart."

Karen slowly nodded in agreement, as the elevator doors opened to the barrels of assault rifles aimed directly at their heads. Before they could raise their arms to surrender, their bodies were riddled with bullets that caused their blood to quickly form a puddle on the floor.

The soldiers swiftly stuffed the bullet riddled bodies into large black bags, and carried them out to an enormous black helicopter that was full of large black bags.

Inside all the other black bags were the deceased corpses of every single person who was found inside The W.M.O. Headquarters. More soldiers then stormed The Supercomputing Centre, searching for more targets.

"China?"

"China is present."

"France?"

"France is present."

"Russia?"

"Russia is present."

"The United Kingdom?"

"The United kingdom is present"

"The United States?"

"The United States is present."

"For the record, it shall be noted that all 5 permanent seats of The Security Council of The United Nations are filled by the aforestated nations in Manhattan, New York, on this, the 14th day, of October 2032."

The Secretarial General nodded his head to the clerk who conducted the roll call, and said,

"Thank you. This emergency meeting was called to direct attention to an ongoing investigation into an international threat to global peace and security. The current threat is not an internal dispute. It's origins are derived from activity that was detected just beyond the orbit of the planet Mars.

"The Hubble Space Telescope discovered the activity and relayed the information to the World Meteorological Organization.

"The W.M.O. immediately forwarded the information to the Swiss National Supercomputing Centre, who confirmed through a series of calculations, that an unobservable force recently caused 3 celestial objects composed mostly of frozen liquid to spontaneously materialize and join the course of the comet, "Temple Tuttle".

"I have been advised that Temple Tuttle is a comet with a course of orbit that causes it's debris to storm down thousands of meteors onto our planet every 33 years, and once a year, we're bombarded with it's weaker debris, because it's debris stretches throughout the entire length of its orbit, so it's head literally touches it's tail.

"The resulting mediocre meteor showers are nothing more than a source of entertainment to those who travel to certain locations to view the event. These 3 additional rocks, that allegedly formed in seconds, from nothingness, present far more than an amusement show.

"The reason we have gathered here today, is to make some determinations about the various peacekeeping forces deployed throughout the world, to prepare the people of the world for the danger being presented by these 3 celestial objects that, according to technologically assisted observations, materialized out of nowhere! To further explain the phenomenon, we have here The Director of The W.M.O. Headquarters."

The Secretarial General looked towards the other end of the table, at an elderly man who was staring down at the table, and said,

"Mr. Director?"

# 4

The W.M.O. Director rose from his seat, and said,

"Yes, thank you sir. As the general stated, we are in fact in grave danger. The individuals who were present at the W.M.O. building, were rendered direct threats to international security, due to the seriousness of the information I am about to relay to you.

"All the individuals who were present at the W.M.O. building, as well as those who were present at the Supercomputing Centre, were rendered imminent and impending dangers to a premature disclosure. They were all thereby terminated on site. The following information is still considered to be ultimately sensitive, and should be designated at your highest level of secrecy, if not beyond."

The W.M.O. Director pressed a few buttons on a small tablet he was holding, which caused the lights in the small room to dim, as a screen appeared on a white wall.

A recording of 3 large comets traveling back-to-back, heading straight towards planet earth, brought an instant uneasiness to the room, that quickly captured everyone's attention.

The W.M.O. Director wiped a few droplets of sweat from his forehead, and placed his handkerchief back into his rear pants pocket.

He slowly looked up, inhaled a large breath of air, blew it out, and said,

"All 3 of these comets will most assuredly collide into the planet. But, by no means could this bring our global civilization to a complete end.

"Nevertheless, there is virtually no way for us to ensure the survival of nearly 9 billion people."

The W.M.O. Director frowned, looked around the room through eye's that showed concern, and said,

"We, unfortunately, do not have the time or the resources to save every single person on the planet."

The Representative of the United States squinted her eyes, and said,

"How much time do we have?"

"In New York, it will be precisely 7 o'clock in the morning, March 22nd, 2033, when the first comet starts entering into the atmosphere."

The people in the room started murmuring amongst themselves, and a few started taking notes, as the W.M.O. Director said,

"People, please. As I said earlier, these comets do not have the ability to destroy the entire..."

The Russian aggressively cut the W.M.O. Director off, by shouting,

"Why is it you took so long to bring matter to attention? Had you informed soon, we could of long ago took step to ensure survival of more people than number it will be because you have given only 5 month to prepare!"

"Sir., the day before yesterday, none of these comets even existed. You see, you have to understand that..."

"Aargh! Stop! You don't want to take responsibility for getting billion of people kill. It was your job to watch for incoming object, and you fail! You miss these 3 like blind man! Now, you try to cover up lethal mistake, but cover is poor! You do terrible job! This is why you kill your own people, and possibly went as far as erasing record, destroying footage, and creating bogus imagery of comet popping up from nowhere!"

The Russian forcefully rose from his seat, and shouted,

"You have said what you said! I heard more than enough! I love my country, I love my people, we are not in collusion with deceptive practices of the West! We do not kill or allow people to suffer and die for no good reason! I go back to country to prepare people for..."

The Secretarial General fiercely cut the Russian off, by saying,

"Sir.! You will not inform private citizens of this danger until we have prepared an appropriate disclosure!"

# 5

The Russian twisted his face with a look of disgust, as he stared into the Secretarial Generals' eye's, and said,

"If you and I can handle news, so can everyone else. This is not secret of war! This event will obliterate whole family, whole neighborhood, perhaps whole country!"

The Russian's eyes grew wide as he realized the danger of his own vision. He quickly charged towards the exit, as the Secretarial General raised his voice, by shouting,

"Sir.! Sir.! You are not permitted to leave! Force will be used against you! Sir.! This final order will not be repeated! Sir.! Got dammit!"

The Russian ignored The Secretarial General while tearing out the door.

The Chinese Representative suddenly looked to the right, nervously looked to the left, slowly pushed himself up from his seat, and rushed towards the exit without making eye contact with anyone. He abruptly stopped at the door, and managed to force out a strained statement, saying,

"China possess sufficient observatory to track danger. China require no assisting. China prepare for collision."

As soon as both men were gone, the Secretarial General pressed the touchscreen on a tablet that was on the table in front of him, from which a voice rapidly shouted,

"Sir. yes Sir.!"

"Detain and sequester the representatives of China and Russia immediately!"

"Detain? Sir., those individuals are diplomats, protected under diplomatic immunity! I do not have the authority to detain them!"

"This is The Secretarial General of The United Nations Security Council! I am designating the representatives of China and Russia to be direct threats to international peace and security!

"I am giving you a direct order to detain and sequester the representatives of China and Russia, and you are to use all forms of force necessary to secure their "immediate" compliance! You are to do the same to "anyone" who resists your efforts! Do I make myself clear?"

"Sir. yes Sir.!"

All 3 representatives who remained in the room, felt like defecating the disturbing feelings they were feeling in their stomachs, as the Secretarial General rose from his seat, calmly walked over to the exit, closed the door, and returned to his seat, while saying to the W.M.O. Director,

"Please Sir., continue."

"Well, okay, let me explain how these comets formed so rapidly, before I speak on the damage they will..."

The W.M.O. Director was cut off by the sound of gunshots, that caused him to dive underneath the table, while everyone else remained seated.

The gunshots ceased as fast as they started.

The voice of the assassin on the tablet broke the silence in the room, shouting,

"Sir.! The Representatives of China and Russia are deceased! Along with all who accompanied them!"

The Secretarial General banged his fist on the table, shook his head to the negative, roughly rubbed his hand over his mouth and his chin, and then looked at the tablet, and rapidly shouted,

"Shut down this entire building! Sequester everyone who heard even as much as a faint popping sound! Scramble the networks!

"Detain "everyone", and do not permit the detainees to communicate with each other or any form of outside source!

"Document, and clean, and sanitize the area of the shooting, and then deliver the corpses to the nearest morgue to be destroyed by incineration immediately!"

"Sir. yes Sir!"

The Secretarial General looked underneath the table, and shook his head to the negative, as he made direct eye contact with the W.M.O. Director, who was balled up in the fetal position, covering his head with both of his hands, whole shaking like a leaf.

The Secretarial General nodded, and said,

"Please Sir., continue."

The W.M.O. Director stumbled out from underneath the table, climbed to his feet, and mumbled,

"Uhhhh... Right... Uhh..."

The Representative from France said,

"You were going to explain the origin of the comets."

"The comets!... Right!... Of course!... The comets!... Of course! Of course!... Umm... Okay okay!"

The W.M.O. Director stumbled to the screen, picked his tablet up off of the floor, and quickly said,

"It's not that they just came from "nowhere". We know "exactly" where they came from! "And" we know "exactly" how they got here! They were formed! Rapidly! But, up until 2 days ago, we never imagined this process of formation spontaneously occurring the way it did, and of all the places in this vast universe that it could've occurred, it just sprang up on a direct collision course with this planet!"

The American said,

"So how could 3 comets just spring up like that?"

"Exactly! Look, we've been wrestling with some very mysterious forms of existences for quite some time now. We actually have no clue as to what "existence", in-and-of-itself, is composed of."

# 6

Everyone looked confused, as the Secretarial General said,

"What?"

The W.M.O. Director inhaled a large breath of air, while looking down at the ground. He blew it out slowly, and then looked back up, and said,

"Everything we can see is only 4 percent of what is really and truly there. We only interact with a tiny fragment of existence.

"Our realm isn't even composed of enough of existence for us to have the slightest idea of what it truly is, or what it's really like.

"We don't even know how anything actually looks. We've only seen 4 percent! We haven't seen anything!"

The W.M.O. Director scanned all the faces lost in deep thought, and said,

"96 percent of existence is composed of what we call "Dark Energy" and "Dark Matter", and we call them "Dark", simply because we have no idea of what they really and truly are.

"All we know is, Dark things exist.

"We know Dark Energy caused The Big Bang. We know it stretches out the fabric of the universe, but we have no idea of what it is! All we know is, it's there, we kind of have an idea of what it's doing, and up until 2 days ago, it never really threatened us, or put us in any danger, even though it's always been a very serious threat."

The American looked puzzled, as she said,

"How do you figure it's always been a "threat"? And how is it threatening us now?"

The W.M.O. Director nodded, and said,

"The greatest astronomical discovery of the 20th century was that the galaxies of the universe are all moving further and further away from the earth, and further and further away from each other, at a continuously accelerating rate. The only force causing the increasing speed of the expansion is something we call Dark Energy."

The American said,

"So the universe is growing?"

"Well, the more appropriate term is "stretching", or "expanding". You see, the universe is actually shaped like a big giant ball, and we're near the center of it. The big giant ball is full of little clusters of stars we call "galaxies". We call our star cluster, "The Milky Way Galaxy", and there are around 400 billion stars in our galaxy. Our sun is just one of those 400 billion stars.

"On top of all of that, the big giant ball, which is our universe, is expanding, at an accelerating rate, like a balloon being filled with air. The accelerating rate of the expansion of the universe is our evidence of the invisible force we call, "Dark Energy."

The W.M.O. Director scanned the confused looking faces, sighed, and plainly said,

"Just imagine a person blowing air into a balloon, using only the oxygen in their lungs.

"Each and every time they exhale into the balloon, it expands.

"Then, they must inhale more oxygen into their lungs, and exhale it into the balloon, to make the balloon expand once more.

"Now imagine that your lungs was the source of oxygen, and you never needed to inhale in order to exhale.

"Not only that, but imagine that the force of your lungs had the power to produce an infinite amount of increasing exhales, as if the force of your lungs kept getting stronger and stronger the more you exhaled.

"You could begin exhaling at a rate of 100 miles an hour, and in 1 second, you could increase the speed to 10,000 miles an hour.

"By the third second, you could increase the speed to one million miles an hour, and so on and so forth, without ever finding the need to inhale in order to continue exhaling.

"Well that's precisely what our universe has been doing for the past thirteen billion years!

It's as if our universe is a big giant balloon, and Dark Energy has some type of super lungs that keeps inhaling into our universe sized balloon at an accelerating rate!"

The Secretarial General frowned through a look of shock and confusion, as he said,

"If this universe is some big gigantic balloon, that is being blown up, won't it eventually just blow up?"

The W.M.O. Director busted out in laughter, as he said,

"Sir., that's common sense! But, keep in mind, we don't have the slightest idea of what Dark Energy actually is, and this ignorance rests on the fact that Dark Energy is the direct cause of the expansion of our universe. So, whatever Dark Energy is, it will definitely be the cause of any such explosion, and in that sense, it will dictate when any such explosion will take place."

The American said,

"What happens when a universe explodes?"

The W.M.O. Director chuckled, and said,

"Based on the fact that the accelerting rate of the expansion of the universe is a direct indicator that Dark Energy very well may possess infinite energy, it just might be the release of such energy, either in to or out of this physical state."

The Secretarial General slowly blinked his eyes, and said,

"What does that mean?"

# 7

Look, we honestly do not know what this universe is made of. But, we do know that our physical realm is composed of only 4 percent of whatever everything is composed of. Why our realm is only 4 percent is a whole other topic of unknown subjects. It is possible, and very likely, that everything we can see is really and truly composed of a form of existence that has infinite energy inherent in it's very fabric, and for some reason, the energy is being withheld under some form of constraint.

"We have no idea! But, the physical construct of this physical form of existence seems to be holding the very fabric of each and every subatomic particle captive, as if this physical realm is some form of particle prison. The release of the captives very well may equate to the release of infinite energy, an explosion beyond the definition of explosion, so much so, instead of "exploding", everything might just be reformed into the purest form of energy that exists."

The American asked,

"What does pure energy look like?"

The W.M.O. Director responded,

"We do not know, because we can'not see it."

As confusion danced throughout the minds in the room, The W.M.O. Director shook his head, and said,

"Alright listen. This understanding should not be too far fetched for you few here who remain, as you are all Christians, and should somewhat be familiar with the oldest Christian document that exists, which is a letter that was written by the apostle Paul to the Church in Rome."

The W.M.O. Director quickly punched some keys on his tablet, and when Bible verses appeared on the screen, he started reading them, saying,

"Just look at this... All else failed to help you comprehend, so hopefully, this may give you an understanding. It's Romans chapter 8 verses 18 to 25. I'll read it,

*"For I consider the sufferings of this present time are not worthy to be compared with the glory which shall be revealed in us.*

*"For the earnest expectation of the creation eagerly waits for the revealing of the Sons of God.*

*"For the creation was subjected to futility, not willingly, but because of Him who subjected it in hope,*

*"Because the creation itself also will be delivered from the bondage of corruption into the glorious liberty of the Children of God.*

*"For we know that the whole creation groans and labors with birth pangs together until now.*

*"Not only that, but we also who have the first fruits of the spirit, even we ourselves groan within ourselves, eagerly waiting for the adoption, the redemption of our body.*

*"For we were saved in this hope, but hope that is seen is not hope, for why does one still hope for what he sees?*

*"But if we hope for what we do not see, we eagerly wait for it with perseverance."*


"You see? Paul's comprehension of physics and matter was astonishingly accurate!

"His instructions to place hope in the unseen reveals his knowledge of the invisible side of existence, which, to his understanding, is a spiritual realm where supreme intelligence exists in some form of mythical kingdom that has everlasting life interwoven into it's very fabric.

"It is clear that the biblical references to "everlasting life" in the "Kingdom of God" are speaking about what we know to be infinite energy in the region of Dark Energy."

# 8

Paul was somehow aware of the fact that this universe, that he refers to as "the creation", is composed of some form of invisible existence, that has intelligence, and has a true form that is completely different from what it appears to be.

"It should really make your skin crawl to know that your skin could possibly have some form of intelligence, or an awareness of its own existence.

"Trillions of tiny sections of your flesh could be aware of the fact that a supreme being, who Paul calls "The Creator", has reduced them to the lesser form from which they are forced to work together to make you believe that they are your skin.

"This would also mean that the universe itself is alive, and is conscious, and is aware of the fact that it is trapped in a mediocre slave state, or in Paul's words, "the creation" has been "subjected to futility".

"What Paul refers to as "the creation" being "delivered from bondage", is a direct reference to this universe being restored to its original infinite state.

"Even more shocking, Paul wasn't the only Bible composer who caught "The Spirit" that led him to such an understanding.

"Peter also revealed his retention of esoteric knowledge, when he made shockingly accurate references to the sequence of events that would lead to the end of the universe as we know it.

"We know that this universe will eventually blow up one day. I mean, it's just a big ball chucked full of little balls of fire, like the sun, balls of gas, like Jupiter, and flammable rocks, like the asteroid belt.

"Fire, gas, and flammable rocks. It kind of reminds you of The U.S.."

The French Representative scrunched up her eyebrows, and said,

"How so?"

"The United States is in many ways structured similar to the universe, and the Kingdom of The Creator, as it is proclaimed to be in The Bible."

The American Representative, then said,

"Not even I know what you mean by that."

The Director sighed hard, pulled a fresh Bible verse up on the screen, and responded,

"Isaiah chapter 33 verse 22,

"For The Lord is our Judge, The Lord is our Lawgiver, The Lord is our King, He shall save us."

"That one simple Bible verse established the foundation of the most powerful government to ever come into existence.

"The Lord is our Judge", became The U.S. Supreme Court, with its 9 Justices who judge the most important cases in the country. They call that The Judicial branch.

"The Lord is our Lawgiver", became Congress, and The U.S. House of Representatives, who writes the laws for the country. They call that The Legislative Branch.

"The Lord is our King, became The White House, The President, and his cabinet. They call that The Executive Branch.

"The country is furthermore likened to the universe, in the sense that it can explode at any moment.

"We all know very well of the 2022 Biden Administration's failed attempt to blow up the country."

The French Representative, said,

"What? No we don't!"

"In 2022, The Biden Administration conspired with China and Russia, to blow up America, by inticing those nations to invade The U.S..

"The U.S. will never become the property of a foreign nation, because, for decades, all sorts of atomic and nuclear bombs have been strategically buried at underground locations all across the country.

"The bombs are there to destroy the country in the event that the U.S. is on the brink of becoming the possession of a foreign nation.

"The understanding is, "If we can't have it, no one will". Every President since Truman has added to the arsenal of destructive forces buried under The U.S..

"If the plan had succeeded in 2022, China and Russia would've staged an invasion that The Biden Administration would've used to justify blowing the country up.

"Like America, The universe is one really big bomb, that can explode at any moment, and quite a few Bible guy's knew it..."

The W.M.O. Director hit a few buttons on his tablet, and a new set of Bible verses popped up on the screen, as he said,

"In Second Peter chapter 3, verses 6 to thirteen, Peter said,

*"...By which the world that then existed perished, being flooded with water. But the heavens and the earth which are now preserved by the same word, are reserved for fire until the day of judgement and perdition of ungodly men.*

*"But Beloved, do not forget this one thing, that with the Lord one day is as a thousand years, and a thousand years as one day.*

*"The Lord Is not slack concerning His promise, as some count slackness, but is long-suffering toward us, not willing that any should perish, but that all should come to repentance.*

*"But The Day of The Lord shall come like a thief in the night, in which the heavens will pass away with a great noise, and the elements will melt with fervent heat, both the earth and the works that are in it will be*

*burned up.*

*"Therefore since all these things will be dissolved, what manner of persons ought you to be in holy conduct and godliness, looking for and hastening the coming of The Day of God, because of which the heavens will be dissolved, being on fire, and the elements will melt with fervent heat?*

*"Nevertheless we, according to His promise, look for new heavens and a new earth in which righteousness dwells."*

"You see, where Peter says,

*"We... Look for new heavens and a new earth."*

"He is clearly making a well informed reference to the fact that this universe will not just be destroyed, but will actually be reformed in to a form of existence that will never cease to exist.

"The universe will become a form of existence that is composed entirely of what we now know to be infinite energy, what the Bible calls, "eternal life".

"Science discovered this through research into the universe as a whole. The Bible composers say the "Creator" revealed the blueprint to them. I don't know.

"But I do know that Science and The Bible have finally reached the same exact conclusion: The universe, as we know it, is about to be destroyed by an invisible force."

The Secretarial General nodded, and said,

"So, how long has Dark Energy been a threat?"

The W.M.O. Director, responded,

"Since the beginning! It's been a threat for over thirteen billion years now! You see, Dark Energy doesn't just "stretch the universe". It moves every object in the physical realm. From the gazillions of stars, to every single subatomic particle, and this is all on top of the fact that "it's" what set all this movement into motion!

"If Dark Energy has enough energy to simultaneously move trillions upon trillions of outrageously humongous suns, all at once, it obviously has more than enough energy to crush our tiny little planet like a giant wrestler smashing his foot down to annihilate one tiny little ant.

"We don't stand a chance! Dark Energy can destroy us without us ever realizing we were on the brink of destruction! The only thing that's been keeping us safe is the fact that Dark Energy has always abided by its own natural laws of physics. But, 2 days ago, it broke one of those laws, on a level that will surely result in the loss of billions of lives."

# 9

The French woman, said,

"Which of it's laws did Dark Energy break?"

The W.M.O. Director nodded, and said,

"Everything in this room is everything in this room and that's it.

"That's a natural law.

"It's a basic law of physics.

"In the science of matter and energy, which is physics, the law of conservation states that in a closed system where neither mass nor energy is added or subtracted, certain measurable quantities will remain constant.

"So let's take this table for example.

"In theory, we can shred it, burn it, boil it, or grind it down to dust and sweep all of it's tiny particles under a rug, and in theory, all of its particles will always continue to exist.

"In the same sense, another table can't just pop up out of nowhere for no apparent reason.

"In our universe, except on a quantum level, nothing ever just pops up out of anywhere for no apparent reason.

"In the same sense, nothing ever just indefinitely ceases to exist, because that's just the way things are, but, the truth is, we know that it isn't impossible for something to just pop up out of nowhere, or completely disappear.

"As long as an invisible thing is fueled by enough energy to materialize into a physical form, by all means, it can, and the invisible thing can suddenly become visible.

"In the same sense, if the invisible source of energy retracts all of it's energy from the occupation of a visible physical form, the physical form may remain visible, but in that moment, all the energy inside the form will cease to exist.

"There is no need to conduct experiments to prove this. Life shows us how energy materializes out of nowhere, inside a womb, and death shows us how, once energy is retracted from a physical form, and it returns to The Source, it is a very tragic event, because there is virtually no way to bring the energy back.

"We can trace the process of life and death but so far. At this point in time, we still do not know the exact point of the source of life.

"Likewise, when someone dies, we can not accurately say where that life goes, because energy comes from and returns to a force we know nothing about, a force we call, "Dark Energy".

"The power that moves flesh and blood through this physical realm, appears and disappears on quantum levels.

"It therefore escapes our understanding.

"The Bible defines life and death as the movement of a "soul" into and out of the physical realm.

"The Bible presents God as being the authority Who dictates when a soul comes and goes.

"Science interprets this as meaning Dark Energy dictates who lives and who dies, and that's pretty obvious.

"We need energy to live, energy ultimately comes from The Source of Energy, and Dark Energy is The Source of energy.

"So that's precisely what's always been our greatest fear of Dark Energy. It's The Source of our lIfe, but we know absolutely nothing about it!

"We do not know what it is, so we have no way of knowing what dictates how it chooses to use, withhold, withdraw, or dispense its energy, which, to us, is life.

"Aside from granting us our own personal portions of everlasting life, Dark Energy has more than enough energy to fill this planet with fire and brimstone in the matter of one split second!

"Dark Energy can transform our universe into torment, torture, and pain, in an instant!

"At any given moment, the physical realm can be swallowed by Dark Energy before anyone could even gasp, and the only reason the universe seems to be in a state that such things wouldn't happen, is basically because everything has been behaving the same exact way ever since as far back as we can tell, and that's all the way back to the beginning!"

The people listening to the W.M.O. Director said, "Hmm", at the same exact time, and the W.M.O. Director continued saying,

"Even the slightest change in the behavior of Dark Energy can be a sign that the universe is near it's end.

"If Dark Energy wants a star in the sky, it doesn't just put a star there. Instead, it follows it's patterns and procedures.

"A cluster of gas and dust must come together to form a nebula that will ignite and give birth to a ball of fire that will surpass temperatures in the sum of 30 million degrees Fahrenheit.

"We've somewhat always been able to trust that Dark Energy would always behave the way its always behaved, ensuring us that we wouldn't wake up one morning to find a sun forming in our backyard, or a black hole forming in our brain.

"Dark Energy was always predictable, but for the first time ever, Dark Energy is breaking it's own laws on a scale large enough to kill us all, if not a few billion."

# 10

We thought we knew Dark Energy's laws, but that never actually meant Dark Energy wouldn't break one of them, by doing something it never did, like preparing to destroy the universe."

The General frowned, and said,

"You make it sound like Dark Energy is aware of it's own existence, like it has some form of intelligence or something."

"Sir., mice have intelligence. Surely you can understand that it doesn't take much energy to manifest intelligence. We say that we do not know what Dark Energy is because it is literally invisible to the absolute sense of the meaning.

"We can not see it. We do not know where it is, and we can not find it, despite the fact that we can clearly see the results of it's actions.

"We have no way of making any observations of whatever it is, because its on the invisible side of existence, so, for all we know, it could be anything, or perhaps, even anyone..."

Eye's popped open.

The W.M.O. Director gave an affirmative nod, and said,

"Not only is Dark Energy obviously aware of everything it's intentionally doing, has always been doing, and will ever do, but it also has far more than enough energy to simultaneously be aware of everything you're doing, and thinking, and feeling, as well as everything I'm doing, and thinking, and feeling, at the same exact time that it keeps it's tabs on all the subatomic particles that form the atoms that form the elements of every single thing in existence under the preeminent dominance of the unseen force."

The American said,

"So, you're saying this thing could be Santa Clause?"

The W.M.O. Director raised his thick bushy eyebrows in shock, and said,

"No mam. I'm saying that the force of energy, that placed this entire planet in jeopardy of an extinction level event, by forming 3 comets in an instant, and placing them on a direct collision course with this planet, that is sure to cause billions of deaths, is the same exact force of energy that brought everything in this vast universe into existence. So it obviously took some form of intelligence to bring intelligence into existence.

"Look, I'm the only one in this room who identifies as an atheist, but that doesn't mean that I'm ignorant to the biblical testimonies that prove contact was made with some form of intelligent life."

The W.M.O. Director sighed hard, and shook his head in frustration at the confused looks on everyone's faces. He pulled up some fresh Bible verses, and said,

"Now I have to teach you what you claim to believe. Imagine that.

"Zechariah 12:1,

*"The Lord, who stretches out the heavens..."*

"Isaiah 42:5-6,

*"The Lord... The Creator of the heavens...*
*Stretches them out..."*

"Job 9:8,

*"He alone stretches out the heavens..."*

"Psalm 104:2

*"He stretches out the heavens like a tent."*

"Isaiah 40:22

*"He stretches out the heavens like a tent."*

"That's 5 testimonies that direct attention to the fact that ancient people possessed knowledge of activities that were transpiring at the edges of the universe!

"They said the Creator, "stretches out the heavens", thousands of years before we had the ability to see the activity transpiring in deep space, to determine that what those individuals called "the heavens", is stretching, just the way they claim their "God" told them it is...

"Don't look at me like that, I'm not saying I'm a Christian or any of that organized foolishness!

"But I do find it interesting that quite a few people living in a pre advanced telescope era all claimed that the "Creator" of the "heavens" told them something they had no way of figuring out on their own, or even with the help of every other person on the planet in those days.

"They had no way of even guessing that what they called the "heavens", which is the universe, is stretching. But, they repeated what they claimed to of heard, despite how ridiculous the assertion may of seemed.

"They believed they were in contact with the Creator, they wrote down what they claimed to of heard, and now, thousands of years later, in the technologically advanced future, where we have the powerful tools to enable us to see things they couldn't possibly of seen, we now know that their implication that the universe is stretching, is accurate!

"Furthermore, they claim that "God" is "Almighty", that "He" has "eternal life", and that it is "He" who "stretches the heavens". I have no idea of who or what their "God" is, and frankly, I can care less. But, what I do know is energy can not be created nor destroyed, Dark Energy seems to be the source of infinite energy, and Dark Energy is stretching the universe."

# 11

So, did Dark Energy contact these humans of times past, and introduce Himself as God? It's quite possible, but I have no clue.

"And, have we simply rediscovered and thereby proved the existence of their God, and unknowingly named Him "Dark Energy"? It's almost obvious, but I can't say, because I do not know Who or What their God or Dark Energy is.

"So anyway, the first comet is so small the sun and our atmosphere will melt it down to a cloud of who knows what is inside that big ball of ice.

"We may see the biggest meteor shower ever, or, we may see a whole lot worse. We just won't know what we're dealing with until the sun peals back enough of it's layers so we can see.

"The second comet is far too large to be completely disintegrated by the sun, and it's currently on a collision course with the Atlantic Ocean.

"We do not know the composition of the comet, so we can not say what will happen when this large piece of ice lands in the Atlantic Ocean, and melts.

"But we do know that the coastal regions of Southern Greenland, East of the Americas, West of Africa, and virtually all of the Caribbean Islands, will be completely destroyed.

"Entire states, and quite a few small countries, will all need to be evacuated.

"Something in the neighborhood of half a billion people will all need to be relocated."

The American began rubbing on the sides of her temples, while staring at the table, shaking her head to the negative, as the W.M.O. Director continued saying,

"The third and final comet is far smaller than the second, but is still large enough to pass through the atmosphere and crash into the crust of the earth.

"It is currently on a collision course with the Middle East."

The French woman said,

"The Russians are going to swear that these comets were somehow created by a group of people right here on earth."

The Secretarial General responded,

"The Russians are free to believe anything they can imagine! But! If any nation, or any nations for that matter, become any form of threat to international peace and security, they will be dealt with accordingly!"

The W.M.O. Director quickly nodded in agreement, and said,

"Finally, the last comet will disintegrate and release unknown substances into the atmosphere. In case of any fallout, all locations within 300 miles of Baghdad will need to be evacuated."

All 3 Representatives shook their heads to the negative, as the woman representing the United Kingdom said,

"They'll never desert their land. The majority Muslim population will refuse to believe that Allah would allow them to see such destruction."

The Secretarial General shrugged his shoulders, and said,

"They're more than welcome to stay put! If they don't believe in The Rock, they can continue on with their day-to-day activities until it lands and converts their whole entire region into believers!"

The W.M.O. Director shook his head to the negative, and said,

"No one will be continuing on with any type of normal activities. You see, the force that created the comets is still with them.

"Before the comets enter the earths orbit, the force will cause some form of cataclysmic disturbance of the earth and atmosphere."

The American jolted her head, and said,

"You mean Dark Energy is coming with the comets?"

"Well, not necessarily "Dark Energy", it's more of it's ghost."

The French woman blurted out,

"It's ghost?"

"Listen, Dark Energy is in an unseen realm. It exists in an invisible form of existence. When it does things in its realm, we experience a form of after affect that materializes in the form of a spontaneous physical manifestation.

"The force I'm speaking of is basically the ripple effect of the comets spontaneous manifestation.

"There will most assuredly be a very powerful forcefield crashing into the earth before and after the comets, and it very well may bounce into the sun and return with a decent amount of it's heat, if not some of it's flames."

The American's eye's widened at the thought of a forcefield of flames crashing into the earth. She looked straight at the W.M.O. Director, and said,

"Is there any chance of survival? Wouldn't we be burned alive in underground bunkers? Should we be launching a preservation group to the moon, or to mars? And what about the space stations? Aren't the astronauts in danger? What about the astronauts?"

# 12

The W.M.O. Director calmly responded,

"Once again, you're shocked, as if the knowledge of these incoming events is new information. As a Christian, you should've already known that 3 comets and a forcefield of flames would've eventually crashed into the earth.

"This should all sound like a coincidence to you, but you're so ignorant of your own "Sacred and Holy doctrine", you need an atheist to show you how your Bible's predictions are apparently about to come true."

The W.M.O. Director put some fresh Bible verses on the screen, and said,

"Comet number 1: Revelation 8:7,

*"Hail and fire mingled with blood, and they were cast upon the earth."*

"Comet number 2: Revelation 8:8,

*"A great mountain burning with fire was cast into the sea."*

"Comet number 3: Revelation 8:10,

*"A great star from heaven burning like a lamp fell upon the rivers and the lakes."*

"The forcefield of flames: Revelation 16:8-9,

*"The sun received permission to burn people with fire. People were burned with intense heat, and they blasphemed God who they knew was controlling the plagues, but they did not repent or give Him glory."*

"The book of Revelation was written in A.D. 90, by a man that was on an island in the Mediterranean Sea, just North of Africa.

"He said God sent him a vision of events that would eventually occur in chronological order, and here it is, thousands of years later, and it's looking like the prophecy is about to be fulfilled.

"Either way, as a Christian, you should feel safe from these plagues, because, before any of these events occur, the Bible says believers will be removed from the earth.

"Apparently, a "multitude" of people are going to be carried out of the universe by what might seem to us to be a global invasion followed by international kidnappings, during the event the Christians have come to call, "The Rapture."

The W.M.O. Director paused for a moment while frowning in deep thought. He then made a, "Hmm", sound, quietly said to himself, "Very interesting...", and then, he looked up and continued to speak, saying,

"So I guess we're about to see how all that goes. As for the brave men and women in the space stations, they have all vowed to keep watch until their posts are destroyed. They request that we use our resources to save the many, as opposed to the few.

"To be safe outside of the planet, a preservation group would need to be further away from the forcefield than we can get them. Everyone will be safer here on earth, and the chances of survival will only increase by being sheltered in an underground bunker, preferably constructed inside or underneath a mountain, or a mountainous region.

"On that note, I'm going to leave you Christians with one final Bible verse, because it's giving me the creeps at how accurate this thing is proving to be, and I think everyone deserves a chance to hear this: Revelation 6:15-17 says,

> *"And all the world leaders, and all the famous people, and all the rich people, and all the military people, and all the gangsters, and all the prisoners, and all the free people, all over the earth,*

*"Hid themselves in the dens and in the rocks of the mountains and said to the mountains,*

*"fall on us and hide us from the face of The One who sits on The Throne, and from the wrath of The Lamb, for the great day of His wrath has come, and who will be able to stand?'*

## Dallas, Texas
## October 15, 2032

"Call me as soon as you reach!"

"Okay mommy. I love you!"

"I love you too sweetie!"

"Come on Jasmine we gotta hurry before your dad locks us out and releases the dogs on us."

The tiny framed 9 year old laughed, and said,

"He was just joking Tiffany, you know we don't have any dogs. But we do gotta hurry because daddy always makes Italian food on Friday."

As Tiffany grabbed her sleep over bag, she said,

"Well thank God it's Friday!"

As they stepped on the driveway of the corner house, they could smell the aroma of Italian spices fuming out of the windows.

Both girls mouths began watering, as they approached the front door with growling stomachs.

Jasmine lifted an imitation pebble from a pile of pebbles, turned it over, and pulled out her hidden front door key.

As soon as Jasmine opened the door, she gasped, dropped her backpack, and bolted into the house in tears, screaming,
"Daddy! Daddy! Daddy!"
Tiffany bolted over to the phone, and immediately dialed 9-1-1.
"9-1-1. What's your emergency?"
Through tears, Tiffany managed to cough out words, saying,
"We just came in from school... And my best friends dad... Is on the floor... In the kitchen."
"Okay okay. Calm down sweetie. Can you tell me your address?"

# 12+1

## Department of Defense
## Washington, D.C.
## One Hour Later

 

 

The Secretary of Defense stood in a large auditorium in front of the leaders of the Army, the Navy, and the Air Force.

He looked around the silent room, and said,

"An international State of Emergency has been declared in preparation for the impending disclosure of an extinction level event."

Slight movements and repositionings could be seen in the crowd, but other than a few throat clearings, not one word was uttered.

The Secretary broke the brief pause, by saying,

"An intelligent, hostile, inter-dimensional forcefield fueled by Dark Energy has rapidly materialized 3 comets and set them on a direct collision course with this planet."

Eyeballs popped out the socket as a wave of shock and disbelief sprinted across the room.

The Secretary continued to invoke fear, saying,

"The first comet will disintegrate down to a cloud that will enter the atmosphere in a form composed of currently unknown substances. The second comet has a nucleus the size of Hawaii, and it will crash into the Atlantic Ocean in exactly one hundred and thirty days."

Every eye in the room was glued to the Secretaries face in desperate search for even the slightest sign of the highly unlikely possibility that he was joking.

The Secretary continued,

"All coastal regions which border the Atlantic Ocean will be completely destroyed, and must be evacuated. Every island in the Atlantic Ocean will be completely destroyed, and must be evacuated."

The Secretary paused, and then said,

"The final comet is the size of Mount Everest, and it will land on Iraq. The Navy will be deployed into the Caribbean Sea to assist with the transport of individuals and supplies from out of lethal zones into designated safety locations.

"The Marines will be deployed into Brazil to assist with the establishment of temporary inland housing units for the displaced.

"The Army and National Guard will be deployed onto American soil to assist with the relocation of something in the neighborhood of 150 million Americans. In conjunction with the international declaration of a State of Emergency, global Martial Law has been instituted.

"All nations have agreed to open their borders and operate their military forces as one united force, except for the following, which have all been designated as hostile combatants: China, Russia, North Korea, Iraq, Iran, and Syria.

"The hostile combatants are the only countries on the planet that have chosen to endure the incoming disasters as individual nations. Once order is established, and all the displaced have been relocated to their inland safety locations, force will be used against the hostile combatants in the event that their methods of preparation are determined to be a danger to the safety and the security of the general population of the people of planet earth."


**Federal Emergency Management Agency (F.E.M.A.)**
**Washington, D.C.**
**October 16, 2032**


"In one hour, the national network of organizations and institutions involved in the imminent effort of safeguarding the United States from the danger currently posed by the incoming celestial objects, will begin directing the dispersement of military forces, in coordination with law enforcement, into public and private streets, to enforce an indefinite curfew.

"Before the general public can be made aware of the magnitude of the incoming danger, every road, airway, and waterway, public and private, must be cleared of all vehicles, aircrafts, and vessels. All civilians must be secured on the inside of some form of enclosed structure.

"Resistance will be met with death.

"Any individual who stands in opposition to any final order shall be designated an enemy combatant who shall be terminated as a danger to global peace, safety, and security.

"Any unauthorized persons found in the streets, flying an aircraft, or operating a motor vehicle or water vessel, shall be terminated on sight without question. Federal and State Constitutions are officially no longer in effect. All buildings, structures, persons, and things, air, land, water, vessels, vehicles, and crafts, are now the property of the United States government.

"Civilians are all ordered to enter into a structure and remain until given further orders. Civilians will have 6 hours to comply with these orders. In 7 hours, any civilian who fails to comply with these orders, shall be terminated."

# 14

"Mam, this road is closed to the public. There are no private dwellings or residential structures down this road. I advise that you immediately find an enclosed structure, enter into the structure, and remain therein."

"That's what I'm trying to do! I own my own home, but my daughters best friend's dad is inside that hospital that's down that road, and according to this ridiculous indefinite curfew thing, he's going to need a ride home, and that's why we're here. So if you don't mind, can you please tell them to raise that lever so we can go get my neighbor and go home?"

The soldier began growing visibly impatient, as he gripped his assault rifle a little firmer, and began shouting,

"Mam! Only government vehicles are allowed access to this road! This road is closed to civilians! You are a civilian! To you, this road is thereby closed! The only way you will come down this road is in the back of an ambulance!

"I am giving you a direct order to cease your non-compliant behavior, by reversing, performing a U-turn, and returning to your residence immediately! This is your final order!"

"Where are your manners? Don't you..."

The soldier dramatically raised his rifle and aimed it directly at the woman's face, causing Jasmine and Tiffany to let out bloodcurdling screams from the backseat, as Tiffany's mother firmly gripped the steering wheel with both of her hands, and screamed at the top of her lungs while staring down the barrel of a high-powered rifle for the first time in her life.

"Soldier! Lower your weapon!"

An older man, also holding a rifle, wearing an identical uniform as the younger man, with the addition of 3 black stripes on his shoulders, walked up to the driver side window, as the younger soldier backed off, and said,

"Mam! What part of turn around and leave do you not understand?

"Did you not hear the announcements? The world is in a State of Emergency!

"This whole entire country is under Martial Law, A.K.A. military rule, A.K.A. you do what we say or die!

"You and those children can be killed for not following orders! This is serious business! What is your malfunction?"

Still gripping the steering wheel in utter shock, through tears, she managed to say,

"I was just trying to pick my neighbor up... He had a heart attack... And was transported here yesterday... In a coma. That's his only child in the back seat."

The man looked at the 2 tear covered faces in the back seat, then looked back at the driver, and said,

"I understand. Now "you" need to understand! No one is permitted to enter into the hospital unless they are government personnel, or they are brought here inside an emergency transport vehicle. Furthermore, no one inside the hospital is permitted to leave on their own accord.

"If your neighbor has been discharged, he will be transported to his residence once the streets are cleared. By being in the streets, your delaying his release."

"But his daughter is staying at my house. How will they reunite if no one can go outside?"

"She looks old enough to take care of herself until her father is carried home. Drop her off at her house."

The woman looked back at Jasmine, and as soon as they locked eyes, Tiffany hugged Jasmine, and said,

"Mommy! We can't just leave her all alone! We don't even know what's happening!"

The woman looked back at the soldier, and went to speak, but before she could say anything, he said,

"Just go to your neighbors house, and... Do you have a partner?"

"No. My husband died from a heart attack 4 years ago."

"Oh, okay. Where's the girl's mother?"

"My Mommy died from ovarian cancer when I was 5."

"Oh. Well, does your father have a partner?"

"I'm his partner."

The man busted out laughing, and said,

"I mean, does your father have a wife, or a girlfriend, or, you know, some type of other?"

Jasmine and Tiffany both laughed, as Jasmine said,

"No. My daddy serves The Lord."

# 15

Just then, an ambulance pulled up behind the woman's car, and the driver of the ambulance stuck her head out of the window, and said,

"Is that Megan?"

The man looked at the driver of the car, and said,

"Is your name Megan?"

As Megan nodded, the man looked back at the ambulance driver, who had hopped out of the ambulance, and said,

"Yes, this is Megan."

As soon as the ambulance driver walked up to the driver side door of the car, Megan jumped out the car, and screamed,

"Oh my goodness, Rebeeca!"

As Megan and Rebecca embraced, Megan looked at Tiffany, and said,

"Sweetie, this is your cousin Rebecca... Don't look at her like that! This is your dad's oldest brother's youngest daughter."

"Oooh! The Florida people?"

Megan and Rebecca both laughed, as Megan said,

"Yea, the Florida people."

Rebecca suddenly got very serious, and said,

"What are you doing here Aunt Meg? Is everything okay?"

"Well, I just had a gun pointed at me!"

The man locked eyes with Rebecca, and said,

"That was a trigger happy youngster. But you know what's happening, and you need to wrap this little reunion up and clear this entrance. This is very serious business!"

"Yes Sir.! Listen Aunt Meg, inside that hospital is about to be a million times more safer than inside your home, especially since you're not a gun owner. Trust me on this, give those soldiers your vehicle and hop in the ambulance with me. I'll get you guys into the hospital."

"Give them my vehicle?"

"Aunt Meg, the world we woke up in no longer exists..."

Rebecca lowered her voice so the girls in the car couldn't hear her speak, as she said,

"In a few hours, there will be dead bodies all over the streets. This curfew will cause widespread civil unrest, and all the people in the streets will be terminated by soldiers and drones.

"Once the killing starts, more people will pour into the streets, starting fires, looting, invading peoples homes, raping women, and doing all types of third world things. Trust me, that vehicle will be burned, stolen, or commandeered by the government by tomorrow morning. Get those girls and come with me."

Rebecca took a better look in the car, and said,

"Who's that Black kid?"

"Jasmine. Tiffany's best friend. Her father lives in the corner house on my street."

"The big 2 story?"

"Yea yea, he's a Conservative Christian talk radio guy, and he's here."

"At the hospital?"

"Yea! He had a heart attack yesterday."

Rebecca's face twisted, as she blurted out,

"Well what are you waiting for? Let's go!"

# 16

**Brooklyn, New York**
**8 Hours Later**


"Su-Wuu!"
"B.B.O.!"
"Cu-Riip!"
"Amor-De-Rey!"
"Wu-Wuu!"
"Boss!"
"O-k-k-kaaayy!"
"This is an unlawful gathering! You are in an unauthorized area! Civilians do not have permission to be in the streets! This is your final order to cease your disorderly actions and comply with the directive to enter into a structure and remain! This final order will not be repeated! If you refuse to enter into a structure, deadly force will be used against you!"

A voice screamed out from the crowd of predominantly Black and Hispanic men and women, shouting,

"We run the streets!"

The entire crowd started chanting,

"We run the streets!"
"We run the streets!"
"We run the streets!"

An Army captain, sitting inside a bulletproof vehicle, radioed in to his general requesting permission to use deadly force.

The general picked up the receiver, and said,
"What does the scene look like?"

"We got about 15 thousand young men and women, several dozen small children, and quite a few infants. All predominantly Black and Hispanic gang members, not brandishing any weapons, marching and chanting in unison, 4 hours past the deadline, refusing to follow all orders.
"A final order has been given, the non compliant behavior continues to persist. We set up a perimeter around the 4 block radius that they are currently occupying. Sufficient destroyer drones are hovering above, ready to begin firing at the targets."

The general rubbed his tired eyes, shaking his head to the negative. He blew a strong gust of coffee scented breath out of his mouth, and then looked at the other generals sitting at the table, and said,
"Usually, we would have some very serious political issues with using deadly force on such a large group of civilians peacefully protesting, especially with all those members of minority groups.

"Regardless to their obvious ignorance of the law, these individuals no longer possess the freedom of speech, or to peaceably assemble.

"We are on the brink of an extinction level event. The whole entire world is in a State of Emergency!

"Every single person on this planet is subject to Marshall Law with zero regard to whether or not they possess even the slightest comprehension of their expectations.

"Constitutional Rights, Civil Rights, The Bill of Rights, even Natural Rights, are officially obsolete! The failure of our educational system has unfortunately produced massive groups of extremely unstable individuals who fail to comprehend the lethal dangers of challenging the authority!

"This failure has thereby presented us with the "worst" type of scenario imaginable!"

As the general raised his voice, the other generals showed signs of empathizing with his outburst of emotion. The general clenched his jaw, blew air out of his nostrils, and said,

"Political issues no longer play a role in the determination of any decisions. Our number one priority is the preservation of life that can only be established on the foundation of absolute order.

"It is our duty to establish and maintain order, and we will fulfill our duty by any means necessary!"

The general quickly scanned a sheet of paper, and said,

"We have 2 options! We can isolate the interior of the perimeter, scramble the communication devices, cut the power, terminate every target, and initiate a rapid clean up.

"Option 2 is to establish a barrier in place of the perimeter, which will include the installation of roofs that would cover all open spaces exposed to the elements.

"In the second option, it will take continuous manpower to maintain the barrier that can in fact be destroyed, if met with enough resistance.

"Option 2 also presents the dilemma of the delivery of food and health supplies, and then worrying if everyone is receiving and being able to utilize their fair share.

"In Option one, we must also consider eliminationg only a fraction of the targets.

"Such action would surely deliver a message to the remainder that such is the fate of those who refuse to follow orders.

"On the other hand, if we eliminate all targets, we eliminate the possibility of retaliatory efforts when the military returns to that area, and others like it, to transport individuals inland.

"We do not want anyone relocating with hostile feelings towards the government that would actually act on their feelings with violent actions."

The General scanned the sheet of paper once more, gave an affirmative nod, and then said,

'Wherefore, on the basis of the current occurrence, and the state of the world, to set a precedent that will establish order in the area in which the request was made, as well as in numerous other areas faced with massive non compliant scenarios, I say we grant the request to utilize deadly force against all who have failed to comply with a final order! All agreed say I!"

All 6 generals at the table, said,

"I."

"I."

"I."

"I."

"I."

"I."

"The decision is unanimous! As said, so shall it be! The request to utilize deadly force is hereby granted!"

# 17

"Yooo! Crenshaw on the block after hours! Ya heard that! Shout-out ta' tha' L.B.C.! Hollywood, y'all got nothing on my movie making skills! This? This right here? This is exclusive concrete jungle footage! Ain't nobody on the block like us! Bringing it to you live on the net! Yooo! Shout-out to you clowns missing this California party!

"Hiding in tha' house? Y'all done got grounded? Ha! 30 40 50 years old and y'all done got grounded! Man my grandma out here somewhere! I bet yours done got grounded by sneak ol' Uncle Sam! Haaa!"

The young black man with bright red dreadlocks flowing down his back allowed his camera drone to fly high above the crowd to show a very large group of people dancing in the middle of the street.

As the drone hovered over a group of drunk women, they got excited and started screaming,

"Look y'all we famous!"

"Heeey everybody! We out here living it up!"

"They done shut down the schools, all the restaurants, all the stores?"

"We can't even buy no food? Are y'all crazy? Not my government!"

"No worries! Rasta-Mon out here cooking and selling all typa-ting!"

"We don't gotta work! We straight! Y'all can shut tha' whole world down! You just better have my money!"

"Whaaaat!"

Over 50 thousand people crowded the streets and set up barbeque grills, D.J. booths, big speakers, and bar tables, where they were selling food and drinks to people who were eating and drinking and having a good time when all the lights went out at the same exact time all the music stopped playing.

Then, all the lights in all the houses and stores that lined the streets went out. There was an immediate silence mixed with an eerie calm crawling up everyone's spines, as the people struggled to see through the pitch blackness.

A voice screamed,

"They jammed the phones! Do anybody phone work?"

Panic exploded into chaos as people started stampeding over each other, trampling those who fell on the ground, tumbling over steaming hot barbeque grills, screaming shouts of terror at the unknown danger in the dark.

2 men latched onto a woman and started tearing at her clothes, as she cried to deaf ears that completely ignored her. Unannounced bright lights made all the madness cease, as the blinding illumination stopped everyone dead in their tracks.

The destroyer drones wasted no time in delivering a monsoon of bullets upon all who stood in the streets. Of the over 50 thousand people who were partying, less than 500 were able to escape into structures by crashing through glass windows and solid doors before the highly sophisticated weapons in the sky were able to track them down, and eliminate them.

# 18

## The White House
## Washington, D.C.

The Secretary of Defense promptly entered the Oval Office with a tablet in his hand that contained the top secret tally of authorized uses of deadly force against civilians found outside of structures in the United States of America. As soon as the Secretary handed ThePresident the tablet, she looked at it twice, and screamed,

"Oh my Lord! This is ridiculous! You mean to tell me my military couldn't convince over 5 million people that they would "kill them" if they didn't go inside? This doesn't even make sense! We didn't give them a license to kill, we gave them an order to clear the streets! It looks like they're just filling it with dead bodies! Unbelievable! It looks like they just went around shooting everyone they saw!

"Did they think they were playing a videogame? According to this, there are less than 2 thousand people left in the streets, in just... Half an hour after the generals decided to start killing?

"Goodness gracious they killed over 5 million Americans in just half an hour?"

"Mam, 99 percent of the civilians who remain in the streets are those who have taken hostages and are fleeing in some form of vehicle, aircraft, or water vessel."

"Don't kill anyone else! Spray them with some form of anesthetics and take them into custody unconscious, but alive."

The President continued scrolling through the tablet, and then jolted her head back, as she said,

"What's with all these slayings of prisoners? They're already inside! Why are people confined in cells being killed?"

"Mam, the prisoners, who were terminated, were either attempting to escape after hearing the announcements, or they received some type of medication that was pertinent to their sanity or survival."

"So, you're killing people who you think will go crazy or will die if they can't get medication?"

"Prisoners mam, prisoners in prison. Many of them guilty of murders in and out of prison. Yes."

"Stop doing that! If they go crazy, you deal with it by placing them in an isolation cell without any property.

"And stop killing people just because you think they are going to die either way, that's just senseless!"

The President scrolled through the tablet once more, shook her head to the negative, and said,

"What in the world? What are all these, "Entrances into structures to eliminate targets suspected of planning to disrupt global security", In America? What type of foolish reason is that to take someone's life?

"And how could anyone possibly determine that someone is planning to disrupt, "whatever", when they're in compliance with the order to enter into a structure and remain?"

"Mam, intelligence was gathered from ongoing F.B.I., N.S.A., A.T.F., D.E.A., C.I.A., and ICE investigations into various forms of security threat groups and fugitives from justice.

"The vast majority of the targets that were eliminated while in compliance with the order to enter into a structure and remain, were members of some form of Crime Mob, Criminal Street Gang Organization, Violent Drug Cartel, Anti-government Organization, Anarchist Group, Paramilitary Hostile Militia, Home Grown Terrorist Organization, Racial Supremacist Group, and quite a few Fugitives From Justice who escaped from various forms of secure detention, such as Prisons, Work Camps, and County Jails.

"Once the precedent was set by the elimination of the almost 15,000 targets in Brooklyn, every single agent in every single agency acted on every single lead they ever investigated.

"Any person found anywhere who was known to be a danger to the Local, Statewide, National or International Community, was labeled a target and terminated in the name of international peace and security."

The President firmly put down the tablet, and said,

"Okay! Are the streets cleared?"

"As of right now, there are several dozen active fleeing to elude situations, where the targets are being pursued but not engaged for the sake of the hostages.

"To accomplish the goal of completely clearing the streets, the generals have requested an amendment to the rules of engagement, whereas, they request to use deadly force with zero regard for the safety of the hostages. Such action would..."

"Absolutely not! No! Let them chase them until they run out of gas, and just negotiate them into custody! If that's the only people left in the streets, the American people deserve to know what's going on.

"Now that the majority of the people are isolated, we are better prepared to deal with any isolated chaotic reactions. I'm ready to address the nation. Inform the United Nations that we will now be deploying our surplus troops into those nations that require our assistance."

"Yes Mam! And about the violent kidnappers, who are currently fleeing with hostages, what shall the authorities do in the event that the hostages lives are placed in danger?"

The President rubbed her forehead, as she shook her head to the negative, and said,

"If the hostage is literally about to die then of course they must kill the kidnapper, but "only" if it will save the hostages life."

The secretary took a mental note of the Presidents words, "kill the kidnapper", and relayed his own interpretation of the Presidents message to the generals.

Ten minutes later, the kidnappers were dead, along with their hostages, leaving the streets, airways, and waterways, in the United States of America, cleared of all its civilians.

# 19

## The Other Side of Existence Beyond Time

"I didn't realize how hungry I was until the provisions appeared."

"Which of the sons have come to be devoured?"

"None. The souls of humans have arrived."

"How many humans remain on planet earth?"

"Just over 9 billion."

"Has the land been divided?"

"It has. The humans have divided it into 196 separate sections. Each section is an independent nation."

"Have they activated the power?"

"They have. But they remain unaware of The source. They refer to him as "Dark Energy.""

"What method do they utilize to receive?"

"The humans have established gods that rule in the form of words they call "Law." All who refuse to abide by the Law are isolated, maimed, or killed!"

"How many humans does the mightiest nation isolate?"

"Look! just over 4 million."

"What is that cluster of states?"

"The United States."

"What do the humans call it?"

"They call it, "The United States"."

"Why does the land look so neat?"

"The majority of those particular individuals have mastered the art of taking better care of the appearance, than that of the actual state."

"Do they call?"

"They call."

"Does He hear them?"

"He hears them, but they are wicked, so He does not listen. The Law commands that the isolated humans receive an abundance of care. The source therefore blesses them with the means to provide an ample quantity of guardianship and attention to those held captive.

"The land that incarcerates the most humans has therefore become the most powerful kingdom to of ever risen on planet earth."

"Have they used the power to establish the foundation of the rise?"

"They have! But not one comprehends the creation."

"Has one been found worthy to unseal the scroll?"

"One has! The Sacrifice has resurrected with authority to initiate the beginning of the end!"

"Behold! Bloody presentiments shall pour out many endings! Time is near the fruit of the end from the root of the beginning! We are now authorized to feast on time! Begin chewing from in the beginning!"

"Daddy?"

Jasmine's father still hadn't awoken from his coma after hitting his head on the kitchen counter during his heart attack.

Jasmine gave him a gentle kiss right on top of the bandages on his head, and then quickly trnee her hed to see Megan and Tiffany smiling at her in the doorway.

Megan quietly said,

"The doctors say he'll make a full recovery sweetie. How about you come on down to the waiting room with us so we can listen to the President's address to the nation together.

"We'll finally figure out what's going on, and maybe later when your dad wakes up, you'll be able to explain to him everything that's been going on, okay?"

Jasmine nodded, kissed her fathers boo-boo one last time, and then joined Megan and Tiffany as they walked down the hallway.

They entered into a crowded waiting room where people were gathering around an enormous T.V. mounted to a wall. The people suddenly got quiet, as the Press Secretary wrapped up her introduction of the President, by saying,

"...And now, The President of the United States of America."

There was plenty of applause on the television, while the crowded hospital waiting room remained silent.

2 Black women walked onto the stage, with their adopted Cambodian daughter, who was born a male.

One of the women approached the mic., and said,

"Thank you, thank you very much. I would first like to thank everyone who complied with the governments request to promptly find shelter and remain within it's confines. Rest assured, our main objective is the safety and security of all of our citizens.

"The protocol we chose to implement was developed through years of meditations on the appropriate actions to take in the event that this planet were to be faced with the form of dilemma that we are currently faced with right now.

"What I am about to tell you will alarm you. Please remain calm. This information will shock you and cause you to worry about whether or not you will survive. As your elected officials, our job is to ensure your survival. In order for us to guarantee your survival, we ask you to continue to follow all orders immediately after they are given.

"Do not question any orders. The authority is working hard to ensure your survival, but we can not accomplish anything without your cooperation.

"As long as you continue to follow all of your orders, you will be led to saftey, and we will come out of this situation as a united force, even stronger than we are right now.

"On October thirteenth, 2032, at approximately 2:52 in the morning over Switzerland, an unusual event transpired. The event was detected by the Hubble Space Telescope, who relayed the imagery to the World Meteorological Organization Headquarters in Geneva.

"The telescope detected the spontaneous rapid materialization of 3 enormous celestial objects just off the orbit of the planet Mars. All 3 comets are on a direct collision course with our planet..."

"What the Hell?"

"Oh my God!"

"We're going to die! We're... We're all going to die!"

# 20

The waiting room broke out in a panic. A man standing in front of the T.V. turned to the crowd and screamed at the top of his lungs,

"That's why we can't go outside? They want us to stay inside and die? But if we go outside we die? No matter what we die?"

Jasmine climbed on top of a small coffee table, and screamed as loud as she could,

"Heeey! Can you all please be quiet? I'm trying to hear what we need to do to survive so I can tell my dad!"

The pint sized 9 year old restored order to the waiting room, and the President's voice could once again be heard, saying,

"...Will completely disintegrate into a cloud of unknown substances, as it enters into the atmosphere, and rains down a trail of mysterious particles beginning in The Bay of Bengal above the Indian Ocean, and then over India, Pakistan, Iraq, Iran, Syria, Turkey, across The Mediterranean Sea, Greece, Italy, Spain, Portugal, and then out into the Atlantic Ocean where it will cease its outpour.

"The second comet is roughly the size of Hawaii, at its nucleus.

"It is expected to collide into the earth at 500 miles off the coast of Ireland, 1500 miles off the coast of The United States, directly into the Atlantic Ocean.

"The tidal wave from the deep impact will be so violent, it will completely destroy every island in the Atlantic Ocean, and every coastal region on the Atlantic Ocean in the Americas, Europe, and Africa. The final comet will land on Iraq.

"Before the comets come close to our planet, we will be hit by a forcefield that the most recent calculations are showing will have the ability to cause a pole shift so severe, the entire crust of the earth may wobble out of place and move to a new location.

"As the points of impact change, we will make the appropriate accommodations to ensure that no one is left stranded in a danger zone."

The waiting room was as silent as all the rooms around the world that were filled with attentive listeners who were hearing about the danger for the first time.

The President's voice continued to pump fear into peoples ears, as she continued to say,

"After the comets hit, the forcefield will bounce into the sun and return to the earth in the form of a colossal solar flare, that may be strong enough to manifest firestorms, that could cause flames of fire to touch down on the earth.

"As drastic as this sounds, we can and will survive. Our plan will work as long as we have your cooperation. Survival of the people of planet earth is our number one priority.

"Please understand that there are millions of people currently working very hard to ensure that you survive this coming disaster.

"We isolated everyone so we could clear the roads and begin the preperations for survival. We must put our lives on pause in order to save them.

"Our goal is to effectively move everyone out of the way of the danger, allow it to devestate portions of the earth, and then reestablish our civilization as we get back on track with our lives.

"The first comet won't enter our atmosphere until March 22nd, but we will start feeling the effects of the forcefield as early as January 20th.

"You must all understand that we have control of this situation, we know exactly what needs to be done, and it's exactly what we are doing.

"Trust your government. The authority is your guardian who will lead you to safety by giving you instructions that you must follow.

"You must follow all orders to be safe from the threat of destruction.

"First, you will need to elect a mediator for your structure. The mediator will be the one person with permission to exit your structure each and every time your food and healthcare rations arrive.

"If your structure has more than 4 stories, no one will be allowed to exit. Your structure will not require a mediator. For those structures with mediators, the mediator will only be permitted to exit the dwelling for the duration of the time needed to retrieve the ration box or boxes and enter back into the structure.

"The boxes are being prepared in every town and city of every state. The government has retrieved useful items from stores all over your state. They are currently putting together generous packages for every person in this country.

"Your government has total control of the food supplies and manufacturing facilities. We will utilize the bulk of these facilities to freely distribute boxes of supplies that will keep you well fed and well groomed while remaining inside your structure."

# 21

**Y**ou will not pay for the boxes, for any water, any light, any electricity, rent, mortgage, or any bills. The United States of America, and everything in it, is now the absolute property of the Democratic Party of The United States government.

"We will utilize our property to evenly distribute the tools that you will need to survive.

"Your structure will be scanned by tracker drones that will determine the height, weight, and approximate age and sex, of all the structures occupants.

"Each and every individual will then receive a ration box for the following groups:

"Pregnant Teen, Pregnant Adult, Infant, Small Child, Adolescent, Adult, and Eldery.

"Please keep in mind, there will be certain healthcare produts inside some of the boxes that are intended for the individuals with the X Y chromosome.

"Due to the scarceness of the supplies, it would be unreasonable for us to include certain products in all of the boxes in the name of gender neutrality.

"We do understand that there will be quite a few women who receive packages intended for men, but please understand, as well as you men who receive women's packages, the determinations are not being based on whether or not you actually are a man or a woman.

"The determinations are being based on whether or not your D.N.A. causes you to require specific healthcare products, and that is all.

"For those dwellings with mediators, your box or boxes will be dropped off in front of the apparent main entrance to your structure by a drone that will sound a very loud alarm as soon as the package is dropped.

"If you are hearing impaired, and you are reading these words on a screen, please be on the lookout for your rations. If you are blind, and you are hearing these words, please listen carefully for the alarms that will blare each and every time a ration box is dropped in front of your structure.

"If anyone is seen attempting to steal your box, the algorithms in the artificial intelligence of the drones will detect that a crime is in progress, and they will kill anyone who leaves the boundary of one structure to enter into the boundary of another.

"If you see your neighbour struggling to retrieve their ration, mind your business and go back into your structure. If you leave your boundary, you will be killed. If you go outside at a time when rations have not recently been delivered, you will be killed.

"Millions of drones will be soaring through the skies searching for wrongdoers. Do not think that this is an opportunity to prey on the weak.

"For those structures without mediators, Armed Forces will enter your structures with carrier drones to make hand deliveries. Please be advised that the government has ultimate power. The Armed Forces are representatives of that power. They have orders to shoot anyone who poses any type of danger, opposition, or even the slightest hindrance to the task at hand.

"Each soldier will be equipped with technology inside their helmets that will tell them which individual receives which package. When they bring you your package, your duty is to accept it in silence. If you argue for a different package you will be killed. I repeat, if you even complain about your package, the soldiers have the right to kill you and any witnesses.

"There is no need for there to ever be any form of communication between the Armed Forces and the recipients of the packages. You can not purchase or receive another package. Not even a million dollars in gold is useful in the face of this extinction level event.

"If you try to communicate with the soldiers, they have the authority to perceive even the slightest "thank you" as hostile, and they will kill you. Please be cautious. Follow your orders and you will not be harmed. Receive your ration in silence or face death.

"If you have any questions, comments, or concerns, there will be a national hotline that you can call to voice your expressions. Do not make a fatal mistake. Accept what they give you and let them leave.

"They will be moving very quickly. They will literally be sprinting through your structures because they have millions of deliveries to make.

"The soldiers have orders to enter and exit within the specified times blaring across the screens of their helmets. They won't even have time to make eye contact with you, so please, take the box and let them go."

# 22

For those of you living in the following states, these arrangements won't last long, as you will be the first ones to be evacuated into inland safety locations:

"Maine, New Hampshire, Vermont, Massachusetts, Rhode Island, Connecticut, New York, New Jersey, Pennsylvania, Delaware, Maryland, The District of Colombia, Virginia, North Carolina, South Carolina, Georgia, Florida, Alabama, Mississippi, Louisiana, and the entire eastern region of Texas.

"In the following weeks, all sorts of vehicles operated by government officials will be coming to your structures to transport you to designated safety locations.

"Some of you will be placed in underground bunkers. Some of you will be housed in above ground shelters.

"There is enough underground bunker space, aboveground housing shelters, food, and supplies, for everyone in this country, and everyone in a few small islands.

"Brazil will house the majority of the displaced individuals from the remaining island countries.

"Loud horns and intercom drones will announce when it will be your opportunity to exit your structure and board your bus.

"The following will be the only personal items that you will be allowed to bring with you: One pair of socks, oone set of pampers, panties, or boxers. One long john set. One shirt, one pair of shorts or pants. One jacket.

"One head covering, one wig, one chain, one watch, one bracelet, one ring, one pair of glasses, hearing aides, an oxygen tank, one cane or walker, one inhaler, one contact lens case with a bottle of solution, prosthetics, no wheel chairs, and one cellular communication device.

"If you can not walk, you will be seated on a movable chair, and a wheelchair will be provided at your safety location. Nothing else will be permitted. When you arrive at your safety location, everything you need to survive will be provided to you. Please understand, survival of the human race is our number one priority. You can not bring any pets.

"Deadly force will be used against anyone who even attempts to violate these orders. If you are found in possession of contraband, you will be killed without question. This is an extinction level event. Entire states, and a few small countries, will soon be completely destroyed. Many will survive, but over 5 million Americans have already perished for refusing to follow orders. This is a very serious situation.

"Many more people will perish for not following orders, so please, the number one priority is the preservation of "human" life, not that of the animals, or property, or any possessions.

"Once all the Americans are safe and secured, we will make space for people who will be coming from foreign countries.

"We do not have room for sentimental items. If you are told to leave something behind, leave it behind or you will be killed along with everyone standing next to you. The Armed Forces are authorized to do anything necessary to ensure that no one stands in the way of the preservation of our overall civilization.

"If you have any medical needs, we will address those needs when you reach your designated safety location. If you are currently in need of any type of medication... Or... Or... Or living assistance... You... You are instructed to call the medical hotline at..."

"BOOM!"

"BOOM!"

"BOOM!"

"BOOM!"

"BAM! BAM! BAM!"

"Ahhh!"

"Ahhh!"

"Oh my God!"

The television went blank, as the President's bloody corpse went crashing into the podium.

# 23

Jasmine bolted off to her father's room, screaming screams that could barely be heard over the chaos that erupted in the waiting room.

As soon as Jasmine reached her father's bed, she buried her tears in his motionless shoulder.

Megan and Tiffany came bursting into the room so terrified, Tiffany closed the door without realizing Rebecca was behind her. The door suddenly swung open, and Rebecca came charging into the room with a male nurse, who slammed the door so hard, Jasmine's father rose up in the bed, and screamed,

"The Lamb took the scroll from God! I saw Him open the seal!"

## Washington, D.C.
## 1 Hour Later

"He was just an overall weird looking strange acting person. I couldn't help but stare!"

The Marine nodded his head at the woman, and said,

"So, you say he was "mechanical"? What do you mean by that?"

"Okay, that's the real spooky part! He arrived with the press. He was on time, he had his press pass and all that, but he walked like a robot and he didn't speak at all! He just walked to his location and stood there like a statue. He stood there like a soldier at attention, staring directly at the podium before anyone even took the stage.

"He looked so dorky, like, everyone was laughing at him, but he just kept standing there all super-focused on nothing. He never applauded, he didn't take notes, he didn't even pay attention to whoever was on stage. The President even noticed how awkward he was, and I made sure to take note of how out of place he seemed.

"He didn't move one muscle, until he suddenly jerked his body so dramatically, the President stuttered when he moved. It was like he was hit with a bolt of energy that made him stuff his hand into his lapel like his heart was hurting. That's when the President stuttered, but he just kept holding his chest, so she kept speaking.

"Then, his whole body jolted again, but that time he pulled out the gun and stood in the same position firing shot after shot until he got shot. He was definitely under some type of mind control, or he was a robot, or a clone or something."

"Thank you. Thank you mam. Thank you for your statement. You're the final witness to this tragic event, so we'll finally be able to wrap this up and get back on track with securing the people of this planet from the incoming threat.

"There's one last step in the process of officially documenting you as a witness, and then you'll be free to leave. Please exit this room through the door that is opposite the door that you entered. You will meet an officer on the other side that will give you final instructions."

The Marine quickly rose from his seat and exited the room through the door that he instructed the woman to exit through. Butterflies danced in her stomach as she nervously rose from her seat, held her head high, inhaled a large gust of wind through her nostrils, boldly walked up to the door, grabbed the handle, and swung the door open to a loud hissing sound in the midst of thick white clouds of smoke blasting directly into her face.

Before she could run she collapsed. As soon as she hit the ground she was dead. The Marine stepped out of the room wearing a gas mask, holding a large black bag in his hand.

He quickly stuffed the woman's corpse into the bag, carried dragged it out of the building, hurled it in into the back of the truck that was filled with bulky black bags, threw his mask into the truck, closed the door, and called his general.

# 24

Right!... Right!... Roger that!... Good!"

The general slammed the secure receiver, looked towards the other generals in the dark room, and said,

"All targets terminated! Currently in route to an incinerator!"

The other generals nodded in silence, as the one who spoke dialed another number, and started shouting into the receiver, saying,

"Has he taken the oath?... Good! What has he empowered us to do?... Right!... Right!... Right!... Good!"

The general slammed the secure receiver, and said,

"The President of The United States has delegated the relocation and preservation efforts to this committee! Unlike the now deceased former President, this President has given us absolute authority to make final determinations about the appropriate actions to be made for the preservation of the global civilization.

"Our first action will be to completely dismantle and permanently abolish the meaningless healthcare services being offered to individuals designated for relocation.

"That'll free up an additional 300 thousand troops. The relocations will begin in exactly 5 hours and 32 minutes. We have more than enough time to instruct the transporters to only transport those individuals that their scanners deem to be healthy and able to reproduce.

"Once the coastal regions are evacuated, the United Troops will sweep across the country in search of healthy and reproductive individuals between the ages of 9 to 35 years of age.

"The entire East Coast will not be evacuated. We will only evacuate those who are healthy and able to reproduce. We will not evacuate any children under the age of 9, any pregnant women, the sick, the elderly, anyone over the age of 35, or anyone who refuses to procreate with the opposite sex.

"In every structure where the healthy and reproductive are located, all the other occupants shall be told to wait on the next bus.

"The Naval Troops are hereby prohibited from transporting any individuals from foreign countries who are unhealthy or unable to reproduce. There shall by no means enter into this country any individual who is unhealthy or unable to reproduce. This shall include, but not be limited to: The blind, the deaf, the maimed, the dwarfed, the diseased, and the mentally ill."

The general picked up the secure receiver, dialed a number, and said,

"The new eagle has landed! Destroy the cellular systems and the electronic communication networks!... Right!... Right!... Good!"

The general slammed the secure receiver, and said,

"In just a few minutes, the general public of the western hemisphere of planet earth will lose the ability to utilize all forms of technological communication devices. The level one Bar-Enash devices will be passed out to every single person in this country on the inside of their first ration boxes. We willll be able to give the survivors orders through their devices."

# 25

## Dallas, Texas

"Surely you were dreaming Robert."

Rebecca raised her arm in protest as she said,

"Hold on Aunt Meg! This hospital conducts some serious studies into this type of stuff."

Rebecca then looked at the male nurse, and blurted out,

"Find the doctors!"

The man bolted out the door as Jasmine sadly looked up at her father, and said,

"Daddy, somebody shot the President. We saw her bleeding on T.V. and now she's dead."

Robert's eye's widened, as he said,

"Look in that top drawer and see if you're see a Bible in there."

Tiffany moved her hand off of Jasmines shoulder, and lunged towards the small table at the side of Roberts bed. When Tiffany opened the drawer, she was so surprised to see a Bible sitting next to a Quran, as she handed Robert the Bible, she said,

"How did you know that was there? Did Jesus tell you?"

Robert laughed, and said,

"No no no. I know there is a group of Christians who call themselves, "The Gideons". They place Bibles in Hospitals, Motels, and County Jails, all over this country."

As Jasmine and Tiffany both said, "Ohhh", Robert opened the Bible and turned to the last few pages. Just as he opened his mouth to speak, the door flew open and an Asian man in a white coat came charging into the room, followed by an Asian woman in a white coat, who was followed by the male nurse.

"Mr. Williams! We hear you might of had an out of body experience!"

Robert made eye contact with the male doctor who spoke to him, and said,

"Not "might of", I did have an out of body experience. I came out of my body, out of this hospital, out of this world, and out of this realm."

The male doctor responded,

"Before you came "out of this realm", which direction did you travel to leave the hospital?"

"I went up."

"Did you look down at your body as you were going up?"

"I couldn't stop looking down at my body as I was going up."

"Other than your body, did you notice anything that seemed strange or out of place?"

"No... Not that I can think of."

Robert frowned and looked down for a brief moment, as he thought carefully, and then gasped as he looked up at the doctor, and said,

"I saw a traffic light!"

Both doctors looked straight at each other with similar looks of shock, as Robert looked up at the ceiling, and said,

"For what it's worth, this may sound strange, but I think there's a traffic light on that ledge way up there."

Jasmine and Tiffany both looked up, as Megan stared at Robert with a look of concern, that instantly transformed into shock, when the female doctor said,

"There "is" a traffic light up there on that ledge! Well, a very large and realistic picture of one..."

# 26

Y ou see Mr. Williams, out of body experiences are

actually a whole lot more common than most people would like to admit. Our physical bodies are electric. You might of discovered that by rubbing a balloon on your head!

"The body of all our electric energy gives rise to another body of magnetic energy.

"The coexistence of the 2 bodies is an electromagnetic body called, "The Astral Body". Within the midst of our Astral Body, we exist in our most fundamental form called the "I-consciousness", which is the most basic essence of who we truly are.

"The I-consciousness is the exact point of our awareness of existence. Right now, we are fully aware of our existence as a physical body.

"This is because of all the electricity within us that keeps our I-consciousness attracted to our physical bodies in such a tight form of occupation, it seems that "we" are the physical body, when in actuality, "we" are the energies within.

"When the electric activity, or, as others like to call it, "Our life", "Our life force", or "our energy", is weakened, for one reason or another, the bond between the electromagnetic body and the physical body is weakened, and the 2 separate. When this happens, the electromagnetic body, which is the Astral body, moves away from the physical body, and hovers at a distance.

"Every time the Astral body detaches from the physical body, the I-consciousness also detaches from the physical body, and "we" literally leave our bodies. Most-times, we are totally unaware of the detachment that takes place each and every time we fall asleep, fall unconscious, fall into a coma, or, on the onset of the final seperation which occurs during the event we have come to call "death".

"Sometimes, we are totally aware of the detachment, and when we detach with an awareness of the seperation, we come into the awareness of our occupation of the Astral Body, just the same as if we were occupying the physical body.

"When people perform the detachment by their own will, the act is called "Astral Projection". When the conscious seperation occurs spontaneously, the event is called an "Out of Body Experience". And when the seperation occurs because the electric energy in the physical body is weakened, due to some form of trauma, the conscious seperation is called a "Near Death Experience".

"Studies into these unseen forces have led to the development of technology that can transfer the I-consciousness from one physical body to another. The current issue is the Astral Body. It seems to have a mind of it's own.

"Each time we've successfully transfered an I-consciousness, the Astral Body detaches from the I-consciousness, and the 2 bodies disappear as the patient dies.

"We are on the verge of creating an artificial Astral Body that will have the ability to transport our I-consciousness into a whole new physical body. In so doing, we will never die! Instead, we will just purchase brand new bodies, move into them, and live forever."

Jasmine looked up at her father, and said,

"Daddy, is the I-con-shis-ness our soul? And the Astral Body is our spirit that we got from God?"

Robert laughed, and said,

"Only The Spirit of God could've revealed such wisdom to you, because I can assure you, these college educated doctors with their doctorate degrees would've never been able to come to such a conclusion in all their years of studies. What she calls an "Out of Body Experience", is what the Bible calls, "Moving In The Spirit".

"She calls the soul the "I-consciousness", and the spirit, she calls it, "The Astral Body". What truly occurs during what she calls an "Out of Body Experience" is simply our soul moving out of our body in the spirit."

# 27

The female doctor gave a nervous smile, and said,

"Well, of course different people speak different languages, and we all have different words for the same thing, and we have different ways of explaining lifes processes, but we all know it's the same thing right?"

Robert shook his head in disagreement, and said,

"No. This Astral Projection that you speak of is clearly the evidence of the existence of our soul and the Spirit of God.

"It's an experiment that anyone can conduct to come to the full knowledge that we are in fact souls that can exist outside of these physical bodies.

"It strengthens the accuracy of biblical testimonies that direct attention to the fact that we are something other than flesh and bones, and we will one day come out of these bodies in full awareness of the departure.

"We will not just go into another body! If you would've said such a preposterous thing to the late great Albert Einstein, he would've called you insane!

"You are a doctor for goodness sakes!

"You have a full comprehension of the existence of your soul, but you think it has nothing to do with what the Bible says will come out of this physical realm to stand before The Terror of The Lord on judgement day? Do you not understand that the day of judgement will be the day of the determination of where your soul will spend eternity?

"Your lack of comprehension is appalling! But you don't stand alone! Most people know nothing of this evidence, and you don't make the widespread state of ignorance any better by using such confusing terminologies that inform without educating and therefore keep people in the dark about their internal evidence of an eternal form of existence!"

The male doctor clasped his hands, and said,

"Mr. Williams, we most sincerely do apologize. We highly respect your religious beliefs that we can see you are very passionate about. We came only to confirm that you did in fact have an O.B.E..

"We know that you did because you identified with accuracy the picture that we placed in this room to test those who claim to of endured such experiences, and with that, we are interested in knowing what else you were able to observe while you were out of your body. I see you are holding a Bible. Is there something you would like to share with us? Do you think your experience might of been some type of divine intervention?"

Robert looked down at the Bible, and began scanning the verses, while saying,

"Revelation chapter 1 verse 10 tells us John was in The Spirit on the Lords Day when he turned around and saw an Angel.

"The Lord's Day is over a thousand of our days. It's the period in which The Lord will destroy His creation. John was, as you would say, "Having an Out of Body Experience".

"While he was out of his body, an Angel approached his soul and revealed the future to him. As his soul received the Revelation, his body wrote it down.

"The first verse in the Revelation tells us God gave it to Jesus. God is in the spiritual realm. When He gave Jesus the Revelation, He gave it to Him in the spiritual realm. Jesus gave the Revelation to His angel, and the angel met with John who's soul was at that time in The Spirit.

"John's flesh was incarcerated on an island in what is now the Mediterranean Sea, North of Africa. John was there in the year A.D. 90, in exile, for preaching the gospel of Jesus Christ."

Tiffany said,

"What's the Revelation Mr. Williams? We never went over this."

Robert laughed, and said,

"We should've, and we will. I promise"


As Robert spoke, a small crowd started gathering at the door, drawn to his thunderous authoritative voice.

As the people listened, Robert said,

"Time is a tiny fragment of our Creators mind. The past is His memory. The present is a figment of His imagination. The future is His will.

"The future is what God wants to come into existence. The only way we can know the future before it becomes the present, is if God reveals it to us.

"God revealed the future to John. John wrote what he saw on a document that became the last book of the Bible, "The Revelation". God showed John so deep into the future, he saw the end, and he even saw far beyond the end, into The Kingdom of Eternity."

# 28

Tiffany asked,

"So what's in the future?"

A man stepped into the room from the small crowd, and began speaking through a smile, saying,

"No one understands the Revelation. It's esoteric. It was only intended to be understood by a few. It's symbolical, allegorical, metaphorical, and way too spiritual for anyone to be able to say anything about it with any type of accuracy. You don't need to understand John's Revelation to be saved. All you need to understand is God's love for us, so you can have the personal relationship with Him that will bring you many forms of salvation from all sorts of life's difficulties."

Robert blankly stared at the man, and said,

"That's why Jesus told us beforehand that the gate is straight that leads to life, the path is narrow, and there will only be a few who find it. The reason is simple; There are only a few who are truly searching."

Robert looked at everyone looking at him, and said,

"Did you hear what this man just said?

"No one can understand the Revelation? It was only intended to be understood by a few? If that foolishness was the case, John would've never been instructed to send it to "7" different churches that, on a map, all pointed to the island that John received the Revelation on."

"Ha!" The man busted out laughing, and said,

"The churches pointed to the island? Is this the crazy ward? Listen man, I'm a pastor, and I hate to break it to you, but you're wrong."

Robert shook his head to the negative, and said,

"Why don't you just do some research? As a matter of fact..."

Robert flipped through the Bible, looking at the maps, and said,

"Here we are!... Let me see that pen."

As the man hesitated to reach for the gold pen hanging out of his shirt pocket, the female doctor promptly handed Robert a pen she had in her pocket.
"Thank you."

Robert quietly drew on the map, and said,

"Today, we call this land "Turkey". In the days when John was on the island of Patmos, this land was called "Lydia", which means "little Asia", or, more appropriately, "Asia Minor".

"You see Patmos in the Mediterranean Sea? That's where John was being held in exile when he received the Revelation.

"Now look at the positions of the locations of the 7 churches that John was instructed to send copies of the Revelation. The first 2 churches, Ephesus and Smyrna, are aligned with the island of Patmos.

"Then, we draw a line from Ephesus to Laodicea, Laodicea to Philadelphia, Philadelphia to Sardis, Sardis to Thyatira, Thyatira to Pergamum, Pergamum to Smyrna, and from Smyrna back to Ephesus. What do you see?"

The man nodded his head impressed, as Tiffany said,

"I see a bow and an arrow!"

Robert nodded, and said,

"Just imagine..."

He then turned to a fresh map of the same region, and said,

"If you think that's something, look at what happens when we draw a line following the order of the churches as they were mentioned in the book of Revelation. We go from Ephesus, to Smyrna, to Pergamum, to Thyatira, to Sardis, to Philadelphia, and we stop at Laodicea. We draw a line from the island of Patmos to the church in Ephesus. What do you see?"

The people at the door started pouring into the room, but everyone stared at the design puzzled. Jasmine finally said,

"Is it a sickle?"

Robert laughed, and said,

"It sure does look like one doesn't it? A sickle is a device that is used for reaping, as in the rapture of a church."

The man frowned, and said,

"The word rapture doesn't appear at all in the Bible."

Robert responded,

"Neither does the word Bible, and who ever said it did? Are you not the pastor of a group of people who follow Christ?

"Was it not Christ who planted the seed of the crop that He will soon return to reap? Is not the event of a reaping called a "rapture"? Pastor?"

# 29

**R**obert shook his head to the negative, while staring at what he drew in the Bible. He raised the Bible towards the crowd, and said,

"Discoveries like this can only be made by doing searches into the truth."

Robert put the Bible down, and continued saying,

"The problem is, most people believe one of the many lies that they have been deceived into believing is the truth, and they therefore feel no need to search for what they believe they have already found.

"Some people just don't understand the truth, and they're too lazy to do the mental work that needs to be done to receive the understanding.

"They really make their fatal mistake when they give up searching for the truth.

"That's when they settle for an abundance of ignorance, or some form of twisted version of the truth, or in most cases, they settle for a boldfaced lie. The unfortunate reality of the matter is most people are simply destined for doom, and the therefore have no desire to know the truth.

"I can assure you, just as the apostle Paul wrote to Timothy in verse 15 and 16 of the Bible book of Second Timothy, all the words in the Bible have the power to make you wise enough to escape death, and live forever, by giving you a burning desire for The Truth.

"All scripture is useful for teaching, rebuking, correcting, and training in righteousness, so the servant of The Lord can be thoroughly equipped for every good work."

Tiffany excitedly said,

"So what's in the future Mr. Williams? What did the angel show John?"

Robert leaned towards Tiffany, and said,

"It showed him a place where heart attacks are extinct! A place where people can't get attacked by their own hearts!"

The crowd gave a roar of laughter, as a voice called out from the hall, shouting,

"Is that Mr. Williams from "The Bible With Mr. Williams" radio show? "I know" I know that voice!"

Robert laughed, held up the Bible, and started quoting his mantra that he starts his show with, saying,

" This Is my Bible! There are many others like it, but this one is mine! I believe in the words of this Bible, all the words of this Bible, and nothing but the seven hundred and ninety one thousand, three hundred and twenty eight words in this Bible. I believe the words in this Bible lead to everlasting life, and all other books lead astray."

The crowd broke out in applause, as Tiffany sunk her head into her shoulders, pouted her lips, scrunched up her face, and sadly said,

"What's in the future Mr. Williams? You promised."

Robert busted out laughing at how Tiffany's little face reminded him of her late father, who was his good friend. Robert frowned into the distance as he inhaled through his nostrils. When the applause silenced, he looked at Tiffany, and said,

"Not one split second will ever cease! You'll no longer shed tears! You'll no longer feel pain! You'll no longer be afraid of anything. There will no longer be anything to fear! You'll no longer yawn. You'll no longer feel tired. You'll no longer go to sleep. No one will ever die. We will always be alive forever. There will never be any night.

"It will be the most beautiful day "forever!" The everlasting day will not be illuminated by the sun, or any man made artificial light. It will be illuminated by the glory of Everlasting Love! You'll see His face, and look directly into His eyes. The Truth will always be present, and happiness will last for all of eternity."

A voice shouted from the packed hallway,

"Man, I can't hear you man! You got people out here wanna hear you and can't hear you man! People thinking the world coming to an end and they wanna get right with God! Can you come out to the waiting room where everybody can hear you?"

Robert put the Bible down and started tearing wires off of his body, as the female doctor said,

"You appear to of made a full recovery Mr. Williams, but we still would like to learn more about your experiences while you were... Uhh... Moving in the spirit."

Robert yanked the last wire off of his body, stood to his feet, and said,

"Meet me in the waiting room!"

# 30

As soon as everyone exited the room, Robert took off his hospital gown, put his personal clothes on, tore the bandage off of his head, and briskly walked out to the waiting room where everyone was facing an empty couch.

As he approached the couch, someone called out from the crowd,

"The chair's all yours Mr. Williams! We've been waiting!"

As Robert took his seat, Jasmine and Tiffany sat on either side of him, as he paused, and started saying,

"Nothing. Absolutely nothing like this has ever happened to me. One second, I was in the kitchen cooking, and then I was vaguely dreaming, and then, I was staring at my body in the hospital bed.

"I was so amazed at the fact that I was staring at myself, I didn't realize I was ascending, until my head was going through the roof!

"That's when I started thinking I died for sure, but then, I heard a voice say,

"Son of man, faithful servant, come and see what The Spirit has to show you!"

"I felt a strong presence, and I couldn't see who was speaking, but I knew that whoever was speaking was pulling me through the ceiling."

Robert looked up, and said,

"Now that I think of it, 2 people died in the same room at the same time."

Both doctors looked at each other shocked to their cores, as Robert continued saying,

"I saw their souls leave their bodies and disappear. When they vanished, I had a strong feeling in my... In my insides, that kind of told me they had both died."

The female doctor spoke in a loud whisper of shock, saying,

"They were in a bad accident. They died at the same exact time, 5 floors above your room, "yesterday", while you were still in your coma."

People silently murmered, as Robert nodded, and said,

"I don't know where their souls went, but I was carried out of the hospital.

"I saw the town, the city, and then, I saw a decent portion of the whole world!

"I was floating in space far above the planet, and the fabric of space suddenly tore and opened right in front of my face, and sucked me into this bright white opening!

"I ended up in a whole other realm! Instead of darkness, as far as I could see, there was bright electrifying light everywhere! The further I looked in the distance, the brighter the light got!

"And there were these enormous balls of light zipping over everywhere! They were like balls of lightning swooping around all over the place like shooting stars!

"They were coming from far away, zipping right past me! They were moving far beyond the speed of light! And there were millions of them! Big balls of white light zipping over everywhere! Everything glistened and shimmered and shined like thin air was made of pure white light that was dense and could be felt!

"I felt like I was floating in the middle of an ocean composed of one great big liquid diamond, if you can imagine such a thing. There wasn't any sky, or clouds, or ground, or grass, or trees, or water, or mountains, or anything like that anywhere! It just seemed like everything was one big ocean composed of the substance of diamonds, but it didn't have a bottom or a surface.

"I was in the middle, everything was in the middle, and all it had was a middle! I couldn't see any edges, a top, or even a bottom! Everything had this glistening glow like the filament of a lightbulb, and I could see straight through the dense glare for what seemed like trillions of miles! I could see the light right in my face, the light in the distance, and I could even see the even brighter lights on the insides of all the balls of light that were zipping through the bright dense light that was everywhere!

"The balls were everywhere! Way down below looking like stars billions of miles beneath my feet! Way up above like stars in the night sky we see here on earth, but more, and they were much farther away, and from that outrageously far distance, I could see each and every one of them just as clearly as I can see all of your faces! They moved so fast..."

# 31

Robert shook chills off of his hand, and continued saying,

"They would be way up there, and then, in an instant, they would be zipping right past me, so close to me that I could've reached out and touched them, but I didn't try to reach out and touch anything because I was so spooked out of my mind, I couldn't move!

"I couldn't wiggle one finger! I was hoping the balls wouldn't hit me, because they looked like miniature suns!

"There was this sound. It was like millions of people speaking at the same exact time in millions of different languages that somehow all made one perfect sound.

"It was this sound.

"I can't think of anything like it.

"I guess, rolling your tounge while screaming in a soft hum?"

Robert rolled his tounge while humming, trying to mimic the sound, only to shake his head to the negative, and say,

"No no no, that wasn't it.

"It sounded like music, but not from musical instruments. And it wasnt anything like the noise those people make when they claim to be speaking in "tounges". This was real music, and I felt so light, I felt like I could fall up or to the right or even forward at beyond the speed of the light! I was hovering in thin... Light?

"I felt so lightweight! I felt like I could fall up at the speed of light, in a place that looked like I would've kept falling up at the speed of light forever! I have no clue as to what was holding me up. I didn't feel tired, I didn't blink, I didn't feel any pain, I didn't feel dizzy or sick, and I can honestly say it was the most terrifying experience I have ever experienced in my whole entire life. I was in four prison riots where I watched people get stabbed to death. This made that seem like a walk in the park.

"I was scared stiff! It looked and felt great, but to be honest, I was afraid I would never be able to get back into my body, or even back into the physical realm. I felt like I had made a big mistake that I had no idea of how to begin fixing. It was like the first day of kindergarten all over again, and I just wanted to go home!

"And I could smell something that smelt like home! I never smelt anything like it. It was such a powerful smell. My insides felt like they were receiving nourishment from inhaling this nonstop gust of something that smelt like warm blankets on a cold winter night. It didn't smell like food, or candy, or baked goods, or perfume, or cologne, or anything like that.

"I really can't say what it smelt like because it smelt like a feeling you could see... I mean... I... I mean... It made perfect sense when I was there... But now...

"It seems impossible to put into words. It felt like how you feel when you're tired, and your back hurts, and you finally lay down, and your like, "Ahhh". That "Ahhh" feeling, is what I was smelling, and the smell was so strong, it was pouring into my vision, and I could see and feel what I was smelling through the senses in my nose alone.

"The scent was so prevalent, and overwhelming, it can only be described with additional senses! If you can understand the feeling of ultimate relaxation, that feeling is how that place smelt.

"But I didn't see or feel what I was smelling, I just smelt it, and it smelt like home! And my arms! I was a ghost! My body was see through! And I could still see it! I had arms and legs and fingers and toes, and they were all in this seeable seethrough form! I didn't even think to check my sexual organ.

"My whole entire body looked like it was composed of brand new glass that was soft as cotton, and as fluid as water. My body also had this slight colorful tint, like the colors you see in soap bubbles. Everywhere I rubbed on my body, I felt a steady stream of fluids pouring out of my being, but I didn't see anything pouring out of anywhere!.

"The whole time I was hovering, I could feel something big coming. It was somewhere in the distance, like the distance of trillons of miles away, and it was coming, fast, and I could feel it!"

"What did it feel like daddy?"

"It felt like warm blood flowing through my veins, but I could feel it in the air, and behind my eyes. As soon as I started thinking of how big it was, nothing else mattered, and I couldn't breathe!

"Just the thought of its size alone was so unsettling, I started feeling like I was dying a death that had no end. I was suffocating and panicking and feeling trapped.

"I was being buried alive, in an everlasting grave. I wanted to escape it, but I could feel it crawling inside my insides from trillions of light years away. I didn't know where I was! I knew I wasn't dreaming, and I was convinced that I was dead."

# 32

I looked down, and out of nowhere, I could see all this nasty oily darkness pumping and growing towards me like a giant heartbeat.

"It looked like a planet sized ocean composed of slimy black jelly that was in the shape of a ball that was growing. I looked, and the ball was the universe in one big image!

"I could see everything! All the galaxies, all the stars, and then, my attention was glued to planet earth, hovering in front the sun!

"I could see right onto the earths surface. From what seemed like trillions of light years away, I could see the surface of the hospital walls.

"I saw straight through the walls, and I could see my body laying on the hospital bed.

"I looked, and I could see the texture of a strand of hair on my chest. I could see through my skin. I saw my heart and my lungs!"

Robert looked down at his stomach, and he rubbed on his chest, as he softly said,

"I was outside my flesh, on the other side of existence, and I was looking at my heart. I looked at it carefully, and I said to myself, "okay". I could see I was breathing, my heart was beating, and in that moment, I knew I would be alright.

"It suddenly came back to me, and I remembered who I was. I remembered my Creator, and in that moment, I knew where I was. I screamed,

"Glory to The Most High God! By the power of His Spirit! In the name of His Word! Let It Be True!"

The waiting room was silent. Every eye was locked onto Robert. Every ear was listening to the words rumbling out of his mouth. Every mind was wondering if what his voice uttered was true. Wondering, if this man really left his body, traveled to this mysterious place, and returned. They were wondering, if they would also have to come out of their bodies, and travel to this mysterious place.

Robert was scaring people, but they were thirsty for knowledge, so they listened as he continued to speak.

A woman pulled out a cellphone, pointed it at Robert, and tried to record a live stream, but she was puzzled when she realized she could not access the internet or social media.

The woman tried to make a call, shook her head to the negative, and stuffed her phone back in her purse when she saw that she did not have service.

A younger woman, who was watching the other woman struggle with her phone, looked at Robert, and said,

"Look, I'm sorry, but does anyone's phone work? My server is like never down, and I haven't been able to get on the web for like the past 10 minutes.

"I think something's happening."

As people started checking their phones, Robert stared at the blank television screen, and said,

"Wasn't that T.V. on when I came out here?"

All the heads turned towards the T.V., as the male nurse walked over to it, and said,

"It sure was! I cut the volume."

The nurse flipped through the channels, confused that none were coming in. He shook his head, cut the T.V. off, and calmly walked back towards Robert, saying,

"Guy's, just relax. Some idiot probably blew something up and destroyed like all the signals in the whole neighborhood or something.

"Who needs T.V. anyway? We got The Bible With Mr. Williams! Come on dude, you saw you were still breathing, then what happen?"

As people gave up on their phones and redirected their attention to Robert, he went back to speaking, saying,

"As soon as my fears went away, I heard something behind me that felt like it was the size of a skyscraper. It was so loud, the balls of light in the distance started dancing to its vibrations. I spun around, and a giant Temple swallowed me into its interior.

The walls were gold that shined like some form of solid gold light. The floor glistened with the same gold dazzle, and in front of me, I could see millions of balls of lights entering into the Temple from evey direction, slowing down to a stop, allowing me to see that they were Angels!

"When they stopped moving, I saw more detail. Their heads were made of lighting, and suns burned in their eye sockets. In the midst of the Angels, I saw God's Throne!"

Megan gasped, and said,
"You really saw God?"

# 33

I didn't see "God". I saw His throne. God was on The Throne, but He was too bright for me to see. It was like staring at the sun, trying to see what's in the middle. It was impossible for me to see Him, but He was there!

"The light around His throne had a light bronze goldish glare with a slightly colorful glow. It was like the color of a brand new penny. If one penny here on earth could shine with just one ounce of the brightness I saw, we would never see darkness.

"That's God's color. He isn't Black like me or white like you Megan. He isn't the color of flesh. He's different! The only thing in our realm that describes the texture of God is bright light, metal, fire, lightning, and jewelry."

Robert looked around, and laughed, as he said,

"I could tell that everything in that realm will last forever. There was no rust, no wrinkles, no scars, no form of decay. Nothing was wearing away! Now that I look at this realm, all I see something God made up! A bunch of stuff He just created! Stuff that will most definitely come to an end!

"Look at your body! It doesn't even look like it can last forever!"

Robert looked around and let out a roar of laughter, saying,

"This realm... Is fake! Its an imitation of God's realm, and it doesn't even come close! Can you imagine being built out of diamonds? That's how my soul looked!"

Robert let out a hard laugh, while everyone stared in silence.

"What do you mean daddy?"

Robert calmed his laughter, looked at Jasmine through a smile, and said,

"Can you imagine? Everything seems real because it's all we know. But when you think about it, you can feel yourself inside your body. Your body is a house. You're up there by your eyes, looking out your windows. Your body belongs to you. It's your's. Those are "your" legs, "your" arms, "your" head, "your" looking out "your" eyes! But who owns those body parts?

"Who is that in there looking out those eyes? Who is moving those arms and those legs? Who are "you?"

"I'm the soul inside the body daddy."

Robert laughed, and said,

'God loves you so much, and you're right. We are souls inside these bodies, and my soul was carried into the spiritual realm."

A voice called out from the crowd,

"Why you?"

"I'm not sure, but I can say this: Ever since Jesus left this earth, every believer has been looking forward to these days that we are about to endure.

"If we survive, we will see the Messiah who most people only know as a character from an ancient book."

People started looking nervous, as a woman said,

"Are you saying the rapture is about to take place?"

A man with his back on a wall snorted, and said,

"The rapture takes place "before" the tribulation. There's no need to worry about anything. Jesus will get us before bad things start happening, just like in Noah's days."

Robert said,

"Call your family and see how they're doing. Turn on the T.V. and find out what's going on with the cellphones."

A different man standing in the crowd, said,

"Oh it's a whole lot worse than that! We can't even leave this hospital!"

Robert's head jolted back in confusion, as Megan said,

"Oh Robert, we forgot to tell you!"

"Forgot to tell me what?"

"Daddy, listen to me carefully. Nobody in America is allowed outside. 5 million people got killed for going outside. We're getting food boxes from the Army people, and they're taking us to bunkers under the ground to be safe from the comets that are going to start crashing into the world in a couple more months. 3 big comets daddy."

Robert leaned forward with his jaw hanging to his knees, he swallowed a large gulp of saliva, and said,

"That's what was on T.V.? That's what the President said before she got shot?"

As Jasmine nodded her head up and down, Robert looked towards the crowd, and said,

"And you don't think this is the tribulation? Let me see the Bible."

# 34

As soon as Tiffany handed Robert the Bible, he began furiously scanning the last pages, as he said,

"This event that John said would take place in the future, is what I just saw. Understand what I'm saying, please! My soul came out of my body, and as a soul, I went into the spiritual realm, to the location of God's Throne. While I was there, I saw The Lamb open the first seal."

"Wait wait wait! Slow down man!"

The male nurse shook his head in confusion, as he lowered his arms, and said,

"What's all that Lamb and seal stuff about? I believe in God, I don't know what the Bible says, but I know I'm a Christian, and I'm a believer, so I need to know what's going on if this is like the rapture or something.

"The one thing I know about the rapture is, "Don't get left behind". So if God's giving you messages or something, break it down, but say it in a way that we can understand, please."

"Alright. Jesus is The Lamb of God."

"So The Lamb is the nickname of Jesus?"

"No. Its the form He appears in, "In The Spirit", to take the scroll from God."

"Okay I'm lost. Totally lost. Anyone else lost?"

As the crowd laughed, Robert said,

"Think of it like this: When you were 3 weeks old, still in the womb, you looked like your pinky. When you were 3 weeks old, outside the womb, you looked like someone you would probably lift up into your arms. And now, decades later, you look totally different than those 2 different forms of the same exact you.

"Now remember, this physical realm is some form of watered down wannabe version of the spiritual realm. We experience changes in this physical realm, but they're nothing like the changes In the spiritual realm.

"In the spiritual realm, spiritual beings experience real changes that don't take weeks or months or years, and they don't just change from looking old to young or young to old. They go from looking like humans to looking like animals to looking like lightning, and their changes can occur in an instant!"

"Woa! So like, tell us some more forms of Jesus man! This stuff is pretty cool!"

"Well, the Bible tells us His original form is The Word of God."

"Aw man! You mean like? He started out like... Like... Did you say, His Word? What does that mean?"

People laughed, as Robert said,

"I mean what I said. Before God's Word manifested in the flesh as Jesus, He was The Word of God in the spiritual realm. Use your imagination to see the words manifest in your mind as thoughts.

"Once "my words" materialize inside "your mind" in the form of "your thoughts", you can see a vision of how what I'm saying actually looks, and you will receive a better understanding."

The female doctor nodded in agreement, and said,

"You are very wise Mr. Williams."

Robert responded,

"Before I was wise, I was praying for wisdom."

The doctor nodded with a smile, as Robert looked at the male nurse, and said,

"Picture God speaking. Picture God as He is truly described in the Bible. The light blaring out of His being. The unapproachable light surrounding His presence. Red hot flames of fire pouring out of His eyes. Can you imagine how God's words look, in a place where light dances? A place where Angels travel at speeds far surpassing their own existence as light, "and" they move unassisted by any form of machine?

"Can you imagine how powerful they must be to blast through an atmosphere composed of diamonds? Angels are creations! Imagine how their Creator looks? Can you imagine how The Words of the Creator look when they move out of His mouth? You can. Imagine a baby coming out the womb. Take the image of the birth of a child, and use it to imagine God's Word coming out of His mouth, alive, fully aware of the fact that its God's Word, and it's alive.

"God's Word can see, it can hear, it can create, and it knows its purpose. Its purpose is to fulfill God's will. When God said, "Let their be light". His Word came out His mouth and conformed the creation to the image of light.

"God's Word came in the flesh to conform humans to the image of God's Word in the flesh. God's Word is His creative force that brought everything in existence into existence, by conforming forms into images of His will."

# 35

Just before a skeptical looking man went to speak, Robert started reading the Bible, saying,

"In the Bible book of John, chapter one tells us The Word was with God in the beginning, and The Word was God.

"It's hard for people to take those words, and transform them into thoughts, so they could fuel their imagination with the images that must be seen in the mind, to understand how God and His Word can be seperate, and still be one.

"The problem is, people try to understand things going on in the spiritual realm, using mental images that are based on things from this physical realm, where people and their words are just flesh and the vibrations of vocal cords.

"It's hard for people to see the vibrations of vocal cords being equivalent to their body. Instead of strengthening their imagination, so they could understand, they settle for lies, and they fail to discover the true identity of God's Word.

"When we look back to the beginning, as it is accounted in the Bible book of Genesis, we see God speaking things into existence. The fact that He is speaking is the evidence that His word is present with Him.

"So, in the very first verses in the Bible, we see God, we see His Word, and as we continue to read, we see The Spirit hovering over the waters."

The skeptical looking man blurted out,

"Oh my God! That's the trinity? Oh my God I think I finally understand the trinity! I can see it in my mind! The Almighty, The Word, and The Spirit? That's what the trinity is?"

Robert nodded, and said,

"The Father is The Almighty, The Son is The Word, The Holy Ghost is The Spirit. Each entity is aware of its own existence, in God, with God, as God. Just the same way we are souls, seperate from our flesh.

"That's the eternal Godhead. The first chapter of the book of John further explains how The Word became flesh, lived as a human being, left the flesh through death, and then returned to the flesh through ressurection.

"When The Word reentered the body of Christ, He rose from the dead."

The male nurse was chewing on his thumb, staring directly at Robert, like a wild eyed madman. When Robert stopped speaking, the nurse spit the tip of his finger nail on to the floor, and said,

"But, doesn't Gods word became flesh just mean people started preaching and teaching about God?"

Robert shook his head to the negative, and said,

"Does that fit with the rest of the scripture?

"Does that statement agree with what the rest of the Bible says? Especially the books in the old testament?"

The male nurse shrugged his shoulders, and said,

"I don't really read the Bible.

"I'm just the nurse man.

"I let the pastor do the Bible thing.

"I do the nurse thing."

"If you seek everlasting life, and you desire to live forever, as opposed to being roasted, you must also do the Bible thing. You can't rely on anyone but God."

The male nurse nodded, as Robert continued to say,

"Before Jesus started preaching, a man named John was preaching God's Word, and he was baptizing people.

"John even baptized Jesus! Jesus studied the Old Testament of the Bible, which was based on the testimonies of Prophets who not only preached God's word, but they spoke to God, and they spoke for Him as His earthly representatives.

"At no time did any of those prophets, or even John The Baptist himself, ever claim to be "God's Word that came in the flesh", nor did they title their preaching as being "God's Word that came in the flesh".

"Based on that comparison, with the rest of scripture, we find that the terminology, "God's Word came in the flesh", is an exclusive title that only describes God's Word entering into this physical realm in the flesh of Jesus Christ.

"You are not the first person I ever heard say that. That comprehension is another one of those bold faced lies lazy people settle for because their weak imaginations can not imagine the spiritual realm.

"They can't imagine God's Word coming out of His mouth in the spiritual realm, entering into this physical realm, and manifesting inside the womb of a virgin to materialize in the form of God's Son, the epidomy of God's Word in the flesh.

"They can't imagine that, while still claiming to have the ability to imagine that same exact word creating this universe. If you can imagine God speaking this massive universe into existence, how is it that you struggle to comprehend how He spoke His Word into one tiny little fetus?"

# 36

The male nurse blurted out,

"I confess! I confess I confess! I have a weak imagination! Man, when I was little, my mom bought me a Barney The Dinosaur stuffed teddy thing. It came with all these old Barney reruns on D.V.D..

"I got hooked! I played those shows so many times, I memorized all the songs! One day, I started thinking about what I was saying when I was singing the introduction song..."

Rebecca said,

"The I Love You song?"

"Not that one. That's the closing song that they sing at the end of the show. I love you too, but the beginning song goes,

"Barney is a dinosaur from our imagination. When he's tall he's what you call a dinosaur sensation. Barney can come be with you whenever you may need him. Barney can be your friend too if you just make believe him." So I understood the first few lines before I got the whole "make believe him" thing.

"One day, I really needed my dinosaur sensation to come be with me. I got my mom to buy me the exact same Barney bear as the children in the show. Every time the show started, they would go to recess, and there would be this magical explosion, and their bear would come to life! One day, I tried to use my imagination to bring my Barney to life, but it didn't work!

"I slowed down the D.V.D. and watched every step carefully. I even paused it and studied the magical twinkles for hours! I held my Barney bear up to the twinkles, I showed him how their Barney bear came to life, I prayed to God and asked Him to bring my Barney bear to life, and nothing worked. I realized I didn't have an imagination, and that's why I wasn't picked to be on the show."

The crowd let out a roar of laughter, and Robert finally said,

"That was an amazing testimony... Uhh..."

"John! My name is John."

"John! Well John, did you ever discover that everything you were seeing on your D.V.D., was actually going on inside the minds of children?"

"I hope so! I mean, I get it now, I think. But I still struggle to just pick up a big book like the Bible and immediately start seeing what I'm reading in my head. Really, I just see the words."

Robert made a "Hmm" sound, and then said,

"Its not that you're only seeing the words. The words are all you're focusing on. You should try looking around the words, or through the words. Look at what they represent."

Rebecca said,

"Man you're deep!"

Robert smiled, looked at John, and said,

"Think of the girl that you love."

John looked straight at Rebecca, which caused her to blush, and Jasmine and Tiffany to laugh, as Robert said,

"What was the first thing that came to your mind?"

"Her name."

"Okay stop right there. How does that name make you feel?"

"Complete."

"Do you really think a cluster of letters, jumbled into a word, has the power to stir your emotions? Or is it something deeper than the words? Is it the thoughts that materialize inside your mind when those words manifest as the fuel to your own imagination? Is it the images that flash through your mind when your brain starts bringing those words to life? Is it the visions you see of her eyes, her laughter you hear in your mind, your memory of how you feel when your staring into her eyes, and she's staring into yours?

"Look beyond the words. Look at the presentation, not the representation. Don't look at the attorney, he's not the one on trial. Look at the defendant, he's the reason behind the proceeding."

# 37

John looked around at all the people listening and

nodding in agreement, and said,

"This is good. Hey man, tell us what you see in your imagination when you read the words, 'God's Word became flesh'."

Robert inhaled a large gust of air into his nostrils, as he stared into the distance, nodding in agreement. He looked at the Bible, flipped a few pages in silence, slowly began reading verses in silence, and then looked back up at John, as he said,

"I see a strong handsome man, hovering in the midst of light that is blasting out of every inch of His being. The light is so bright! The man is so mighty, so strong! The light is erupting even out of His face at beyond the speed of light. The form of His face is perfection. The surface of His face is shining like lightning. His head and hair is glowing with the glisten of shooting stars. His eyes look like suns that won't stop exploding out his sockets! When He opens His mouth, smoke pours out, and in the midst of the smoke, I see  metal.

"A silver Word proceeds out of His mouth, rippling like the water on the surface of the ocean.

"The edges of the Word are sharp as razors. The Word tears through the midst of the smoke like lightning.

"The razor sharp Word is applauded by billions of creatures, as it tears through the spiritual realm, being trailed by the white Smoke, which is The Spirit of God.

"The Word moves it into the physical realm, where it takes on an invisible form, as it materializes into the oxygen that the virgin breathes into her nostrils.

"In the form of oxygen, possessed by the Word of God, He enters into the blood that pumps Him into the womb where an egg is penetrated the same way a sperm would've entered the egg had it of been a natural birth.

"The force that causes the immaculate conception is composed of what later generations will call "Dark Energy."

A woman sitting on the floor with her back on a wall, said,

"Wait a minute! I caught a story coming out of Moscow that was informing people to not believe the lie from the West that the comets were a creation of Dark Energy."

A man standing close to the woman, said,

"Yea? And who can trust anything the Russians say? They're the definition of master deceivers to the masses. They'll say anything to push an agenda."

Another female said,

"Russia's not the only country saying that. China says it. Iraq, Iran, and North Korea are saying it it too."

Another man who was standing by the T.V., said,

"Wars been brewing with those countries ever since they started building The New City, The New Jerusalem."

Robert frowned, as he asked,

"The New Jerusalem? What is that?"

Tiffany said,

"You never heard of The New Jerusalem? All you gotta do is look up... Oh, I forgot. The internet is down."

The woman on the floor with her back to the wall, said,

"New Jerusalem isn't what you're thinking Mr. Williams. I'm familiar with the Bible talking about a future New Jerusalem and all that, but this is a real place that people are building "right now". Everything in The City will obey the commands of the people who live in it. It'll be the first smart city! It'll be the dwelling of the gods, and it'll even be in the sky!"

Robert said,

"In the sky?"

The man standing by the T.V., said,

"I'm surprised you haven't heard of this. It's the biggest thing happening in the Christian community. It will be a holy place. It's being constructed exactly how The New Jerusalem in the Bible is described. It has thirteen levels, and it's in the shape of a pyramid. They followed the pattern in the Bible to give all the glory to God. Every week, The City will hover over a different country. So every 4 years every country will get a chance to see it hovering over their country for an entire week. It'll be way up in low earth orbit, and the  floor, all the way on top, will be the transmitter for the Bar-Enash system."

Roberts head jolted back, as he said,

"What's the Bar-Enash system?"

Rebecca said,

"How long have you been in a coma?

"This stuff has been developing for months!"
Megan said,
"I never heard of Bar-Enash."

Several other people said they hadn't heard of Bar-Enash either, and the crowd started murmuring, as the man by the T.V. raised his voice, saying,

"Bar-Enash and New Jerusalem go hand in hand. New Jerusalem will be the city of the world. It will be the capital of the global government, and instead of a bunch of incompetent money hungry bafoons, it will be ran by the most powerful artificial intelligence ever constructed. The supercomputer that will rule the world will have 20 million cores that will enable it to have a top speed of 200 hundred petaflops. That means it will have the power to do 200 hundred quadrillion floating-point operations per second.

"That's what will be balancing the global budget, and that's what will be making the decisions when the world has the marriage."

John said,

"What marriage? Are they making a decision about whether or not people can marry animals?"

# 38

No of course not! I'm not talking about that
foolishness! Haven't any of you studied deeper into
Bar-Enash than just the smart city?"

A woman standing next to Rebecca, said,

"The smart city is the only thing that's interesting about
it. Well that, and The Chip of Allegiance."

Another woman said,

"I'm familiar with The Chip, but I haven't heard of any
"marriage" either."

The man by the T.V., said,

"Well you all need to do some more studying! This is
way more than some fancy new gadgets. It's the gateway
to the next stage of the evolution of our species! This will
unite the world."

An elderly woman sitting in a wheelchair, said,

"Does anyone know what "Bar-Enash" means?"

Rebecca said,

"That's easy! It means "Human" in Aramaic.

"It's all holy and spiritual and biblical. It comes from the
Bible."

The man who was standing by the T.V., walked over to Robert, and said,

"Can I check that out for a sec'?"

Robert promptly handed the man the Bible. The man quickly flipped to the first few pages, and said,

"Here we go! Genesis chapter eleven verse one,

*"Now the whole earth had one language and one speech."*

"Then, verse five and six, says,

*"But The Lord came down to see the city and the tower which the sons of men had built. And The Lord said, "Indeed the people are one, and they all have one language, and this is what they begin to do now nothing that they propose to do will be withheld from them."*

"You see! God told us how to become Almighty! All we gotta do is get the whole world to unite, speak the same language, and speak with the same intent of heart, and nothing we set out to do will be impossible! We can set out to bring the dead back to life, to live forever, and to populate the universe with our descendants that we can all live with for eternity! That's what Bar-Enash will do! Bar-Enash will unite all the people in the world into the system at the apex of New Jerusalem, and the supercomputer will teach us how to speak and think as one."

Robert was listening to the man very carefully, and when the man finally stopped speaking, Robert asked him,

"Exactly what is The Chip of Allegiance?"

"It's everyone's key to paradise! It's the only way to connect with New Jerusalem, to maintain a personal relationship with BarEnash. Bar-Enash will have the accumulation of all known knowledge.

"Everything that has ever been on the internet, on the darknet, on google, and so much more, will all be known to Bar-Enash.

"When you plug in to the system, your brain will be uploaded to the supercomputer, and everything you ever knew, saw, heard, thought, smelt, or felt, will be known to Bar-Enash.

"Bar-Enash will use that information to create order out of chaos by organizing the thoughts of all the people in the world. Bar-Enash will be able to connect us to our perfect matches to every aspect of our lives.

"Every person on this planet is a piece to the global puzzle. Bar-Enash will assemble the puzzle, and like God promised, we will succeed at doing everything we imagine to do!"

The old woman sitting in the wheelchair, said,

"Now how can a computer promise all that?"

The man by the T.V. responded,

"Its not the computer granny! It's us! God told us we have this power! All we gotta do to activate it is unite! We "will" unite! Every person on this planet will take The Chip of Allegiance or they will be destroyed!

"You all have something inside your minds that every person on this planet needs.

"You know what you know and I know what I know and Mr. Williams here knows what he knows, and "that's" the problem!

"The knowledge is divided into billions of different sections on the insides of billions of seperated people. The Chip of Allegiance will go inside us, to capture and send our piece to Bar-Enash. Bar-Enash will unite all of our knowledge, and it will send one collective thought back into our minds so we can all agree and think as one. When we unite, we will be what God wanted us to be from the beginning, which is love, because God is love."

# 39

Jasmine looked at her father, and said,

"Daddy, is that true?"

Robert looked Jasmine directly in her eyes, and aggressively said,

"If you take the Mark of The Beast, your soul will be tossed into an eternal Lake of Fire and Brimstone, where the smoke of your torment will rise forever.

"There will be no rest, day nor night, for any of those tormented souls that disregard the threats of Revelation chapter 14. They will suffer an endless pain for trillions of years and beyond for infinity.

"Jesus and His angels will be present at The Lake of Fire, and they will never remove any of those doomed souls from their..."

The man by the T.V. harshly cut Robert off, shaking his head, saying,

"That's what I don't get with you kooky extremists! You really think our loving God would just toss people into an oven and leave them there to burn and suffer forever? Are you insane?

"You think Jesus, and all those angels, would actually stand there and watch without "ever" doing anything to help souls that are suffering?

"Come on man, I know you don't believe Jesus could ever be that cruel. He wouldn't even authorize the stoning of a woman caught "in the act" of adultery!

"And Jesus was the first preacher to start preaching the peaceful messages of "turn the other cheek", "love your enemies", and "bless those who curse you".

"You think He would just morph into an almighty hypocrite, and just stand there and do nothing as the souls that He loved so much He died for, are suffering right in front of His face?

"Be for real! It doesn't even matter what the Bible says! Everyone knows a loving God would never let His people suffer forever. Even if the prophets said God said He would, even the prophets knew He wouldn't really do it.

"That's common sense! Even if God does toss souls into the lake of fire, after a few years, or even a couple thousand years, He'll soften up, and Jesus will talk Him out of it, or just be the savior He is and take away the suffering.

"Heck, He might even create a seperate Heaven for all the people who fail judgement.

"Either way, God obviously went a little over the top with the whole suffering forever thing, and when He really sees the suffering, He'll end it, that's love."

After carefully listening to the man, patiently waiting for him to finish speaking, Robert said,

"For the love of His brothers and sisters, Jesus will always be present at The Lake with an army of Angels.

"He will be standing as a gurantee that none of the doomed will ever escape their place of torture, to bring their cowardly, hateful, unbelieving, abominable, murderous, sexually immoral, vile and disgusting way of life into The Kingdom, to defile it with their filth and nastiness.

"God's love is everlasting, and so is His wrath!

"The man who the country "Israel" was named after, had a son named "Judah".

"Judah's firstborn was a man named "Er". Er was wicked in God's eye's, so God killed Him. "Onan" was told to impregnate Er's wife, so the children could be considered Er's children, and Er would have descendants.

"Onan had sex with his deceased brothers wife, and he intentionally ejaculated on the floor.

"God killed Onan for his wicked act.

"The account of how and why God killed Er and Onan is recorded in the Bible book of Genesis, chapter 38.

"Moses was the Hebrew prophet who God used to deliver the Israelites from Egyptian slavery.

"Moses was adopted by an Egyptian princess, and raised by his biological mother, who was the slave of the Egyptian Princess, the daughter of the Pharaoh.

"Moses had a brother named "Aaron", who had 2 sons named, "Nadab" and "Abihu", both of whom were burned to death by God Himself, when they tried to offer unauthorized fire to God.

"God killed them with the same fire they tried to offer Him.

"The story of how God roasted Nadab and Abihu is in the Bible book of Leviticus, chapter 10.

"In the Bible book of Deuteronomy 32:39, God Himself said,

> "Now see that I, even I, am He,
> And there is no God besides Me. I kill and I
> make alive. I wound and I heal. Nor is there
> any who can deliver from My hand."

"The story of all stories about the terrorfying wrath of God is found in Genesis chapter 6, where it tells us how God killed pregnant women, small children, blind people, deaf people, old people, young people, all people who weren't "Noah", his 3 sons, and their 4 wives.

"God drowned every single person on the planet, and there very well may of been almost a quarter of a billion people living on the earth in those days.

"Truly, all those people God killed could've easily been brought back to life, like Lazarus, or even Jesus Himself, but I can assure you, God killed those people to show us how serious He is about His Word."

# 40

Goad has destroyed many people, many kingdoms, many nations, and He is surely going to destroy many many souls with a form of destruction that will last forever.

"God allowed His Word to come into this world to suffer and die so no one would have to go to that awful place, but make no mistake!

"Those who do not believe in that place, will end up trapped there forever.

"Those who do not believe Jesus died, so they would not have to go there, will end up being held there by Jesus Himself.

"And those who do not believe Jesus rose from the dead, and entered back into The Kingdom from which He came, they will end up isolated from that kingdom for all of eternity."

Robert made eye contact with the terrified looking faces, and said,

"I do not know what happened in these past few weeks with New Jerusalem, Bar-Enash, or any Chip of Allegiance.

"But, along with the state of this world, and what I experienced and witnessed when I came out of my flesh, it sounds like what the Bible prophesied about The Kingdom of The Beast."

The old woman sitting in the wheelchair, said,

"Are you saying Bar-Enash is The Antichrist?"

Robert shook his head to the negative, and said,

"That's another one of those Bible subjects people twist into their own dark misinterpretations. The Antichrist is an evil spirit that manifests inside the hearts and minds of humans in the form of feelings and thoughts that move the human into confessing a disbelief in The Word of God coming in the flesh as the prophesied Messiah, The Son of God. Look..."

Robert motioned for the man to hand him the Bible back. The man looked at his watch, forcefully shoved the Bible back to Robert, and left the waiting room, saying,

"I don't have time to argue with you. There's 2 things you never argue about: Politics and religion. It's about time for me to go any way! Good luck!"

As the man disappeared down the hallway, Robert found the verse he was looking for, and said,

"The only writer who mentions "The Antichrist", is the apostle John in his 2 letters that he wrote to a group of believers who lost faith in the doctrine of Christ.

"They felt it was impossible for a good spirit to inhabit human flesh, which was evil. In the Bible book of Second John, which was the second letter John wrote to the group, John warned about false teachers who were spreading lies. The word "Antichrist" appears in the Bible a total of 5 times.

"In the Bible book of First John, which was the first letter John wrote to the group, the word "Antichrist" appears 3 times in the second chapter. The letter was written almost two thousand years ago describing a misconception about The Antichrist that people had way back then, that still continues to persist to this present day."

Megan said,

"What do you mean Robert?"

"Just listen. In first John chapter 2, verse 18, we see the apostle saying,

> *"Little children, it is the last hour, and as you have heard that The Antichrist is coming, even now many antichrists have come, by which we know that it is the last hour."*

Megan blurted out,

"Now that only confuses me even further! I thought The Antichrist was going to be Satan in the flesh, The Beast that causes everyone to take his mark."

John said,

"Yea! Isn't that like The Devil's trinity? The Beast, The Antichrist, and The Devil? And the triple 6! Isn't that when The Antichrist will be ruling the world and he'll force everyone to take his mark of 666 on the hand or the head? Break that down for us man because I don't even know how I know that!

"I know for a fact I didn't read it in the Bible, but you always hear about it. What does it all mean? It's so spooky."

# 41

Robert nodded, and said,

"The problem most people have with scripture is they don't treat the Bible like a dictionary. When you open a dictionary, and look up the definition of the word "drench", it might say, "to wet thoroughly".

"From then on you will firmly believe to the point of "knowing for a fact" what the definition of the word is.

"This is because people see the words in the dictionary as being authorative definitions of existence.

"When it comes to the Bible, most people just don't see it the same way.

"Who here ever thinks of a Bible as being similar to a dictionary? How often do you reach for a Bible to define something?

"Most people don't even believe they are creations, and they therefore do not believe the words in the Bible.

"The Bible is a very unique book. When it comes to the Bible, most people have mixed emotions about it.

"The Bible invokes The Spirit of Love into the mind and heart of the reader.

"Love makes people uncomfortable, because it's an extremely revealing emotion. The Bible speaks on subjects that give rise to the reality of an unseen presence that judges your secrets.

"It's like reading a book, and all-of-a-sudden, you realize the words in the book can see you, as if every letter on the page is an eye!

"All those eyes staring up at you. Little cameras with the power to see directly into your mind as you read them! Imagine if every letter on the page was a serial killer who killed book readers, and the letters of the words had the ability to blast off the page and poke out your eyes!

"The Bible brings things into an opposite perspective. Love puts you on a stage in front your greatest fears, and it forces you to face them.

"Who can do that?

"Who can boldly dive to the bottom of an ocean composed of slimey spiders, gooey roaches, and plump juicy flesh eating leaches and maggots?

"You stand at the shore quivering in disgust, and you can't dive in, but behind you, lions and tigers and alligators and bears are quickly approaching to devour you if you don't dive in!

"If something you need is on the bottom of the ocean of creepy crawlers, or inside the heart of one of the man eating monsters, it's a very difficult situation to be placed in. Instead of diving in to search the ocean floor, covered in roaches, or struggling with the bloodthirsty beasts.

"The safest thing to do is close the book and occupy your mind with something far less unsettling. Some keep reading, avoiding the difficult parts.

"Others redefine what they can't understand, and accept the views that best fit their own interpretations.

"No one wants to dive into the ocean of bugs, and only a few will turn around and fight the beasts. Sadly, of the few who fight, far less will overcome.

"Understand, The Antichrist is the spirit living inside the mind and heart of everyone who does not believe that God's Word is The Creator of everything that has ever existed, who came into this earth in the form of Jesus Christ, the prophesied Messiah, died, resurrected, and entered back into the Most Holy Place, where He now sits at the right hand of God Almighty."

# 42

**A**nyone who denies any portion of the gospel, is indwelt with the spirit of The Antichrist, and they themselves are Antichrist, just the same as the antichrists who John said were on the earth almost two thousand years ago. Anyone can be an Antichrist, just the same as anyone can be antiwar, antislavery, or antipotatoesalad, like Jasmine!"

Jasmine leaned her head into Robert's shoulder, smiling, as Robert continued saying,

"First John chapter 4 verse 3, and second John verse 7 both continue on in the comprehension that The Antichrist is a spirit that anyone can possess, where the verses say,

> "And every spirit that does not confess that Jesus Christ has come in the flesh is not of God. And this is the spirit of The Antichrist, which you heard was coming, and is now already in the world."

"Remember, this was written almost two thousand years ago, the other verse says,

*"For many deceivers have gone out into the world who do not confess Jesus Christ as coming in the flesh. This is a deceiver and an Antichrist."*

John said,
"So what's the difference between Satan, The Beast, and The Antichrist?"

As people nodded their heads in agreement that they were also confused, Robert said,

"We've established that The Antichrist is an evil spirit, roaming around the world, slipping into peoples minds and hearts, moving them to hate, oppose, and deny the doctrine of Christ.

"There are currently billions of Antichrists on this planet. In the holy book of the Muslims, that they call the "Quran", in book 4, 157, it clearly says that Jesus Christ did not die on the cross.

"The Quran even goes as far as saying Jesus is not the Son of God, and was nothing more than a prophet.

"This is why Muslims, who carefully adhere to the teachings of the Quran, do not see Jesus as being The Son of God in the flesh.

"Where the Quran denies that Jesus died on the cross, and is "not" the son of God, the Quran makes itself out to be an Antichristian doctrine.

The Qur'an boldly denies the most fundamental teaching of the doctrine of Christ.

"The word "Christ" means "Messiah". To say "Jesus Christ", is to say, "Jesus The Messiah". "Messiah" means "Anointed One", which means to be "consecrated for religious service".

"This means Jesus was The One Who was prophesied to be set aside to perform the sacrificial death that would bring salvation to the world by shedding the blood that would bring forgiveness of sins."

John shouted,

"I thought His last name was "Christ"! So Mary and Joseph weren't "Mary Christ" and "Joseph Christ"? Are you sure?"

As everyone laughed, Robert said,

"I'm positive John. The word "Christ" is a title. Anyone who does not believe in the meaning and definition of that title is Antichrist.

"Any Muslim who does not believe that Jesus died on the cross, is an Antichrist, because they oppose the doctrine of Christ that teaches Jesus is the Messiah. Humans are Antichrists.

"Humans are the ones who manifest the desire to destroy the Christian church. Even many Christian pastors and preachers, are Antichrist, because they mislead people with so many false teachings, they actually do destruction to the Christian church. "Satan" is a totally different form of wickedness."

# 43

Robert flipped to the last few pages of the Bible, and said,

"Here in Revelation, chapter 12, we see that a war took place in Heaven. Going down to verse 7, it says,

> "And a war broke out in Heaven: Michael and his angels fought with the dragon, and the dragon and his angels fought, but they did not prevail, nor was a place found for them in Heaven any longer.
>
> "So the great dragon was cast out, that serpent of old, called The Devil and Satan, who deceives the whole world, he was cast to the earth and his angels were cast out with him.
>
> "Then I heard a loud voice saying in Heaven, "Now salvation, and strength, and the kingdom of our God, and the power of His Christ have come,

*"For the accuser of our brethren, who accused them before our God day and night, has been cast down.*

*"And they overcame him by the blood of the Lamb and by the word of their testimony, and they did not love their lives to the death.*

*"Therefore rejoice, O Heavens, and you who dwell in them! Woe to the inhabitants of the earth and the sea! For The Devil has come down to you, having great wrath, because he knows that he has a short time."*

John asked,

"A short time for what?"

Robert responded,

"The Devil knows about The Lake of Fire. It was prepared for him and his angels. He knows he will suffer I'm The Lake forever, so his purpose on earth is to bring as many souls with him as he can.

"He only has a short time to ensure that he doesn't suffer alone."

John nodded in silence, as Robert continued saying,

"We know the war in Heaven took place "after" Jesus died on the cross because we see Michael and his angels using the blood that was shed on the cross to defeat The Devil.

"This is one of the only parts of Revelation that refers to a past event. It's a recap of events that have already transpired.

"The recap revealed The Devil's role on earth, by showing us that he was thrown down with a motive to deceive people into following him into The Fire.

"The Devil and his angels were thrown into The Sea that is in the middle of this physical earth, but they are trapped on the invisible side, where we wouldn't be able to see them even if we were to travel there, just the same way you wouldn't be able to see your soul, even if you sent a camera into your insides.

"Our souls are coexisting with these physical bodies from the other side of existence.

"We operate this flesh from a location that doesn't even seem to exist.

"The Sea is also called "The Abyss", "The Bottomless Pit", and "The Great Gulf between Death and Hell".

"A form of tangible darkness in the spiritual realm keeps The Devil and his fallen angels trapped in The Sea, just the same way our souls are trapped in these physical bodies, so secure, most people don't even believe they are souls inside flesh.

"This realm is a delusion.

"Furthermore, the same way I escaped my flesh, and this doctor was able to identify the event as being an "Out of Body Experience", The Devil is also able to send his spirit out of his body.

"The Devil performs, a form of Astral Projection, and so do all his wicked angels!

"From their hidden location in the darkness, they send their spirits into the world to manifest inside humans, to move them into rejecting God's salvation, and influencing others to do likewise.

"The spirits of the fallen angels are the entities that we in this day and age call "demons". "Satan", is the spirit of The Devil.

"The demons are also the "Principalities", the "Powers", the "Rulers of The Darkness", the "Spiritual Hosts of Wickedness", the "Princes", and the "Kings", that are stationed all around this earth as invisible guards who rage hostile war on the Angels of God anytime they try to intervene in human affairs.

"The Devil is a red dragon with 7 heads that cascade from the top head in the middle, to 3 heads on the left and the right. The Devil's 7 heads are symmetrical. The Devil has power and authority over this world, and he is empowered and authorized to do a lot.

"The Devil started the war in Heaven when Jesus was dead, deceiving the angels who followed him into believing the kingdom was vulnerable. But, when Jesus rose from the dead, Michael and the holy Angels used The Blood of The Lamb to defeat The Devil, because the life in the blood is the power of The Word of God. As Jesus ascended to The Throne, He watched The Devil get kicked out of Heaven for the very last time."

# 44

John shook his head in wonder and awe, as he said,

"Man! My imagination is working! I can see it all in my mind!"

Everyone laughed, as Robert continued saying,

"When Jesus left the physical realm, God sent His Spirit into the world to comfort the church of believers who join the Body of Christ through baptism."

John blurted out,

"Yea! Break that whole going under the water stuff down! I never did that. I never got the point."

"It's the initiation into the Body of Christ. The only person that ever did what needed to be done to sit with God on His Throne is Jesus.

"Jesus Christ is therefore The Only One going to The Kingdom of Heaven.

"The only way we can get in, is by joining The Body of Christ, and you do that through baptism."

A man in the crowd, said,

"Sit on God's Throne? Where do you get an idea like that?"

"Revelation chapter 3 verse 21 plainly offers the right to sit with Christ on His Throne to anyone who overcomes, it says,

> "*To him who overcomes I will grant to sit with Me on My Throne, as I also overcame and sat down with My Father on His Throne.*"

"God's Throne is the Most Holy Place, and Jesus is our High Priest who has entered into that Most Holy Place with His own blood. He used the blood to bargain for our forgiveness.

"Jesus is the only one who ever obeyed God from the womb to the tomb, without sinning even once.

"Jesus was perfect, and that's why He was the perfect sacrifice. Jesus had The Word in His flesh from birth, so it was impossible for Him to disobey Himself.

"Jesus followed The Word His whole life, and He was therefore the only begotten Son of God, The One who was the Son of God from birth.

"Everyone else becomes Children of God after they come out of their mother's womb, hear the gospel, believe, confess their sins, get baptized, and follow The Spirit.

"Jesus came out the womb the Son of God, and that's what made Him the Messiah, our Saviour. Baptism is the only way into the body of Christ. When we go under the water, we die to the life that leads to death, and we stop following the evil desires that lead us to sin.

"When we come out the water, we start living the life that will never have an end, by following the spirit that never had a beginning. Baptism carries your soul into a spiritual death, so you can have a spiritual birth."

People nodded silently, as Robert continued saying,

"The Spirit of God came into this earth to give gifts to believers, so the Children of God could be equipped with the power they would need to follow The Spirit to the source of eternal life.

"The Devil has been raging war against the Children of God ever since he came to this earth, and his angels follow him in his hateful wickedness."

John looked around, and said,

"So where are they? I've never seen a "demon", or even an Angel of God for that matter."

"And chances are you won't. They're spirits! Spirits are composed of a substance that our senses are too weak to detect without superior assistance. We're like radio waves, or cellphone signals."

Rebecca said,

"Not even a cellphone can detect a cellphone signal right now."

Everyone laughed, as Robert said,

"And that's exactly how most people are! They're like dead cellphones in a world full of signals constantly zipping in, zipping past, and zipping right through them. Signals they can't detect! The Beast is another mysterious entity, but it's identity has also been revealed in the Bible."

Megan looked surprised, and said,

"If it's identity has already been revealed, why are so many people still being accused of being The Beast?"

John added,

"Yea! I heard The Beast was like The Pope or Illuminati and Skull and Bones and a bunch of Freemasons all tied into this big New World Order conspiracy. If this is really like the last days or whatever, why aren't we hearing all about The New World Order and all that stuff?"

# 45

First of all, Illuminati has received a measure of opposition that is so intense, it could be compared to the Nazi Holocaust and The African Slave Trade combined.

"Illuminati was a group of German scientists who set out to prove that the words in the Bible were absolute truth.

"To make their case, they used scientific findings as evidence that strengthened the Bible's claims.

"The illuminati taught the Bible in classroom settings, abandoning the meaningless rituals that were becoming infamous with the Catholic Church.

"Before class, the students prayed in the name of Jesus Christ, by the power of The Spirit of The Most High God.

"The Holy Spirit was invoked into the classroom, and scientific findings in fields such as astronomy and archeology, were compared with scripture.

"No one could argue against their conclusions, because their method was supreme.

"The Catholic Church felt the illuminati was becoming too effective in its ability to convince people.

"The Church felt people would turn to illuminati to lead them to God, and in the process, they would be led away from The Church.

"The Catholic Church initiated its destruction of Illuminati by spreading lies about its members, which deceived people into believing they were Devil worshippers.

"That's why the world hates them even to this day, regardless of the fact that most people know nothing about them.

"The Catholic Church eventually started killing the members of illuminati, which drove them into a level of secrecy that was so isolated from society, they couldn't defend themselves against the lies the Church was spreading.

"Today, so many wicked people have claimed to be members of Illuminati, and so many evil people have been falsely accused of being members, the world is convinced that the largest union of Children of God to of ever come across the face of the earth, is a satanic organization.

"The power of the Catholic Church lies not in what it can do to peoples bodies, but what it can do to their minds. Vatican City has less than a thousand inhabitants. The country where The Pope lives, is a little country in the middle of Italy, that doesn't even possess nuclear weapons.

"The Vatican has an international banking system, but The Pope and the bank are separate entities. The theory that a Pope can take over countries that possess nuclear capabilities, without using any nuclear weapons, or even a massive force of soldiers and drones, is laughable.

"Publicity will keep your cause relevant, regardless to whether or not the publicity is good or bad.

"The Catholic Church has always been surrounded by some form of appalling scandal that, good or bad, has kept the church spoken about and relevant for centuries.

"The well known information about secret societies and global takeover conspiracies are distractions that were constructed by the secret societies themselves.

"The vast majority of the known knowledge about secret societies and their activities is composed entirely of disinformation that was designed to keep nosey people out of private peoples dealings.

"Most secret societies, that have been accused of playing some type of major role in the establishment of the kingdom of The Beast, are really and truly unions of greedy people who have practices that would drive the average person insane.

"In order to persist with their struggles to retain power, control, and influence over the masses, they carry out their true dealings in secrecy, while revealing false information that would inform people of their existence, without giving the slightest clues of their true inner workings, that are oftentimes illegal.

"They advance untrustworthy members into their ranks, and give them false information designated as one of their best kept secrets, and when the secret is leaked, as they expected, their true secrets remain shrouded in even more secrecy.

"Secret societies are indeed the ones behind the mass dumbing down of the population, with an outpour of fashions, fads, sports, and celebrities.

"The desire to amass meaningless possessions, give in to all sorts of perverted desires, and the abnormal infatuation for the knowledge of the activities transpiring in the lives of others.

"As long as people have their minds focused on "people", they will never manifest any form of above average critical thinking that would make them more difficult to scare, keep in fear, and thereby control.

"If The Devil hopped out of a volcanoe in the form of a goat walking on it's hind legs, who would honestly follow him back into the lava? He is a master deceiver, so you better believe if there are over 9 billion people on this planet, more than 8 billion will be deceived.

"Jesus Himself told us the gate that leads to life is narrow, and only a few will find it, because many are deceived! Most people will fall victim to the delusion, because the delusion isn't being sent by the deceiver, it's being sent by the Creator!"

People in the crowd twisted their faces in confusion, as John said,

"The Creator? Who? God? You're saying God is the one sending the delusion?"

"God is The Creator of everything. Of course He's the one sending the delusion. God is sending a very strong delusion!"

# 46

As people began murmuring and shaking their heads in disagreement, Megan said,

"Robert, you usually make sense, and I usually trust that what you're saying is in the Bible, but you're going to have to show me that one in the Bible.

"I need to see where it says God sends some "delusion". I never heard you or any preacher say anything even remotely close to that, except for this Satanist who saw us visiting his prison, and he kept hollering out his window, "Jesus is dead!", but actually, not even he accused God of sending a "delusion."

"Here it is! Second Thessalonians, chapter 2, verses 9 to 12,

> *"The coming of the lawless one is according to the working of Satan, with all signs, and lying wonders, and with all unrighteous deception amongst those who perish,*

184

*"because they did not receive the love of the truth, that they might be saved. And for this reason God will send them strong delusion..."*

People started gasping, as Robert continued,

*"...that they should believe the lie, that they all may be condemned who did not believe the truth, but had pleasure in unrighteousness."*

Fear reverberated throughout the crowd, as all eyes were locked on Robert, and the people silently waited for an explanation.

The silence was shattered by the loud sound of helicopter blades slicing through the air.

"John bolted over to the window, looked out, and shouted,

"Oh shoot! We got company!"

Other people crowded the windows, and started watching the swarm of large black military helicopters landing on the roofs of the hospital's buildings, as a convoy of black vans and dump trucks were tearing up the roadway, quickly pulling up to the entrances, and soldiers were jumping out, charging into the buildings.

John turned on his heels, looked straight at Robert, and said,

"Hostile government takeover!

"A forceful transfer of power from the administrators of this facility, to the military!"

John swallowed a large gulp of saliva, looked straight at Rebecca, looked back at Robert, and said,

"So what's the story on The Beast?"

As Robert started giving the explanation, John charged over to Rebecca, put his lips in her ear, and started whispering, as Robert said,

"In order to understand the identity of The Beast in Revelation, you must first understand the 4 beasts in the book of Daniel chapter 7."

As Robert flipped through the pages of the Bible, Rebecca rushed over to Megan, and whispered in her ear.

Megan's eyes exploded with fear, as she immediately walked over to Tiffany, leaned over to her ear, and quietly said,

"Sweetie, let's take a bathroom break."

Tiffany said,

"Okay.",

stood up, looked at Jasmine, and said,

"Jasmine, let's take a bathroom break."

Megan politely smiled at Jasmine, and said to Tiffany,

"I'm not sure if we all can fit Tiffany."

Tiffany immediately sat back down and crossed her arms, saying,

"I'm not going anywhere without Jasmine!"

John quickly raised his voice, shouting,

"Okay folks! How about we take a break! The government has arrived with rations and supplies, so let's move around and meet back up a little later so we can hear more from Mr. Williams once we've gotten situated!

"Some of us might be on our way home!"

As people started stretching and thanking Robert, a young man bolted over to him, and said,

"Can I have this Bible?"

Robert handed it to him, and said,

"Sure, you can keep it."

John grabbed Rebecca and started dragging her down the hallway as Rebecca looked back at Megan, aggressively motioning for her to come along.

Megan leaned over the couch where Robert and the girls were sitting, and harshly whispered,

"The 3 of you better come with me right now!"

Megan bolted down the hallway behind John and Rebecca so fast, the crowd briefly went silent, as she hurried past them without saying a word.

Tiffany and Jasmine looked at each other confused, grabbed Robert's hands at the same exact time, and hurried off with Robert to catch up to Megan.

John led them through a door at the end of the hallway that led to a staircase, where he rushed everyone in and slammed the door.

# 47

John abruptly stopped moving, as the sounds of combat boots could be heard storming into the building from the top of the stairs.

John hushed everyone as shouting could be heard, that was followed by gunshots.

Reality rose above Megan's head like the sun rising at dawn to chase the darkness out of her ears.

Megan yanked the girls from Robert, and crouched to the ground with eyes as wide as her mouth.

Robert's attention was glued to the top of the stairs, where the gunshots were coming from.

An arm suddenly fell on Robert's shoulder.

"Robert!"

It was John's hand, getting his attention.

"Don't move Robert. No noise! I'll be right back!"

John grabbed Rebecca's shoulder, and said,

"Keep everyone right here! I'll be right back!"

As soon as John stepped foot on the eighth floor, the door swung open, a bullet hit him in the stomach, and he tumbled over the rail as soldiers poured out the door.

Rebecca screamed,

"Noooo! That's Captain Shaw's little brother! You just shot John Shaw! You shot Captain Shaw's little brother!"

Rebecca flew up the stairs as more soldiers poured out the door pointing rifles at her. As Rebecca got closer to the soldiers, the one in the front screamed,

"Identify yourself!"

Rebecca stopped dead in her tracks, and screamed,

"Llama! Alpha! Wednesday! Ralph! Echo! November! Charlie! Echo! Lawrence! Rebecca Lawrence! Bar Enash level 3! Clearance level 5! The man you just shot is John Shaw! My fiancee! Captain Shaw's little brother! You just shot Captain Shaw's little brother!"

A soldier in the mob shouted,

"Captain Shaw confirms that his little brother John Shaw should've been here waiting for an extraction with a female with level 5 clearance!"

The soldier who shot John, shouted back,

"What's the status on John Shaw!"

"He's bleeding profusely! And he's unconscious! But he's alive!"

Rebecca bolted through the mob as the rest of the soldiers poured down the stairs, pointing rifles at Robert.

"Identify yourself!"

Robert raised his arms, and shouted,

"Robert Williams! Servant of God! Covered in The Blood with a name in The Book!"

"What? I said identify yourself! That's a direct order!"

Rebecca screamed from the top of the stairs,

"Get those rifles out of their faces! I'm using my clearance for each and every one of them!"

The soldiers stormed past Robert, poured through the door to the hallway, and started shooting. Rebecca screamed,

"Come on you guys!"

They ran up the stairs and started panicing when they saw John's blood pouring down the stairs.

2 soldiers were lifting his lifeless body off of the ground, to carry it through the eighth floor door.

When they stepped into the hallway, a strong metallic odor crashed into their nostrils and turned their stomachs before they realized they were smelling the gallons of blood that was stretched all over the floor.

Megan grabbed the girls and turned them around so they wouldn't see the pile of corpses that was the source of the blood. 2 blood covered doctors stepped out of a room, carrying a corpse. One of the doctors said,

"We got about... Oh!"

One of the soldiers responded,

"Those civilians are cleared with level 5 clearance!"

"Fine. Where did this corpse come from?"

"This man is not deceased! He suffered a close range gunshot wound to the abdomen! He is the fiance of a female with level 5 clearance, the younger brother of a Captain with level 5 clearance! If he dies, you both die!"

The doctors dropped the corpse they were carrying, and led the soldiers into an operating room where they directed the soldiers to lay John's limp body onto a bloody operating table where they went right to work.

Megan led the girls out onto the staircase, to get them away from all the death, only to turn around and rush them back into the horror scene.

Dead bodies were being carelessly tossed over the railings of the staircase, falling all the way to the bottom floor, where they splatted before being stuffed into a black bag.

More soldiers came to the eighth floor, and left wity the dead bodies.

By the time the doctors finished operating on John, the hospital was cleared of all unhealthy and unreproductive humans.

Just being a patient in a hospital, for whatever reason, deemed the human unhealthy and unable to reproduce, and so, all who were found were terminated along with any civilian who was close enough to hear even the slightest sounds of gunshots.

When the black vans and the dump trucks left, and all the helicopters departed, just 8 soldiers were left behind to operate the hospital full of doctors, nurses, and other health care professionals, who were busy cleaning and desanitizing the buildings, because they no longer had any patients.

# 48

Rebecca walked up to Megan, and sat next to her on a small bench in front of the room where Robert, Jasmine, and Tiffany, were sleeping, and said,

"Did you figure out how to work your Bar-Enash device?"

Megan looked at Rebecca through a face of grief, shock, and despair, as she replied,

"I'm trying to figure out what happened to America! I don't understand how or why they could just murder all those innocent people like that.

"This is like Nazi Germany, only a thousand times worst! If you weren't here..."

Megan started crying, as she said,

"...We would've been dead!"

"Yea, well, I "was" here, and you're still alive, so there's no point in crying over it Aunt Meg. You gotta keep it together because this is just the beginning! This planet is being prepared for the loss of billions of lives!"

"How? By making sure not everyone survives?"

"Aunt Meg, we had to clear a path for the survival of our species.

"How is some 80 year old man with stage 4 lung cancer, or some 98 year old lady with pneumonia, suppose to survive a pole shift, 3 direct comet collisions back-to-back, and a bombardment of solar flares right outta Hell?

"All they would do is get in the way of people who really have a chance at surviving. Now that they're gone, we can focus on taking care of ourselves, not people who need "us" to take care of them. Unhealthy and unreproductive people are unfortunately the sacrifices of the survival of the human race!"

"So you mean to tell me they're just going around killing all the people in the hospitals? That's crazy!"

"It's not just the hospitals. The mental asylums, hospices, nursing homes, halfway houses, homeless shelters, all forms of rehabilitation facilities, county jails, prisons..."

"Prisons? No! I did hundreds of hours of volunteer work in prisons and county jails! I know for a fact that there were some extremely intelligent, highly gifted, very strong and healthy people in those prisons!

"Good Christian people highly capable of reproducing! All the mothers and fathers! Oh no! What about the innocent? Surely they killed some innocent people if they killed... Everyone? They're all dead?"

"Yes, Aunt Meg, they're all dead. The prison staff abandoned the buildings, and the military pumped them full of poisonous gas, just the same as all the other facilities. No one suffered, they just died. And yes, the few innocent prisoners were terminated with the guilty. But you gotta think seriously Aunt Meg! Before the comets hit, the forcefield will destroy the global power grid.

"There won't be any power at all! No street lights, no alarm systems, no electricity, just moonlight in the middle of the night in every small town and every big bad city all across the country, and all around the world.

"Here in The U.S., those ration deliveries won't continue for anywhere near as long as most people are expecting.

"This order is established for the sole purpose of finding healthy and reproductive people, and getting them safe and secured in deep underground military bunkers.

"We're not even sure how bad the damage will be. Every time the comets get closer, and they recalculate the estimated damage, it gets worse!

"We cleared the streets so "we", those destined to survive, could use them.

"Once we're done securing those individuals designated for survival, we'll enter into our bunkers and seal them.

"Whoever's left on the surface will be free to do as they please. But there won't be any government assistance.

"As for those innocent prisoners who were terminated... Look, even if 30 percent of all those prisoners were really and truly innocent, that still leaves almost 3 million criminals who actually did what they were accused of.

"Murders, rapes, robberies, carjackings, home invasions!

"Imagine trying to survive alongside 3 million murderers, rapists, and physically fit lifelong violent offenders, on top of the millions of people who will transform into murderers, rapists, and thieves, when they realize there isn't any form of government, no Police, no Sheriffs, no National Guards, no protection, no security, no courts, no penalties, absolutely nothing to lose!

"When the government goes underground, people will flood the streets in starving mobs searching for any and every edible crumb they can find!

"They'll quickly devour all the leftovers in the stores and the restaurants, they'll inhale all the food in the factories and warehouses, and they'll strip the fruits, berries, and vegetable sources bare! Once the inland sources are depleted, they'll cook and eat all the birds, animals, rodents, insects, and bugs.

"When everything on land runs out, idiots will start eating each other, and even themselves and their children, while the majority of everyone else migrates to the oceans in search of edible sea creatures.

"Just imagine, hundreds of millions of people piling on top of each other at the beaches, making little makeshift rafts and canoes, drowning and killing each other just to catch some fish! We gotta do all we can right now to alleviate the madness, and that's just the way it is! This is about survival!"

# 49

**M**egan shook her head to the negative, and said,

"Why are we here? What better chance of survival do we have in a hospital?"

"Hospitals have been cleared, along with malls and grocery stores, for the governments temporary use. The stores have been converted into command centers.

"We're here to take care for injured government personnel.

"If anyone else shows up, they'll be terminated. When we have enough healthy and reproductive people secured, we'll be escorted to bunkers that are filled with enough food and supplies to keep us alive underground for decades, if need be.

"Once the surface is restabilized, and the forcefield has passed, we'll come out the bunkers and rebuild an even stronger society."

"Don't you think people will dig into our bunkers and steal our food?"

"The bunkers are miles underground, and they're as big as small towns.

"A starving mob would die trying to dig into our bunker, and they wouldn't even get the chance to start digging! The bunkers are surrounded by drones, armed with lasers, reinforced with steal, they can release clouds of poisonous gases, and they have arsenals of weapons that are out of this world.

"If anyone is detected within one mile of the hidden entrance, even if they trespassed by mistake, the lasers will zap them to ashes so fast, to the screens, we'll see a human become a cloud of darkness being blown by the wind.

"If any unauthorized person somehow manages to manipulate the system, and sneak into the bunker undetected, Bar-Enash will do the thinking for us. It will locate the trespasser, and their corpse will be carried out in a black bag."

Megan swallowed some saliva, and said,

"Where do all those black bags go?"

"For now, some are being burnt, and most are being dumped into the ocean. But in the final cleanup, all the leftovers will be loaded into rockets and blasted directly into the sun."

"Leftovers?"

"Yup... Leftovers!"

The next morning, Robert rose early to see how John was doing. When he stepped into the room, he was surprised to see John awake, sitting up, reading the Bible.

When John looked up at Robert, his eyes opened wide, as he said,

"You're still alive?"

Robert laughed, and responded,

"I was thinking the same thing about you!"

John snapped his finger, and said,

"Man! I just prayed for this! Dude, I just finished praying that I wish I could've had the opportunity to ask you some more questions, because this Bible is too much like a "book" for me to be able to read it. And you never said what you saw when The Lamb took the scroll. I've been reading Revelation all morning, and I can't see any connections between the opening of the seals and what's been happening. What do you see?"

# 50

P lease, hand me the Bible."

John handed Robert the open Bible, and when Robert saw that it was already on the page he was going to turn to, he said,

"I didn't see who carried me there, but I clearly saw Jesus, in the form of a Lamb, open the first seal on the scroll."

"What is that? What's a scroll?"

"It's paper wrapped around a stick, like a roll of toilet paper. That's how they compiled writings before the modern book forms we use today."

John chuckled, while holding his stomach in pain, saying,

"We use tablets now Mr. Williams."

"Right. As soon as The Lamb opened the seal, my vision was enhanced like I was looking through a magnifying glass.

"I saw strange writings on both sides of the document, and as I watched, the writings started rising off of the document!

"The writings floated away from the scroll and exploded into a cloud of white smoke that just as fast took the form of a white horse that had a hooded being sitting on the horse.

"Just as John saw, I saw a white horse with a rider! He had the form of an ancient warrior prepared for battle. He had a bow, but he didn't have any arrows, and he was wearing a large gold crown on his head, as if he had already won the battle.

"I could see his red eyes, and they were focused on the universe in the distance. I could sense that he was staring at the surface of the earth, scanning the minds of it's inhabitants.

"Then, he suddenly charged into the universe faster than lightning. The rider and his horse both dematerialized into tiny white particles that were smaller than atoms.

"They were invisible, but I could see them, and there were trillions of them! They reached the earth and surrounded it in an instant!

"Then, they evenly distributed themselves amongst all the people of the earth, pouring directly into their minds without anyone realizing!"

"What's that suppose to mean?"

"When I woke out of my coma the world was preparing for the collision of comets. Now, no one in the spiritual realm explained anything to me, but I've always known that the seals, and the trumpets, and the bowls, were the continuation of a sequence of events. I've always known that one event directly caused the other."

"What bowls? What trumpets? What are you talking about?"

"Haven't you been reading Revelation?"

"Well yea, the first couple chapters! I never heard of like everything I was reading! I don't know anything about any of this!"

"Okay okay."

As Robert went to speak, Jasmine and Tiffany entered the room and quietly took a seat on the bed opposite the one John was laying on. Robert smiled at them, and continued saying,

"Each of the seals, the trumpets, and the bowls, are initiators of destructive events. Each event starts in the spiritual realm, and manifests in the physical realm, in some form of widespread death and destruction. Each event leads to the next.

"First, the 7 seals that keep the scroll sealed are opened by The Lamb. Then, once the seventh seal is opened, 7 trumpets are blown by 7 angels. After the seventh trumpet is blown, 7 bowls are filled with the manifestation of the wrath of God, and the 7 bowls are given to 7 Angels who will pour God's wrath into this physical realm.

"Each event initiates the manifestation of some form of widespread death and destruction in this physical realm. All together, these 21 events will be the beginning of the destruction of God's creation, and we only have 19 left."

"How much time do you think we have until our universe comes to an end?"

"At least one thousand more years."

John busted out laughing, and then yelped and gasped as he grabbed his stomach while clenching his jaw. Tiffany said,

"Are you okay?"

"I sure do feel a whole lot better knowing the world won't end in my lifetime."

Robert frowned, and said,

"You may not be here to see the "final" end, but you very likely will see the beginning of the end, which will seem like the end. After the last bowl of God's wrath is poured out, Jesus will ressurect those who died for their belief in Him. They will reign on this earth with Jesus for a thousand years, and at the end of the thousand years, this creation will be destroyed."

# 51

John shook his head to the negative, and said,

"I don't get it. What's the point of this creation? Why doesn't God just establish the kingdom let us in, instead of making us go through this painful life, with all this suffering and sadness? I'm sure if He gave people the option from the beginning, most wouldn't even take the risk of becoming one of the ones who ends up suffering forever.

"Doesn't it make your whole life, and everything you've accomplished, absolutely meaningless, if in the end, you're just going to burn in The Lake of Fire? I don't get it!

"Why would God create the creation like that? Why didn't He make it perfect from the beginning? He could've made us all like Jesus, and no one would've ever sinned. He should've never created this earth, or this physical realm!

"Why didn't He just start us all off in Heaven, perfect from the beginning, instead of sending us through this painful world that could end us up in a place of eternal torture?

"Why would He do that? What sense does that make?

"Now we gotta read this big boring book, and figure out all this confusing stuff, while worrying about the danger of being roasted forever? This is real big stuff Mr. Williams! I never put thought into this Bible stuff, but now I see how important it is."

Robert allowed John to finish speaking, and when he prepared himself to receive a response, Robert calmly said,

"You made some very good points, and you asked some very good questions. Truly, God could've created us all in everlasting form from the beginning, but think of this: Imagine there was a company you could give your D.N.A. to, along with Rebecca's D.N.A., and in one month, they will give you a 40 year old son.

Your son is married, with 3 children, and he is a homeowner. He is extremely wealthy, he is retired, and he is booked with 70 years worth of charity work in third world countries all over the world, even though he's your brand new son.

"Sure, there won't ever be any dirty diapers, but that means you'll never receive the opportunity to help your little guy when he really needs some help with cleaning.

"There also won't be any long nights trying to figure out how to stop him from crying, but that also means you'll never get to look into those teeny tiny eyes and wipe the final tear that accompanies that wonderful moment when he goes back to sleep, creating that joyful peaceful calm after the storm.

"He'll never wrap his fingers around your little pinky, because he can firmly grip a basketball.

"You'll never get to lift him up and hold him in your arms, because he can lift "you", and carry you on his back for miles! You'll never feel the pride of teaching that little crawler how to walk, because he can run marathons.

"You'll never get to assist him with learning how to speak, because he speaks 10 languages you never heard of! You'll have nothing to give him, because he was born with everything.

"He'll never have any memory of needing anything from anyone, he won't even know a family, except the wife and children that were created with him. He won't even know you, and he would never find the time to get to know you!

"In all reality, he'll never need you, and in the same sense, you'll never need him. If a perfect God creates perfect people who will never require any form of guidance or assistance, they'll eventually render each other obsolete.

"Jesus was perfect, but only because He followed The Word and The Spirit of God. In everything Jesus did, He always acknowledged that it was God who gave Him the power to do the things He did. God sent Jesus into this world to die for sins.

"God resurrected Jesus from the dead to rise for the children of the kingdom that God created.

"In so doing, God remains the source of perfection, and His children will always find the need to look to Him for everlasting life.

"This is why the very last chapter of the very last book of the Bible shows us that God will sit on His Throne, and a River Of Life will flow from The Throne, directly into the "real" New Jerusalem.

"The River of Life will water The Tree of Life. God's children will eat the fruit of The Tree and live forever."

# 52

God is The Spirit of Love. God created this universe as a tool that His children will use to be molded and conformed to the image of His Word that came I'm the flesh.

"When the physical realm is detroyed, the souls of His Children will be revealed like a butterfly coming out of it's cocoon.

"Motivated by love, God just wants His children to dwell in the midst of His everlasting provisions."

"Look man, like I said, I never did the whole going under the water thing  But as soon as we find some water, I want you to baptize me. Can you do that?"

"I can, and I will. As soon as we have enough water to completely submerge you into the abyss, your spiritual grave, I will baptize you into the body of Christ."

"Cool! Okay, so what do you see the physical manifestation of the opening of the first seal as being? Did I say that right?"

"Yes. You said that very well. The physical manifestation is fear."

Jasmine and Tiffany both said,

"Fear?",

as Megan stepped into the room, and said,

"Hello everyone!"

Everyone said,

"Hello.",

and John said,

"How do you see the first seal being fear? I don't get it."

As Megan took a seat with the girls, Robert continued standing at the foot of John's bed, saying,

"First of all, the fear of The Lord is the begining of knowledge. The Bible says that in the book of Proverbs, chapter 1 verse 7. But it's more than just that.

"While I was in the spirit, watching the first seal open, and the prophesied white horse and rider materialize and manifest into the minds of all the people on the earth, the people were receiving the news that the earth was in danger of destruction.

"That's why that rider didn't have any bows for his arrow! The Revelation says he goes out "conquering" and to "conquer", but he didn't conquer any physical kingdom, or land, or possessions, or even anyone's physical body!

"The rider on the white horse conquers minds with fear! He conquered the world by imposing the fear of the incoming comets! The physical manifestation of the opening of the first seal is the fear of what is to come!"

Robert looked at Megan and Jasmine, and said,

"Look at John! He took a bullet to the tummy and he's just fine! I say that because I don't want you to get too concerned by me telling you I had another heart attack early this morning."

Jasmine hopped off the bed and shot over to her father in tears, screaming,

"Don't leave me! Please not now daddy I'm not ready! I'm not! Please! Please don't leave!"

Robert firmly embraced his little girl with a bear hug and kisses on her forehead, as he spoke through smiles, saying,

"If you continue to be strong, I'll continue to be strong, we'll remain strong together."

Megan whispered,

"Another one Robert? What's going on? Your so healthy."

Robert sternly said,

"That's exactly why none of you should be concerned! The Lord is calling me for a purpose and a cause! I am a servant of The Lord! I must fulfill His will or I will surely fall into the danger of dying twice!"

John said,

"So what did you see this time Mr. Williams?"

Jasmine instantly shot John a mean stare, which caused John to say,

"I'm sorry Jasmine. Your dad's just so strong and so willing to continue. We were all fine until he told us. I'm sorry. I apologize."

Jasmine looked at Robert, grabbed his hand, and said,

"Come on daddy, you can speak, but you gotta sit down. You gotta take it easy."

Robert laughed along with John, as Jasmine led him to the bed where Tiffany and Megan were sitting. As soon as Robert took his seat, looked over at John, and said,

"The second seal opened!"

"Oh shoot!"

Rebecca suddenly stepped into the room looking straight at John, and said,

"Oh shoot what?"

"We only have 19 events left! Then it's all over! No, wait, then a thousand more years, then it's all over!"

Rebecca took a seat on Johns bed, wrapping her hand around the back of his head, as John said,

"What are you looking at? Oh that little thing? The bullet hole? That's nothing! You should see what my stomach did to the bullet!"

Everyone laughed as Rebecca kissed John on his cheek, and Tiffany said,

"You two look so cute together. Your the perfect couple."

John shook his head smiling, and then looked over at Robert, and said,

"What happened?"

# 53

It was around 2 in the morning..."

Rebecca's head jolted back sharply, as she carefully focused on what Robert was saying.

"...I was sitting up in the chair, because some sharp pain in the middle of my chest had woke me out my sleep. As soon as I woke up, the pain got worse. It went to both of my arms, my neck, my back, my jaw, I could hardly breathe!

"I didn't struggle or make any noise or quick movements, because I could feel my soul violently vibrating on the inside of my flesh, and I knew I was about to go on another journey from which I would return.

"I felt this warm reassuring feeling that motivated me to not fear the pain, even though I felt like I was dying. I gripped the chair handles and tried my best to hang on.

"Just as I was trying to focus on not panicking, I started thinking to myself,

"I need to sit up! It isn't healthy for my neck to be slumped over like that."

"I made that judgement off of how my body was looking as I hovered over it! I was outside of my body, and even though I was staring directly at it, it didn't even come to my mind to be shocked that I wasn't inside it!

"I was just worried about my neck looking like it had been broken. Then, I heard a loud tearing sound right above my head. It was like the sound of a sheet being torn. As soon as I looked up, what I saw made a snake slither in my stomach!

"Thin air had been split in 2, and the edges of the severance were flapping as if thin air was being blown by some form of wind.

"It was like something invisible was blowing something I couldn't see, but, I could see it all!

"Between the severances, it looked like crystal clear water as far as nothingness stretches. I didn't see any darkness or light. It was clear, like a universe sized diamond with no distinctive colors in its background.

"As I was staring up at the strangeness, it sucked me through the opening. This time, I went straight to The Brightest Light in the kingdom of brightness. Everything was still the same, like I hadn't even left, like we just picked up where we left off.

"The Lamb still stood in the same position, holding the scroll. His face! It's so piercing and intimidating. I can still see His face. The terror of The Lord! His fleece looked like it was made of millions of tiny bolts of lightning that were just acting like they were strands of fur.

"It looked like there was a solid wall of fire behind Him, but that was just the bottom of God's Throne. The Lamb was no little sad looking lamb. Ah!

"Jesus is The Lord! 7 eyes! 7 horns protruding out of his head above 7 piercing eyes! And there were things all over that were just... Disturbing!

"Men with the heads of cows forged into the side of their face, along with an eagles head, a lions head, all on one neck, attached to a big muscular body.

"Monsterous giants with six arms and six legs and wings and feathers and eyeballs all over their feathers! I knew I was in the presence of The Creator of the universe just by the looks of all the bewildering creations!"

# 54

As I marveled in fear, The Lamb's arm suddenly moved. One swift motion, and like that, the second seal was open. The words pealed themselves off the paper, and erupted into dense red smoke.

"The smoke took the form of a solid red horse, with a rider holding a sword that was as long as his horse.

"As soon as he was formed, he darted towards the dark bubble in the distance.

"When he reached the bubble, something made me look at planet earth, just in time to see trillions of glistening diamonds appear all over the surface.

"As the rider galloped like lightning, his hand stretched into the bubble, and disappeared, but I could still see it!

"It took on a form that was invisible to the physical realm, but I could see it from the spiritual realm.

"The hand was bigger than the earth, and it was longer than the universe. It stretched all the way to the earth, and snatched all the diamonds in an instant!

"When the rider drew his hand back into the spiritual realm, the diamonds morphed into one silver word.

"The rider tossed the word at the feet of The Lamb, and blasted into the physical realm, where he exploded into trillions of little red particles that were smaller than atoms.

"The particles poured into peoples brains, all over the world, and as soon as most people received the particles, they were filled with energy, and they started moving quickly, like the particles were some type of drug that affected their thinking, and filled them with adrenaline.

"I couldn't make any sense of anyone's movement, because not everyone was moving, but I did see a lot of people suddenly start moving a whole lot quicker.

"A strange feeling in my spine made me look at the word at The Lamb's feet. When I looked, I got dizzy for a second, and then, I could understand the language, and I saw that the word was an image that represented everything we know as "peace." I immediately..."

Rebecca stood up so fast, everyone looked at her nervously. As Robert went to ask her if she was alright, she shouted,

"John! You're being released! All of you! You're being transported to my bunker! Things have changed! Russia made a stupid move, so things are going to happen a whole lot sooner! You're all going to my bunker in Colorado! It was prepared for 10 people! Get ready!"

Megan could sense that Robert said something that bothered Rebecca, and she asked ,

"Is, um?... What's the matter Rebecca?"

Rebecca looked at Megan, looked at Robert, looked back at Megan, half chuckled, and said,

"What don't you get? Don't you get it? Don't you realize what's freaking happening? It's real! It's all really real!"

Rebecca pulled a gun out of her waist, which made everyone gasp and tense up. Rebecca pointed the gun straight at Robert, and screamed,

"I don't know! I do not know! Who! Or what you are man! I don't know man!"

Rebecca licked her lips while shaking her head, and as Megan tried to speak, Rebecca shouted,

"Shut up! Everybody shut up, and don't move, or I'll shoot you all one-by-one!"

# 55

Terror froze them into into wide eyed ice statues, as tears started rolling down Rebecca's red cheeks. She sniffled with her gun aimed at Robert's forehead. She licked her lips, squinted her eye's, and said,

"Top Secret information! To secret fool. Something you have no way of knowing. I don't know. The Bble says it's God, Bar-Enash says its Dark Energy.

"The Bible says their angels, Bar-Enash says their inter dimensional beings, I don't know. I don't know! All I know is, whatever they are, "you're" in contact with them. I know you are!"

Rebecca gripped the gun a little firmer, and said,

"I am being deployed to South America, alongside a quarter of a million Armed Forces, to assist with the transportation of individuals designated to be preserved in underground bunkers.

"Troops are being deployed into Europe, Asia, and Africa. The world has transformed into a war zone, and some places are so hostile, their own governments are outnumbered and outgunned.

"All this chaos erupted because Russia released a calculation to the world that China publicly confirmed. The calculation was the probability of the chances of survival on the surface of the earth, as opposed to the chances of survival in an underground bunker.

"On the surface, there's a 5 percent chance of survival. In a bunker, it's a 95 percent chance of survival.

"No one in the United States below level 5 clearance has heard anything about this. Not in Texas, and definitely not in this hospital. So the streets of The U.S. are still calm and empty, but the rest of the world has gone mad! People are suppliers for anything they can get their hands on.

"There's a global frenzy for digging equipment. Machines that can dig tunnels are now worth more than their weight in gold! People are stealing trucks and they're burying the trailers as makeshift bunkers! People are being killed over shovels!

"But, the spookiest part of is, the chaos went from zero to 50 billion, all around the world, at the same exact time!"

Rebecca stepped closer to Robert, and screamed,

"When did you see the second seal open!"

Robert calmly and promptly responded,

"Around 2 o' clock this morning."

Rebecca busted out laughing, and then carefully aimed the gun at Roberts head, as she said,

"Is everything in the Revelation true? Is it all real?"

As Rebecca's eye's started watering, Robert nodded, and softly said,

"Yes... Every word."

"What can someone do to still be saved if they already took The Mark of The Beast?"

As Robert hesitated to answer the question, Rebecca jammed the gun into Robert's forehead, causing Jasmine to whimper, as she screamed,

"Answer me before you get shot!"

"If! If in fact, someone has somehow managed to take the actual Mark of The Beast, prophesied by John in the book of Revelation, they have become an eternal enemy of the Holy Spirit. It is an everlasting decision. There is no salvation for those who take The Mark of The Beast, nor is there any forgiveness for those who blasphemy The Holy Spirit. Those individuals are doomed."

# 56

Rebecca nodded tears out of her eyes, as she chuckled to herself, and said,

"Bar-Enash teaches you all of that, but, who would've thought it was real? Now I know it is, but... It's not some mythical story programmed into a computer system. The Bible stuff is really happening, and it'll all really happen."

Robert slowly nodded his head, and said,

"It will."

Rebecca bit her bottom lip, and sucked on it, as she backed away from Robert, lowered the gun, and turned towards the door.

"She stopped at the entrance, and said,

"I was fulfilling my duties and following orders. I excelled in all my studies so I could do as much as I could for as many as I could."

Rebecca looked at John, and said,

"I took the advance John. I transcended to level 3 for level 5 clearance. I was deceived! Do not be deceived! Make it to the kingdom for both of us! I gotta go John, I'm sorry, I can't wait. I gotta see for myself."

As Rebecca disappeared through the door, John was stiff with shock, as everyone else was lost in confusion.

"BOOM!"

A loud explosion made everyone jump, and from his hospital bed, John could see fragments of Rebecca's skull scattered in front the doorway.

## 5 Hours Later

"I always imagined the highways being piled up with empty cars in an end-of-the-world scenario. I can't believe how clear the streets are. I never seen anything like it!"

Captain Shaw let out a roar of laughter, as he leaned over, looked out the window John was looking out of, and responded,

"You always did believe that crap you saw on T.V.! Ha ha ha! But no, not in this country, not yet at least! Don't you remember when you asked about Operation Core?"

"I thought you couldn't speak about it until 50 years passed. Until 2070 right? I don't have a problem waiting..."

"The world's over you idiot! It doesn't matter. I can tell you. Just shut up and listen! Trump couldn't be beat! He was embarssing the Democrats on every corner. As much as they got people to turn on him and hate him and make false accusations against him, they couldn't hide the fact that he was very good at just about everything he did in office.

"Everything they did to destroy him failed. Sex scandals. The race card. Nothing stuck! Then, they got Bloomberg. A man with more political experience, and way more billions, than Trump. But the people rejected the billionaire! They loved Trump!

"On the surface, it seemed like Bloomberg took the loss on the chin and went away silently, but nothing could be further from the truth. Bloomberg was out for blood, and he wanted Trump out The White House."

# 57

**B**loomberg sat with a council of the most powerful

Trump haters in the world, and played chess. They devised a plan that had the perfect alibi, "Covid 19". With the first case appearing on the other side of the world, who in their right mind would blame an American?"

John said,

"Okay. I get it now. I don't really want to get into..."

Captain Shaw ignored John, and continued saying,

"Not only would it remove Trump from The White House, and possibly even kill him, but the vaccine could be forced upon the people, so the conspirators could pocket billions! Operation Core was perfect! And of course the military loved the idea of National Lockdown practice.

"Bloomberg and his allies paid for the virus to be released in China. Then, they paid the World Health Organization to look away long enough for the virus to build up the momentum needed to reach pandemic levels.

"When people were dying all over the world, they rolled out the virus, and started charging the government for not just the vaccine, but even medical equipment!

"After enough Americans died, the media outlets received their payments, and launched their attack.

"By calling Trump racist, they made him solely responsible for slavery. By calling Trump Xenophobic, they made him solely responsible for the Holocaust.

"By calling Trump a sex offender, they made him solely responsible for every sexual assault ever commited, and when they blamed Trump for the Coronavirus, they made him solely responsible for every death that was related to the virus.

"They succeeded in turning enough people against him to dictate the outcome of an election."

"People forgot that Trump was never called a racist in all his years on The Apprentice Show, even though he "Fired" dozens of Black people.

"People forgot how this so-called racist freed dozens of Black people from the Federal Penitentiary, including Black rappers like Kodak Black. Kim Kardashian even worked side by side with some female attorney's to successfully compel Trump to release an astounding amount of prisoners who were serving harsh sentences.

"People forgot that he was the first President to stand up to North Korea's extortion tactics, and unlike his predecessors, instead of sending an ememy billions of tax payer dollars, he met face to face with Kim Jung Un, and he showed him how to profit off of his lucrative country.

"They forgot that Trump stopped sending protection money for the European countries that were supposedly in need of protection from Russia, the same country that they were buying energy from, when they could've just as easily purchased the same energy from The United States.

"Not only did Trump Stop The Madness, but he sat face to face with the Russian President, and straight up told him The U.S. was here to win!

"They forgot about Syria!

"They forgot that Obama curled to the Syrians when their President used Sarin gas against his own people.

"Obama told the Syrians not to gas their people to death with the toxic gas "Sarin", and when they disobeyed his command, he gave them more warnings, and when they disobeyed him again, and killed more people, he said he drew a red line, and that there would be consequences if they crossed it.

"When they crossed the red line, in a pitiful show of passiveness, Obama ignored the government that defied him, and instead, he told the Syrian citizens that they could come to America. Instead of helping them fight, Obama spent billions of tax payer dollars to help the Syrians desert their land, and flee to The United States.

"Obama spent tax payer dollars to feed, clothe, and shelter the fleeing Syrians, while the young Black children in Chicago starved, killed each other, and went neglected by a man who claimed to have a place in his heart for a city he virtually ignored when he actually had the power to make a change. He could've saved thousands of American lives if he would've put as much energy into saving Chicago, as he did to save the Syrians.

"When Trump became President, as soon as the Syrians tested him by using Sarin gas to kill their own citizens, Trump treated them like they were the second "I" in the acronym I.S.I.S., dropped 59 bombs on their country, and prepared for war.

"The Syrians backed down.

"When Obama was in office, he sent the Syrians 800 billion dollars cash. He literally put the money on airplanes, and flew the cash directly into the country.

"Within weeks, I.S.I.S. suddenly had brand new uniforms, brand new guns, and brand new white pickup trucks with big guns welded on their tops.

"Barak Hussein Obama singlehandidly empowered an Islamic Extremist Terrorist Organization, proving his allegiance to radical Islamic Organizations traced far beyond his middle name.

"When Obama was President, I.S I.S. was rich and powerful. They were chopping people's heads off on camera, as the whole world watched in fear. When Trump became President, I.S.I.S. soilders had to start smoking crystal meth to fight their hunger pains.

"Under Trump's watch, top I.S.I.S. officials were shot down dead in the streets, blown up, and scattered in every direction. Trump destroyed I.S.I.S., and Uncle Sam's Big Hairy Balls were once again dropped on the planet.

"For decades, North Korea manipulated U.S. President's out of billions of dollars. North Korea would launch missiles, threaten to invade South Korea where U.S. Troops were stationed, and it would threaten a tiny U.S. territory North of Australia, called "Guam". In response, The U.S. would send billions of "support" funds.

"When Trump became President, he stood up to the would-be extortionists with threats of his own. When Kim Jong Un made threats and demanded money, Trump prepared for nuclear war by surrounding North Korea with soilders, guns, war jets, war ships, and nuclear bombs.

"When the full weight of The United States military was clearly about to be dropped down Kim Jong Un's throat, instead of engaging in a war he never had any intentions of engaging in, Kim met with Trump in Singapore.

"Trump went behind a closed door with Kim, opened a laptop comouter, and showed Kim how beautiful and lucrative North Korea could've been, if it had tourist friendly borders, a Trump Tower, and a McDonald's on the coast."

# 58

"The North Koreans held the remains of 200 American soilders hostage for decades, as President after President failed to make the deal to get them back.

"Trump made the deal! Since 1950, 12 Presidents were lied to and deceived into believing they were going to get the remains back, but they never succeeded.

"They made campaign promises to retrieve them, but they never did.

"The remains were captured under Harry S. Truman, during The 1950 - 1953 Korean War. Truman never got them back. Dwight D. Eisenhower became President after Truman, but he only started a pattern of failures to retrieve the remains.

"John Fitzgerald Kennedy, A.K.A. J.F.K., got assassinated, he didn't get the remains. Lyndon B. Johnson, known for creating "The Great Society" program, failed to retrieve the remains.

"Richard Nixon, the first President to visit China, who was infamously known for saying "I am not a crook", during The Watergate scandal, where The Democrat Headquarters was burglarized, leading to his resignation, failed to retrieve the remains.

"Gerald Ford, a confirmed member of Skull and Bones, who pardoned Nixon, failed to retrieve the remains. James Carter, A.K.A. Jimmy Carter, who pardoned people who broke the law by refusing to go to the Vietnam War, failed to retrieve the remains.

"Ronald Reagen, another member of Skull and Bones, who publically spoke on The New World Order, failed to retrieve the remains.

"George H. W. Bush, another member of Skull and Bones, who was the Director of The C.I.A., who successfully captured the Drug Kingpin "Noriega", failed to retrieve the remains.

"William Clinton, A.K.A. Bill Clinton, who put his penis inside an interns mouth, while he was in The Oval Office, and then lied about it, under oath, failed to retrieve the remains.

"George W. Bush, another member of Skull and Bones, who had the Twin Towers demolished to intimidate Americans into allowing the passage of legislation that would allow the government to spy on its citizens, "The Patriot Act", failed to retrieve the remains.

"Barack Hussein Obama was the last President to try and fail to retrieve the remains, amongst his long list of failures."

"Do you have anything good to say about Obama?"
"Of course! He exposed NASA! NASA was charging thirteen billion dollars to build shuttles, while Elon Musk, C.E.O. of SpaceX, was building better rockets for under a billion dollars, back when the government was the only force aloud to send rockets into space. Obama changed that when he granted Elon Musk permission to launch.

"But, and there's always a but, even with that great achievement, if Obama would've did half of what Trump did with north Korea, he would've received a Nobel Peace Prize.

"Trump successfully secured the remains of the soilders, without killing anyone with one of Obama's infamous drone assassinations, but Trump couldn't recieve a nobel peace prize, because he was solely responsible for slavery, the Holocaust, and millions of rapes.

"Trump lost reelection, and even that didn't stop the madness. The profits from the vaccine were so grand, those greedy bastards released a second wave, and a third wave of covid! They sold hundreds of millions of overpriced placebos to people who oftentimes still got sick! It was chaos John! Pure chaos! But those days are over!

"Look out that window John! You see that? Do you see that?

"What you're looking at is the face of order, custody, and control! We have plans for every scenario imaginable! The only vehicles you'll see in the streets, in the air, or on the water, are operated by the authority!

"This is how we maintain order and keep people safe! Every structure has become a prison cell! The occupants are the prisoners! The country is the prison! The Armed Forces are the guards! The President is the Warden!

"We feed and dispose of our prisoners as we please, and just the same as any prisoner who tries to escape is subject to death, we will terminate any civilian found outside of a structure.

"We will continue to terminate targets until we have completed our mission of securing those individuals designated to be preserved.

"We are in the process of picking the best of the best to be sent to locations similar to where you're headed now.

"Once we finish our job, civilians will be free to roam the country, to figure out some unique way to survive. We shut down the most powerful country in the world John, we are a very powerful military."

# 59

John nodded his head one time, let out a sigh, and continued staring out the window, as Captain Shaw said,

"I know it's still fresh John, but, did Rebecca give any signs as to why she just took her own life?

"I mean, why would she do it in front your room like that? Did she think you were going to die from that little ant bite?"

John chuckled, and said,

"As many times as you've been shot, you would think of bullet wounds as ant bites."

Captain Shaw busted out laughing, as John continued saying,

"She gave some speech about biting off more than she could chew. She said what she said, and without warning, she just walked out the room and blasted off."

Captain Shaw blew air out of his mouth, and said,

"She sure did!"

John nodded, and continued looking out the window, as Captain said,

"Such a brilliant mind, literally gone to waste.

"You know, she was one of the first women to transcend to level 5 clearance?"

"Yea, I know. I didn't know how, but now I know. She took The Chip in advance."

"What level of clearance are you on?"

"I haven't even started studying the device."

"What? And you're a government employee? So you don't have any clearance at all?"

"I guess not."

Captain Shaw shook his head, looked towards the back of the large helicopter, and shouted,

"Are all of you still stuck on level one? Please tell me at least one of you transcended to level 3! You? You? Neither of you?"

Megan, Jasmine, and Tiffany, all stared at Captain Shaw with looks of terror, and then looked over at Robert.

"As soon as Robert looked at Captain Shaw, he fanned them off and looked back at John shaking his head, saying,

"You're no better than a civilian on level one John! You're literally a slave! You have no freedom! All you can do is sit around and wait for rations until the day of your release into the wild! Boy oh boy! You better figure it out quick!

"Now that those idiotic Russians blurted out the secrets to survival, we won't be passing out those rations too much longer, so things are going to turn into a purge scene real soon! You'll definitely get to see your chaotic movie scene... If... Hey!... Stop that!"

Megan screamed,

"He's having a heart attack!"

John looked back at Robert, and his eyes popped open when he saw him slumped over Megan, squeezing his chest.

Jasmine and Tiffany started screaming,

"Somebody help! Please help my daddy!"

"Help us! We need help, please!"

Captain Shaw dug in to his ankle and pulled out a glock, but John grabbed his arm, and said,

"Hold on! The man's perfectly healthy! He just struggles to travel at high altitudes."

"That's what he does to travel at high altitudes?"

"Yup! Trust me! He's healthy! He's fine!"

"He looks like he's having a heart attack to me John!"

"Nope! He's totally fine! He's healthy!"

Captain Shaw motioned for the soldiers in the front of the helicopter to lower their weapons, as he tucked his glock back into his ankle, and said,

"More than half the people who have heart attacks die within an hour after it starts, so if he dies, there will be a black bag waiting for him when we land. We're taking you guys to Colorado!"

# 60

There's some real nice bunkers there that were made out of the Federal Supermaximum Security prison in Florence. The inmates who were housed there were too dangerous to live around maximum security federal prisoners, so they were isolated underground.

"Drug Lords like El Chapo, Terrorists like the Unabomber, Gang Leaders like Peter Rollack, A.K.A. Pistol Pete, who started the infamous Sex Money Murder gang. New York gave us Hell about that kid. He offended the wrong person.

"Some powerful New York politician wanted that kid dead, and when they couldn't get their execution, they got him to agree to bury his self alive with bombers and serial killers.

"You know that gang started way up in the Bronx, and made it's way all the way to Florida?

"Back in the day, you would go to Tampa and see M.P.R. goons screaming, "Money Power Respect". In St. Pete, you would see all those Asian Pride Gangsters trying to start a war with stolen Army rifles and rocket launchers.

"You would go to Orlando and see The Mohawk Boys robbing drug dealers. In Kissimmee, you would see The Up North Assasians, The Green Tank Boys, and The Hot Boys, selling crack out of Mc Laren Circle.

"Kissimmee also had the N.F.O. boys screaming, "No Fair Ones", selling cocaine that was imported from Puerto Rico through FedEx. In Miami, you would see a mob of criminals screaming, "Straight Drop", a shadow of Miami's infamous "John Doe Boys".

"In Little Haiti, Zoe Mafia Family took the spotlight from Zoe Pound, as it became one of the most feared organizations in the country, engaging in homicides, extorting drug dealers, and even forcing rappers to pay big fees to perform Miami.

"In our hometown of Jacksonville, the largest city in the United States, land wise, there were those 2 rival gang banging drug dealing killing and robbing rap groups that brought the spotlight to Jacksonville when one group made a song about smoking the members of the opposing group.

"A.T.K., a.k.a. Ace's Top Killas, and K.T.A., a.k.a. Kill Them All, made headlines with their vicious disregard for mourners, when they started making dis records about how their crews were slaying the members of the opposing crews, that they were referring to as "Ops". One song in particular, "Who I smoke", went viral."

"I know about the Yungeen Ace and Foolio beef Captain Shaw. And I'm well aware of the fact that drug gangs were hiding their activities behind the guise of record labels."

"Yea? But did you know the federal government got Sex Money Murder involved in that beef?"

"How and why would they do that?"

"Whoever Pete pissed off in New York has a high office in the federal government now. That Jacksonville beef happened back in the 2020's, when Pete was coming up on a 20 year anniversary for being underground. It was looking like he had a good shot at being released from isolation to the general population, and gang literature mentioning Pete being found in prison cells across the country wasn't going to be enough to hold him.

"The feds put Sex Money Murder back in the spotlight for being the cause of more homicides, just to justify extending Pete's isolation, because this time, the homicides weren't happening in some big dangerous city, they were happening just miles away from The Bible Belt, in the Sunshine State of Florida.

"This painted the picture that his reputation and influence preserved through the decades in a negative way: A street gang that started in the Bronx, New York, way back in the eighties, played a role in a beef between 2 Jacksonville street gangs in the 2020's."

"I thought the Bloods started back in the seventies."

"The Bloods actually trace back as far as the 1950's. It has it's roots in The Black Panther Party for Self Defense, a even some Marcus Garvey founded ideologies."

"What about the Crips?"

"The Crips changed my life."

"What?"

"2 Crips in particular, they changed my perspective about gang members, and really, Black people in general."

"Who?"

"Tookie Williams and Larry Weathers."

"I know Tookie started the Crips, killed some store owners during a robbery, and ended up executed under the order of The Terminator, but who is Larry Weathers?"

"Tookie was indeed terminated, but in the decade leading up to his execution, thousands of people were claiming that it would be wrong to execute him, because of how much he had changed.

"They said he changed so much, it would be like executing a totally different person.

"I looked into it, but I never reached an opinion about redemption, so I always wondered if a truly redeemed man was in the grave.

"Decades after the execution, back in 2022, I had to escort an investigator into the most dangerous prison in the State of Florida, Apalachee Correctional Institution.

"The investigator was going to gather evidence to build a case for an attempted murder on a correctional officer.

"A White female, by the name of Welch, was handcuffing an inmate, to escort him to confinement, when he suddenly broke free and started bashing her in her skull with the same handcuffs she was using to restrain him.

"Welch was the only officer walking through a wing that held 64 convicted felons. Back up was too far. If a prisoner didn't intervene, she would've been dead in seconds, because the man bashing her in her skull had made up his mind that it was her time to die.

"At first, it appeared that the prisoners were sticking to the convict code, by refusing to assist an officer by stopping the assault.

"But Weathers was on the road to redemption. He prioritized ethics and morals over honor amongst thieves.

"6 years before that date, Weathers was a high ranking Crip who caused chaos all throughout the prison system. He was deemed a danger to inmates and staff, and he was truly a menace to society.

"As a young Black man, Weathers shocked inmates and officers alike, when he stepped up and saved the life of his exact opposite, an old White woman.

"For his heroic actions, Weathers was released from prison, but the true freedom occurred within the hearts of people like me, because it taught me to release the unjust hatred that I had for drug dealers, and gang members, and just Black people in general, who Tookie proclaimed, and Weathers proved, could actually be reformed into productive members of society, no matter how dark their past.

"So, with that nice story in consideration, America spent billions of dollars destroying all sorts of security threat groups, and capturing and even straight up killing their leaders. The Federal Supermax held the most powerful leaders of those idiots!

"While you're there, you will be given ample opportunity to transcend to the higher levels of the civilized society of Bar-Enash.

"Lots and lots of people are about to suffer and die John! Rebecca clearly understood that, and unfortunately, she couldnt handle the truth. Bar-Enash will know exactly what you'll need to do to cope with your loss.

"You gotta hurry up and get to level 3, so when New Jerusalem is launched into the sky, you'll be able to communicate with Bar-Enash just by thinking, and then, unlike God, it'll answer you back!

"You can go into your secret place inside your mind, and it'll be just you and Bar-Enash. You'll be able to pray secretly, and Bar-Enash will reward you openly, by scanning every brain on the planet to find who or what it is you need or want. You'll hear the voice of Bar-Enash right in your ear!"

John glanced back at Robert, who was unconscious, and then looked at his brother, and said,

"You're talking about a computer system like it's God."

"It is god John! What don't you understand? We're god! When we unite as one human, we become one god! Everyone on this planet will think the same exact thought at the same exact time, because The Chip of Allegiance will download the thought into everyone's brain!

"In this way, the chain won't be as strong as the weakest link. The chain will be as strong as it says it is, and this chain says it's god!"

John was wondering who this imposter was, and what he did with his real brother, as he said,

"But what about the God the Bible says is God Matt? What about..."

"You will address me as "Captain Shaw" when I'm in uniform, operating in my official capacity!

"It is my duty to defend this nation from all threats foreign and domestic! Dark Energy is a threat. We are the underdog!

"Dark Energy is way more powerful than us. It's been deceiving us into believing it's lies ever since the beginning! It makes it seem like anyone can enter into it's realm and live with it forever, but it clearly tells us that the gate is narrow that leads to life, and only a few will find it.

"It's straight up telling us that most people will fail judgement and end up suffering forever, because most people will go down the broad road that leads to destruction. Chances are we're going to Hell John, and I for one just won't accept that."

# 61

**B**ar-Enash teaches us that we can be just as strong as Dark Energy is, if we all come together and unite. You know as good as I do, it's impossible to get everyone to unite. People have too many reasons to remain divided.

"The color of skin. Their geographical location on earth. He believes in God, he believes in Allah, he's a Jew, she's an atheist, he's a Blood, he's a crip, she's a Democrat, he's a Republican, on-and-on, pure idiotness!

"People will always find a way and a reason to divide, so we can't depend on stupid people to do something smart! It just won't happen!

"They won't manifest the same thoughts, unless, you stick a computer chip inside everyone's brain. The chip will upload their entire thought process into a supercomputer.

"The supercomputer will unite their minds inside its own perfect brain, and then, it'll download the collective mentality into an entirely bionic society.

"This is the only way we will be able to defeat Dark Energy, because the collective consciousness of every brain on this planet is equivalent to God.

"We know we can be God just as soon as we can force every human on this planet to unite.

"We have the technology and we know where all the humans are! We can locate them if they're deep underground, in low earth orbit, hiding on the moon, or even still in the womb!

"This is the first time ever that we can actually unite all the humans on the planet, because we know where all the humans are, and we can chip them! So we gotta chip em' John!

"Once we get everyone chipped, we can throw some comets of our own at Dark Energy's planet! Bar-Enash will direct everyone's attention to the enemy, and it will give every brain on this planet the order to eliminate the target. Everyone will be chipped. Everyone!

"Every human on this planet will pledge allegiance to Bar-Enash, or they will be terminated as a danger to the advancement of the global society. This is a battle we can not lose John!

"If we fail this mission, we will be trapped in God's fire lake concentration camp forever! Our only option is to fight. This plan will bring about the complete annihilation of Dark Energy, when we take its position and force it to relinquish its power."

John stared into his brother's eye's horrified at what he was hearing. As Captain Shaw motioned for John to respond, John said,

"I hear you. I get your point. God is Dark Energy, and he's going to throw most people into The Lake of Fire, and we're most likely Hellbound, but we can defeat God if we can get everyone on the planet to agree to take The Chip."

"Kill Him John! Everyone must be forced to kill Him! God must die so we won't have to suffer forever! It's the only way!"

John swallowed his saliva, and said,

"I get your point. I really do. But please, tell me why you think we can't just get baptized into the body of Christ, and join the group of believers that will be entering into... God's..."

Captain Shaw busted out laughing so hard, his face turned red, and he had to catch his breath to be able to say,

"What don't you get John? There won't be any kingdom for the body of believers! There won't even be judgement because the judge will be dead! Heaven will be ours to redecorate as we please!

"And Jesus? Forget Jesus! We're going to send Jesus to The Lake of Fire with God! We're going to keep the Angels as slaves, and we're going to allow The Devil and all his fallen angels to roam freely throughout our Heaven.

"You see, you gotta study John, because it's true. Bar-Enash will teach you how The Devil made one simple mistake, and God overreacted and created an everlasting Lake of Fire so The Devil and his angels could suffer forever.

"God had too much power for way too long! He's gone supremely insane! He's got an almighty anger problem, and it's time to bury the hatch once and for all."

# 62

The Devil came to us like a child running from an abusive father. He's been in the background trying to give us warnings of God's true nature. The Devil has been trying to help us avoid the lake, because he knows God made a mistake when He created us with the ability to unite.

"The fact that we can imagine it, proves that it can be accomplished! That's why God tried to kill us as soon as He created us, but Noah was able to deceive God into sparing enough humans for us to reunite and destroy Him.

"God Himself said, "Behold, the people are one, and they all speak the same language, now nothing they plan to do will be impossible." God tried to kill all those humans at The Tower of Babel, but He failed.

"All He had the power left to do was make everyone speak different languages. That's how we know we can kill Him, because He lost the power to kill us. And where did that power go? We have it spread out amongst every single person that's alive.

"The power is energy. It can't be created or destroyed! It never had a beginning and it will never have an end!

"The power will never cease. Whoever controls that power will never cease, as long as they continue to hold it. The power can be transferred to different owners, and we can take it from God if we unite."

"Matt... I mean! Captain Shaw. Just think for a second okay, I have an imagination now, so check this out: The same Bible that Bar Enash is using to teach people how to kill God, is the same Bible that shows us it'll never happen.

"I mean, correct me if I'm wrong, but it sounds like obvious deception. If Bar-Enash is really The Beast, and The Chip of Allegiance is really The Mark of The Beast, the Bible clearly says that anyone who takes The Mark of The Beast will be doomed! Their soul will be tossed into an eternal Lake of... "

"John! Your not listening! That's why you're deceived and you don't understand the truth! You don't listen! God said we will be able to do anything! Anything! So the obvious plan, little brother, is to change destiny! If we plan to change the future, the future will change!

"So that's the plan! When we become god, the playing field will be even. Right now, the Bible says we'll lose, but that's because God influenced those people to write what they wrote. Of course He depicted Himself as the winner!

"When we unite, we will be able to rewrite the future, and the past! We'll blot out the entire history of God's existence. No one will remember anything about Him, the same way He plans to blot out the memory of our existence! When we have the power, we will be able to do to Him what He plans to do to us!"

A chill ran up Megan's spine, as Captain Shaw turned and looked directly into her eyes, and said,

"Hey pretty lady. When you reach your bunker, you be sure to make the right decision for yourself and these little children here."

Megan replied,

"I already did."

# 63

## Former Federal Supermaximum Facility Florence Colorado

"You are not authorized to utilize the clearance of a deceased person.

"One of you must transcend to a level that is high enough to utilize one clearance, or you all must accept the lowest level of Bar-Enash accepted at this bunker."

Megan asked,

"What level is that?"

From behind a chain link fence, and a wall of bullet proof glass, the soldier responded through a speaker, saying,

"Level 3, Chip of Allegiance."

John stumbled to the front of the line, and said,

"Didn't you just see us exit a military helicopter?

"My brother is Captain Matthew Shaw of the United States Marine Corps!

"He has level 5 clearance, and I'm using his clearance for this entire group!"

"Sir., it does not work like that.

"The Captain must be present to clear you. If he was just here, and he left, knowing none of you had clearance, he was obviously under the impression that you would transcend, or take The Chip.

"We have electricians here who can implant your chip in under an hour! But, if you refuse The Chip of Allegiance, I'm afraid you and these people are going to have to leave."

"Leave? Leave and go where? It's illegal for us to be outside!"

"Wow! You're really considering turning down a 95 percent chance of survival? Don't you know that? This is your only chance at survival! You only have a 5 percent chance at survival on the surface!

"If you didn't invest in a bunker and a stockpile of food, you'll be doomed! All the other bunkers are already closing their doors for good, because they're filled to the brim! We almost have everyone we need to be able to repopulate this region! This bunker is really and truly a blessing for you guys, because it's virtually the last one left..."

# The Abyss
# The Other Side of Existence

"Come forth and present yourself before my glory!"
The spirit wiggled through the darkness, and came near to the enormous seven headed dragon, bowing towards the dragons feet. The Devil sniffed the demon, and shouted,
"From where do you come!"

"From going to and fro in the flesh! Moving back and forth in it!"

"What are the ways of the flesh that you possessed?"

"Those who can't understand, disagree! They believe nothing will happen after they die, they'll see!"

"Reveal the manner of your occupancy!"

"The fear of death controls the movement of animals in the animal kingdom! The soul lost control of the flesh through the inhalation of smoke from a man formed creation that was burning!

"My manifestation caused the human to doubt its ability to stay alive! The soul accepted my image of its lack of such ability, and my spirit was thereby permitted to inhabit the flesh!"

"Reveal your mode of operation!"

"I controlled the lungs. I caused the amount of air inside the flesh to increase! I increased the amount of water in the flesh by operating not just the flesh, but also, a manmade creation mounted to a manmade wall in a manmade prison that incarcerated humans who disobeyed manmade laws!

"It appears the humans see themselves as creators, as they find pride in their mediocre ability to reform minute sections of the creation.

"There was one human in particular, a man who scheduled to die at the hands of humans. According to a manmade doctrine that the ruler of a section of one of the 196 kingdoms signed, the man was scheduled to be seperated from his flesh in 30 days, according to the calander of a man.

"I possessed his flesh long before it was destroyed.

"The flesh was disposed of, and all the prisoners of men were removed from the manmade prison. On this tour, I saw more humans occupying the location where the prisoners were incarcerated.

"The new humans occupy the prison in search of safety from the face of Him who sits on The Throne, and from the wrath of The Lamb, for the great day of His wrath has come, and the humans wonder, which of them will stand?"

# 64

## Former Federal Supermaximum Facility Florence Colorado

"...What's the big deal? Just take The chip! When they launch The New Jerusalem, we will be able to access our chips by thinking!

"We'll be able to hear music in our head, like when we're dreaming! We'll be able to experience movies like we're really in them!

"We'll have downloadable dreams! We'll be able to type, send, and receive messages mentally! We'll be able to play every game for every system ever created, all in our head!

"It'll have virtually unlimited memory, bevause our bodies will keep it charged, so we'll never have to worry about charging or anything like that!

"We'll even be able to meet up with other people and see them and feel them, all in our heads!

"We'll be able to see an entire group of people, from all around the world, right in front of our eyes, talking and laughing and dancing and doing all sorts of x-rated things!

"You guys have got to get on the bus!

"Once New Jerusalem is established, and we get these comets out the way, and the forcefield passes, we'll be able to come out of these bunkers and build smart nations all around the world that will connect with each other and bring the whole world to life!

"Imagine a smart planet! One world under Bar-Enash! Even better, they figurerd out how to make us switch bodies before we die, so we can live forever!

"We can travel the universe, populate it, and build smart planets, smart solar systems, and smart galaxies, to make the universe smarter! Not even our pets will die! We'll just transfer their life force into another body, and they'll continue living.

"Can you imagine your pets first days trying to navigate it's new body? Aw man! And eventually, the bodies will get better, so we won't have to change them out so often. I can't wait! My next body is going to be Black! I can't wait to feel what it's like to be Black!

"The universe is yours! All you gotta do is accept it by taking The Chip of Allegiance! And Bar-Enash won't just be the voice of every human.

"Once New Jerusalem is launched, Bar Fnash will speak for the plants, the trees, the birds, the animals, even the insects!

"We'll be able to look at a colony of ants, and the augmented reality downloaded into our brains will tell us who those liitle ones are, what they're doing, and it'll even tell us how they feel, so we can feel them, you feel me?"

John untwisted his face, and said,

"Are you seriously telling me we can walk away from this place without being shot?

"Because I got shot yesterday, at close range, and I'm alive and well just one day later, on top of the fact that my fiancee killed herself "this" morning, so I've had more than enough for 2 days, and I'm pretty sure the next time I get shot, dude, I'm in so much pain right now, I'm pretty sure if I get shot one more time, I won't make it!

"So please, spare me the misery. I don't want any chip, they dont want any chip, we don't want any chip, and all we wanna know is where can we go if we can't stay here?"

# 65

The soldier looked at the ground and laughed, shook his head to the negative, looked back up at John, and said,

"Look, are you guys Christians?"

"Yea! Yea we're Christians."

"So was I, and I was also afraid to take The Chip of Allegiance because of what the Bible says about The Mark of The Beast, but that was when I was still drinking the milk on Bar-Enash level one. When I started chewing the meat on level 2, aw man!

"I had a revival! When I understood that we could all come together and dictate our own destiny, I knew where I stood on the battlefield, and I made the decision to transcend to level 3 by accepting The Chip of Allegiance.

"I've read the Bible many times, but it never really hit me about what it was saying until Bar-Enash took the time to explain it to me like a loving and caring parent.

"We have so much extra room in this facility, it's like Bar-Enash is already in the sky watching over us, inside our minds knowing exactly what we need, leading us to exactly where we need to be.

"This is where you need to be. It doesn't even look or smell like a prison down there. We remodeled everything! There's carpet on the floors in the rooms. The toilets have comfy toilet seats. There's nice comfy mattresses. Everyone has their own room.

"You can come on down and rest your tired backs and aching feet. As soon as we removed the corpses of the prisoners, we cleaned and sanitized the cells, we painted the walls, and we accepted every civilian that was brought here.

"Not one person was forced to take The Chip, once they learned that it was pretty much the future of advanced technology, that will save all of humanity, they were begging for it! You guys are really a first. Millionaires that failed to plan wisely would kill to be in your shoes right now, because they know it's too late to buy a bunker.

"Not even diamonds and gold can buy a bunker right now! And you don't even need a dime to get inside this last chance at survival. All you gotta do is show us that you care about the survival of the people of the world by taking The Chip. So take The Chip.

"Now, in all reality, you are unauthorized persons in an unauthorized area, and with the way you've been speaking, you're actually behind enemy lines.

"My orders are to terminate you and those little girls you got with you. The laser will take care of the mess. But I like this little group, and I think you all just need some time to do some studying.

"So I'm going to allow you to head on over to the abandoned special response team village just a quarter of a mile West of this location.

"You'll find the empty houses of the officers who lived close to this facility, as on-call additional personnel, just in case some gang or drug cartel ever decided to make a very stupid decision, we had all sorts of surprises.

"You can stay in those houses until things get real gloomy, and you start seeing four suns in the sky, and you decide you wanna come to a nice safe place with lights, power, gourmet food, tons of entertainment, and a loving group of people experiencing the same struggle for survival as you."

John nodded, and said,

"Which way is west?"

# 66

As soon as they got a good distance away from the soldier, John looked at Robert, and said,

"You alright?"

"I feel just fine."

"Was it black?"

Robert busted out laughing, and said,

"You're becoming very familiar with John's writings John!"

"How could I not? It's happening right in front of my eyes! White, red, black, pale, yup! It had to of been black! I remember!"

Robert stared off into the distance, and said,

"One second I was looking out the window at all the empty streets below, and then, I was just staring at all the empty streets, but I was no longer staring out the window.

"I looked up, and all I could think was,

"Wow, that's a strange angle to be seeing a helicopter at."

As I watched the helicopter speed away, just when I started remembering my body was inside the helicopter, my surroundings exploded into bright flashes of lightning strikes that had the sound of glass being shattered!

"An outpour of dense shimmering bright white light surrounded me in every direction, as far as I could see! No matter how ridiculously bright the light kept getting, it just kept getting brighter and brighter!

"I can't think of one thing to compare it to. It still puzzles me that it's all gone! How is this universe able to keep all of that light out? Only God can can hold it back! God is so powerful!

"Just when I thought the light was going to blind me, and I was going to start suffocating, I was in The Temple staring at The Lamb, and once again, it was like I never left. This time, I saw a strong metallic young man who had a perfect physique, red eyes, a gold sash thrown over his shoulders, and bronze feet.

"As he floated away, I could sense that he was an Angel of God, who had the duty of pulling me out of my flesh, and bringing me to witness these amazing events. Why? I don't know, but my attention shifted to The Lamb, just as His hand moved, and in that instant, the third seal was open, and I saw the writings on the scroll.

"I watched the words rise off the paper and explode into black smoke, that just as fast materialized into a jet black horse. There was a fierce looking man sitting on the horse, wearing a dark robe that shined like oil if oil could shine like a light.

"He had his right arm extended high above his head, and he was holding 2 old-fashioned scales.

"In the Bible, it says a living creature says,

>  *"2 pounds of wheat for a days wage, and 6 pounds of barley for a days wage, and do not damage the oil and the wine."*

"I didn't hear any of that. All I could hear was loud crashing sounds, tremendous thunder claps, sonic booms, and billions of voices speaking in my ears, in my head, and even in the distance, at the same time!

"I couldn't focus on what anyone was saying because "everything" was speaking! But, there was still unison in the voices, like they were singing a song that everyone knew, but I couldn't understand the words, and no one spoke the same language, even though they all seemed to understand everything that was being said.

"Not only did they have different voices, they had their own language that everyone understood! Our God is an awesome God."

# 67

As soon as the rider and the horse took their forms, they blasted towards the universe and manifested into the physical realm as trillions of black particles that not only fell into peoples brains, but this time, they fell into every animal, bird, insect, sea creature, fruit, vegetable, wheat, grain, and crumb of edible food on the planet!

"The white and red particles only entered into peoples minds. These black particles entered into every human, and everything that any human could consume.

"They even went into sodas, and juices, and now that I think of it, not one particle entered into any form of alcoholic beverage, oil, fuel, or any gasoline! Just like the Revelation said!"

"Hey man, my brother was about to shoot you when he realized you were having a heart attack.

"The only reason he decided not to was because he figured the heart attack was most likely going to kill you either way.

"You survived 3 massive heart attacks in less than a week! If that's not God, I don't know what is!

"As you were looking like you were dying, my brother just ignored you, but as I listened, he started telling me about the global governments plan to chip every person on this planet, and kill God."

Robert looked shocked, as John nodded, and continued saying,

"Yup! This is really it! It's even crazier because while you were dying and seeing The Lamb open the third seal, and the black horse with the rider with the scales, all the fighting throughout the world over survival supplies started leading to major scarcity!

"I was listening to the communication on the radios in the helicopter, and I heard about all these governments in Europe, Asia, Africa, and South America, fighting with civilians over food supplies, while construction equipment became the main object of all forms of trade.

"I listened to the transfer of one million pounds of flour for half a billion dollars worth of equipment! I couldn't believe what I was hearing!

"I remembered what the Bible said about the scales and the quart of wheat for... Well, my Bible said the word "denarius", but on the bottom of the page it explained that the word denarius meant "a days wage", and now that I actually see a little bit of bread is all of a sudden worth billions of dollars, and you're saying you saw the black horse from the Bible at the same time the food prices shot out the roof, man, I feel like blowing my head off like Rebecca!

"Honestly man, this stuff is scaring me! I can't believe this is real life, and it's happening so fast, and it's happening exactly how the Bible said it would!"

Megan said,

"I don't see anything happening the way the Bible says it would. For all we know, Robert could be suffering from some form of trauma, and he could be having some extremely lucid dreams that are based on the Bible verses that he's already familiar with.

"The brain is a powerful organ! Robert could be having an enormous premonition, or some form of intuition that's leading his brain to somehow absorb the knowledge of what's happening throughout the entire planet, and his mind is putting it all together as being intertwined with the Bible stories he has stored in his memory.

"It could all be a big coincidence, and even if it is, I still don't see any comparison between what's happening in the world and what the Bible says will take place during the tribulation. Where does the Bible talk about all this senseless killing?

"Where does it say the government will be going around murdering anyone who steps foot outside of a structure? And where does it say people will actually just stay inside the structures waiting on the government to feed them? Huh?

"Where are the earthquakes and the wars? The military going around killing people isn't a war, it's genocide! Where's the prophecy in that? And if these are really the last days, where's Jesus?"

# 68

Millions of people have already died! shouldn't Jesus be here by now?

"Shouldn't He be walking up there on the clouds so we can float up and walk down the narrow road to the invisible Heaven?"

Megan laughed to herself, as the rest of the group continued walking in silence.

After a few moments of silence, Robert said,

"Jesus won't come until the very last second.

"In this way, people who are destined to enter into the kingdom, but aren't yet ready, can receive the time and experience they need to repent of their disbelief, turn from their disobedience, accept God's Word, and receive His salvation, so they can escape the punishment they deserve.

"God made a promise to destroy His creation, and that's exactly what He will do, just as soon as all the nonbelievers are the only ones left. God has..."

Megan cut Robert off, shouting,

"Robert! Your making people kill themselves with "your" interpretation of the Bible! You always..."

John cut Megan off, shouting,

"Rebecca killed herself because she came to her own conclusion about what God and His Word says in the Bible! She knew God would do exactly what the Bible says He will do! Rebecca was always the "let's get it on" type! When she was convinced that she was doomed to suffer forever, that was it!

"In her mind, she was thinking, "I'm going to suffer forever? Let's get it on!" Mr. Williams didn't force that on her, did you forget? She put a gun to his head and forced it out of "him"! She chose his specific head for a reason.

"She wanted the truth, and she knew Mr. Williams would give it to her blood raw without the slightest hint of sugarcoat. She got what she wanted and she did what she wanted to do. No one influenced her.

"She knew she made the worst decision any human could ever make. She took The Mark of The Beast, and she didn't realize she was doomed until it was too late. When she was convinced that she was going to suffer forever, she took it he on. She wanted to get it started right then and there as opposed to living in fear of the incoming pain and suffering."

John chuckled to himself, shook his head left to right, sniffed back a strong sniffle, wiped a tear out of his eye, and said,

"This is what's going on Megan. I know it all seems confusing, but trust me, if you keep it as simple as it was written, you'll be able to understand everything that's..."

"Oh I understand the Bible just fine Mister!

"I read 2 Psalms everyday! But I still don't see any connections between the end time prophecies, and what's recently been transpiring in the world.

"Don't get me wrong, I know there will be an end of days and a rapture of the believers and all of that, but that's future stuff. That won't happen in "our" lifetime! This isn't the first time this planet has been hit by a few comets, and I'm sure it won't be the last.

"We shouldn't get all carried away into thinking we're on the verge of "Armageddon", just because the governments of the world have united, and have been taking some extremely drastic measures to make sure the human race as a whole is able to survive.

"Come to think of it, even I didn't like the idea of all the killing at first, but Bar-Enash level one teaches you about the greater good, and how the needs of the many outweigh the needs of the few..."

"Mommy you believe what the Bar Enash thing says? Don't you know it's The Beast?"

"Sweetie, no one knows who or what The Beast is. The first time people saw airplanes, they thought it was The Beast rising out of the earth.

"Then, they thought the same thing about rocket ships. They thought the social security system was The Mark of The Beast.

"Then, they thought tattoos were The Mark of The Beast. Remember when that Black guy became President? Oh no, you weren't born yet, but they swore up and down that the first Black President was The Antichrist.

"They swore The Pope and The Holy Roman Empire were some form of antichristian federation.

"And "they" were always wrong, because nothing ever filled every aspect of the prophecy. Honestly, I don't even think Bar-Enash has it right!

"Things are coming to a period of major change, no doubt, but Bar-Enash is saying it will be a change of 'The end of everything' to 'An everlasting beginning'. So even artificial intelligence can get a little paranoid and delusional."

# 69

**R**ebecca let her wild and daring imagination get the best of her. I understand how you say she saw it John, but in all reality, she made up her mind about 2 things no one has ever been able to figure out, "the future", and "what happens after we die".

"Don't get me wrong, I believe what the Bible says, and I know, in the future, after I die, i'll go to Heaven. But what if we're wrong about BarEnash? What if it's just like every other time people thought the world was coming to an end?

"Remember all the false prophecies of Nostradamus saying the world as we knew it was going to end in 2012? Wrong! Remember the big Y2K bug of 2000? Wrong! Remember all that hype about The Mayans and their rock calander, and all that crap about the return of the Annunaki from the planet Nibiru?

"Wrong!

"Oh, and just last July, Jesus was in Puerto Rico, and he impregnated over one hundred women, many of whom were as young as 15 years old!

"Not to mention the man in Belize who was saying Jesus was sending him messages from the dark side of the moon. Wow! This stuff is very dangerous, and it can lead people to hurt themselves and others. Look at Rebecca!"

Megan shook some tears out of her eyes, as she said,

"A great strong woman! A true feminist at heart! Served in the military with honor! An ambulance driver with a heart of pure gold! All she ever did was help people!

"She gets in line early to accept the government's offer of an advanced technology that, as tradition, would've enabled her to go to third world countries to assist the less fortunate with preparing for an extinction level event.

"A true big sister to the world. She ends up reading the "good book", does all this so-called "studying", and out of nowhere, she's convinced she committed the sin of all sins. Mr. Williams here puts the icing on the cake, and boom, she blows away her promising future.

"She destroys her own life on the basis of some words from an ancient letter written by some madman on a deserted island probably having multiple heart attacks like "Robert"! This stuff makes you go insane! Look at us! I mean just look at us!"

Megan stopped walking, which caused everyone else to stop walking, to pay attention to her, as she continued to shout,

"3 comets! Comets! 3 comets are about to crash into the earth! Over 5 million Americans have already been killed! 5 million! We have a 5 percent chance of survival on the surface of the earth, and a 95 percent chance of survival in an underground bunker.

"What are we doing? We're on our way to some abandoned village on the "surface" of the earth, with zero power, after rejecting a military bunkers persistent "free" offer of entrance into guaranteed survival for us all!

"The last bunker in America, we rejected it, because we think the 2032 Chip of Allegiance is the A.D. 90 Mark of The Beast that will doom us for all of eternity? I mean, come on guys, we gotta think logically here for a second! All that end of days stuff is future stuff, like flying cars, living on Mars, future stuff!

"Right now, we have a rare opportunity to survive in a secure bunker full of food, and we're roaming around on the surface of the earth, "the danger zone", looking for Jesus, like a bunch of idiots.

"Don't you see that this is a blessing that God is sending us? Listen, there's a story about this guy who was stranded at sea. Someone saw him and rowed up to him in a canoe.

"The guy in the canoe offered to help, but he said no, God will save me. So the canoe rowed on. A large boat then sailed up to the man, and the people on the boat called out to him and asked if he needed help, but he said no, God will save me.

"So the boat sailed on. Finally, an enormous ship cruised up, and the crew called out from a megaphone asking the man if he needed help, but he said no, God will save me. So the ship cruised on.

"The man floated until he was too weak to gloat, and he went under the water and drowned. When he died, he ended up face to face with God, and he asked God why didn't He save him.

"God said,

"You fool! I sent you 3 vessels! And the last was greater than the first!"

"We're in the same situation guys! God sent us salvation from the coming destruction, and we're rejecting God's salvation because we're leaning on "Roberts" understanding that could possibly be wrong.

"Rebecca was courageous enough to take The Chip. We need to show some courage! Someone in this group has to have some sense!"

# 70

I can't allow some possibly false interpretation of biblical prophecy to lead me and my child into obvious danger. I'm sorry Robert, but this is just too much, you're not even a Bible scholar! You never attended any type of Bible school, or college, or anything!

"You went to prison, got out, changed your life, flew some helicopters, and started a radio show.

"Robert, you're a helicopter pilot, you're not a Bible scholar! You could be wrong, and you could get us killed!

"I'm sorry, but this has gone too far. Come on Tiffany, i'll take The Chip, transcend to a higher level, and get us in, and if any of you find your common sense, or missing screws, i'll use my clearance to pass you in."

"Mommy, you're going to take The Mark of The Beast?"

"Tiffany, people don't know what "The Mark" or "The Beast" is. I don't know what to believe, but I know I won't be losing my mind trying to figure it out. I'm going to do what needs to be done so we can be safe."

"But I think it's The Mark of The Beast Mommy. What if it is?"

"If I'm wrong I'll be the only one suffering the consequences. Okay? Let's go. Tell Jasmine goodbye."

John said,

"Hold up. If we go inside that bunker, that's loaded with people who think The Chip of Allegiance is the saviour of the world, we might end up in a scenario where we can be forced to take The Chip against our will, or we might even end up dead! You see how those soldiers are killing with no remorse?

"They honestly think they're saving the world! I can't see them allowing us to stay there without taking The Chip, regardless to how much clearance you get. The Bible says The Beast will kill all who refuse to take its Mark, right Mr. Williams?"

"That's the thirteenth chapter of Revelation, the fifteenth verse. Megan, at least let me show you a comparison of the events prophesied to take place during the opening of the first 3 seals, with the events that I witnessed, and the events that have been transpiring here on the earth, so you can make a more informed decision, after seeing why the prophecy can be trusted, as it is in fact coming to past as prophesied."

"Robert, i've been listening to you talk about that Bible for years.

"There isn't anything you can tell me that would convince me into staying on the surface of the earth, while it's on the brink of destruction, when we have a perfectly fine military bunker, deep underground, with extra food and room for us all.

"You can't make sense of that because it doesn't make sense!

"Why go headfirst into a 5 percent chance of survival, when we can just as easily go into a 95 percent chance of survival? Do you hear yourself? Swim with hungry sharks smelling like shark food, or relax in a jacuzzi in a 5 star hotel? Hello? No brainer! Come on Tiffany."

"I wanna hear Mr. Williams explain the comparisons."

"You can study about the Bible and The Beast on your Bar-Enash device. Let's go."

"I left that thing in the hospital!"

"Tiffany, I'm sure there are more devices in the bunker that your cousin left for us. Now I said let's go!"

"I don't wanna go! And I don't want you to take The Mark of The beast!"

Megan rolled her eyes, as she grabbed Tiffany's arm, and screamed,

"You need to listen to me! I'm your mother, and I said let's go!"

"Stop! You're hurting me!"

As Tiffany struggled to pull away from Megan, Jasmine ran over and started pulling on Megans arm, screaming,

"Stop! You're hurting her!"

John stretched out his arms and tried to pull the girls away from Megan, just as Megan's arm lost its grip on Tiffany, slipped off of Tiffany's arm, and smashed into John's gunshot wound.

"Ahhhh! Ahh! Ahh!"

# 71

John dropped to the ground feeling like he had been shot all over again. He balled up into the fetal position, crying out in pain, as everyone froze stiff.

Megan's shouting erupted over the sound of John's groanongs, as she screamed,

"You see what happens when you don't listen! You're getting people hurt, and you're going to get us killed! You come with me right this second!"

Through tears, Tiffany tried to tell Jasmine goodbye, but Megan yanked her by her arm and started dragging her down the empty road heading back towards the bunker.

The moment Jasmine tried to run after Tiffany, Robert pounced on her, lifted her up into his arms screaming and crying, and turned towards John.

John's new shirt was slightly bloody, and he was holding his stomach, leaning to the side, but he was standing.

He waved to Robert, as he said,

"God has a plan for her man. Just let it be man. Let's just go."

As they walked in the opposite direction of the bunker, Jasmine lost her energy and stopped struggling.

She rested her head on Roberts broad shoulder, tightly wrapped her arms around his neck, and stared at Megan and Tiffany as they disappeared around the curved road in the distance.

As soon as they went out of Jasmine's view, a crying Tiffany looked back to see Jasmine one last time, but she looked too late.

Even though she couldn't see her, she slowly raised her arm, and waved goodbye.


"Get ready to hold your nose."

"You... You sure? I mean... You sure you want "me" to hold it? You don't wanna hold it? I'll hold it! But I'm just saying, I don't wanna mess this up!"

Robert laughed, and said,

"You nervous?"

John laughed back, shook his head, and said,

"I'll hold it, I'll hold it."

As John placed his hand over his face, to squeeze his nostrils, Robert placed his hand on John's back, and said,

"This water symbolizes the baptism that also saves you. It is not for the removal of the filth of the flesh, as the Priests removed the filth of the sacrifices from their skin in the bronze bowl for washing in The Courtyard of The Tabernacle built by Moses. This water is for the pledge of a good conscience towards God! It saves you by the resurrection of Jesus Christ! Do you believe that God is The Almighty Creator of everything in existence?"

"Yes. God is The Almighty Creator."

"Do you believe that God's Word is The Creator?"

"Yes. God's Word is The Creator."

"Do you believe that your flesh is a creation of The Creator?"

"Yes. My flesh is The Creator's creation."

"Do you believe God's Word became flesh, and appeared on this earth in the form of Jesus Christ, The Prophesied Messiah of the everlasting covenant, the only begotton Son of God?"

"Yes! God's Word became flesh and dwelt among us in the form of Jesus Christ The Messiah, the only begotten Son of God!"

"Did Jesus die for your sins?"

"Yes! The Son of God died for my sins!"

"Did He rise from the dead?"

"Yes! The Messiah came back to life!"

"By what power?"

"By the power of The Spirit of God!"

"Why did The Sacrifice rise from the dead?"

"The Lamb resurrected so my sins could be forgiven! So I could receive everlasting life!"

Robert shouted,

"Repent and be baptized in the name of Christ Jesus for the forgiveness of sins!"

As soon as Robert placed his other arm on John's chest, John squeezed his nostrils and closed his eyes, as Robert splashed him under the water, and brought him right back up so fast, water splashed out the bathtub and landed all over the floor in the tiny bathroom.

Robert shouted,

"You are a new creature! Follow The Spirit of God! Rise and pray so you will not fall into temptation!

"Welcome to your new life in the body of Christ! Your rewards await you in the Kingdom of Love!"

# 72

Jasmine started smiling and clapping as John laughed, and said,

"Robert's voice really makes this all the more sacred."

Robert smiled, as he nodded and said,

"It is. Pray."

As Jasmine stepped into the bathroom and placed the change of clothes she found on the top of the sink, she said,

"You'll no longer look like a nurse, but we'll still know your a nurse. Pray."

Robert and John both laughed, as Robert and Jasmine exited the bathroom.

As soon as Robert closed the door, John screamed,

"Hey! Don't go too far! I still wanna hear your comparison of how the seals are connecting!"

"We'll be in the living room!"

10 minutes later, John stepped into the dim living room, and shouted,

"Whooooa! Thou shall not steal!"

Robert and Tiffany both busted out laughing, as Robert said,

"Would you believe we've been searching for a Bible all this time, and we still haven't found one?"

"Maybe they were atheists! You know alot of people were becoming atheists, or some form of secular humanist. People just started opening their minds so far open, entire legions of demons were marching in!"

Robert shook his head to the negative, and said,

"Sadly, you might be right. You guys hungry?"

John blurted out,

"I totally forgot about food!"

John bolted off to the kitchen, ran up to the pantry, opened the skinny sliding door, and said,

"Jackpot!"

Jasmine ran up behind him, and said,

"What do they have?" "We, have, chips, peanuts, crackers, cookies, peanut butter? I thought peanut butter was supposed to be kept in the fridge!"

Robert said,

"In prison, we kept peanut butter in lockers under our bunks. If it smells good, it isn't rotten."

"Peanut butter rots daddy?"

"Hmm... Come to think of it, I don't know. That's a very good question Jasmine. But, if it doesn't look, smell, or taste bad, I don't see why we can't eat it."

John and Jasmine carried piles of snacks over to a table they found in a small dining room.

As Jasmine and Robert took their seats, John ran over to the fridge, saying,

"I almost forgot!"

As soon as he opened the door, he slammed it back shut so fast, glass jars could be heard clanging into each other on the inside of the fridge. John quickly moved away from the foul stench of rotten food, saying,

"We don't need drinks. Tap water will do just fine."

As soon as John sat down, Robert looked at him, and said,

"Would you like to say a prayer?"

"For what? I never saw the point in praying for something we already received. I never pray for food that's right in front my face. I mean, am I wrong? I thought a prayer was a request."

Robert sighed, and said,

"You see, the world portrays this false image of God. They picture themselves as being God's master, and without realizing it, they make God out to be their slave. They see God as being their own personal servant.

"A magical genie who's sole purpose is to grant their wishes. Without realizing what they're doing, they're trying to force God into fulfilling "their" will, by making God give them what they want for their own pleasure and happiness.

"That false comprehension is what leads most childhood believers into disbelief. There are so many church leaders, pastors, and preachers, who tell these boldfaced lies about having the ability to force God into answering them with an audible voice.

"They make it seem as if every time they pray, God responds as if He were under their authority, and He had a duty to answer their every question, and grant their every wish.

"Then, when people pray, and they hear nothing, they think God either does not want to speak with them the way He speaks to others, or, they believe He does not exist, and the people who claim to hear from Him are lying.

"Most people just stop believing altogether, while some start lying, claiming to also hear the voice of God in their head."

"Yea man! That's so true dude! I had this one guy at my church that taught the Sunday School, and he would always talk to God out loud, right in front of us!

"Then, he would tell us how "God" would be responding, and he would tell us what God would be saying, but none of us kids could ever hear this "voice".

"When we asked why, he would say, "Oh, you're not patient enough to hear the sound still voice of God." But then, we would read all these verses in the Bible that say God's voice is like thunder and rushing waters. It never made sense."

# 73

Let's call the President of The United States and see what she has to say about this."

"She's dead daddy."

"Oh yea! I forgot she got assassinated. Bad example. But I wasn't implying that we would've actually been able to speak with her. My point was, it would've been impossible for us to just pick up the phone and call her, unless we were members of her elite inner circle, and that's the way it is with God.

"People believe God freely gives "everything" anyone asks for, but they twist the scripture into blatant misinterpretation, where it says, if we ask for anything in the name of Jesus, we will receive it."

"Okay yea! So I always thought that was like the holy postage stamp! Like, you gotta say, "in Jesus name" at the end of your prayer for it to like reach Heaven for consideration."

"And that simple miscomprehension is why most prayers go unheard. God simply does not listen to the prayers of those who refuse to obey His will.

"This is why ignorant and unstable people say God will answer their prayers on "His time", when they don't see immediate action.

"What they fail to realize is their prayer was extended in disobedience to God's Word, and it therefore went unheard, and was denied.

"All prayers get answered before their even completed because God knows what we need before we even come to the realization that we're in need!

"Most people have no clue as to what they need. They're like infants crossing a highway, not seeing the truck.

"Not that many people feel like they're in danger of being roasted in The Lake of Fire, and they therefore don't feel the need to seek salvation from the wrath of God, because they don't even know they're in danger!

"We need everlasting life in The Kingdom of Heaven.

"God's will is that His kingdom will be established forever.

"When we seek God's kingdom, He will give us the tools that we need to receive it. Luke 12:31 says,


*"But seek the kingdom of God,
and all these things shall be added to you."*


"As long as you're seeking the kingdom that will never come to an end, you will be moved to pray for the things that will conform your soul to the image of an everlasting existence in the flesh, and you will receive all those things from God.

"But, if you ask for the things that will cease to exist, the physical things that will please the desires of your flesh, you will not receive anything from God, just as the scripture says in James 4:3-4,

> 'You ask and do not receive, because you ask amiss, that you may spend it on "your" pleasures. Adulterers and adulteresses! Do you not know that friendship with the world is enmity with God? Whoever therefore wants to be a friend of the world makes himself an enemy of God.'

"That's the part people get twisted! They think God is there to give them what they need to fulfill "their" perception of happiness, but God knows what we really need, and that's the form of an existence that transcends everything we can imagine.

"We're like children asking for ice cream for breakfast, chocolate candy for lunch, and two pounds of sugar for dinner, for the rest of our life!

"We don't know any better! When we ask God to make our boss give us a raise, and we firmly believe we will receive the raise without any doubting, and the next day our boss says "No!", it's not that the raise will come "at a later time", the answer to the prayer was no!

"People are so deceived they believe God doesn't say no. Perhaps by receiving the raise we might end up in some form of danger that we can't see.

"The danger would be the manifestation of some form of distance between our soul and the kingdom of God. Perhaps the struggle will produce more patience and wisdom needed to follow The Spirit that leads to The Kingdom of eternal life.

"When most people receive something, they get attached to it, and it usually moves them further away from other things, and other people. Do you know where your childhood toys are? Where are all your childhood friends? Are all those things and all those people still the same? What changed? Did you move further away from them? Did they move further away from you?"

As John and Jasmine both pondered Robert's questions, Robert continued saying,

"To pray in the name of Jesus, you must first understand what His name is, by comprehending "who" He is."

John blurted out,

"He's Jesus Christ, the Son of God! Uh... Yashua? Is that it? We gotta say His name in "Hebrew" for it to be heard?"

"Of course not. God is the one who caused people to call on Him in many different languages when He confused the languages at the Tower of Babel. God understands all the different languages just fine."

"So what is it? What does praying in the name of Jesus mean?"

# 74

Jesus is The Word of God. His name is "Faithful and True". Our faith, which is our desire, must be based on the kingdom of Heaven, as it is revealed in the Bible.

"God's Word shows us God's will by showing us what God wants for us, and what we must do to receive His gifts. God reveals His will to His prophets, His prophets share the vision with His people, and God's people receive the knowledge of what is to come.

"By knowing the future, "The Kingdom and The Lake", we can prepare for it by asking God for the tools that we need to be prepared for what is to come. God's kingdom is coming to your heart, and to your mind.

"You will need the tools that will give you the power to work on your heart and your mind, so they can be prepared to receive the kingdom. By asking God for the tools to shape our souls into the form of a receiver of His kingdom, we can rest assured that we will receive it, because that's God's will."

"Okay, so, the faith of the Bible is just trusting and believing everything it says right?"

"No. That's another miscomprehension that lazy people settle for because their weak minds won't do the hard work of digging deep into the scripture until they hit solid rock, so their desire can be reformed into solid faith.

"Faith is the substance of the kingdom of love, it's the evidence of the everlasting existence. If you desire to enter into the kingdom of Heaven, the kingdom will manifest inside your soul, in the form of your desire. Your desire will transform into your faith.

"This is why Luke 17:20-21 says,

*"Now when he was asked by the Pharisees when the kingdom of God would come, he answered and said, 'The kingdom of God does not come with observation, nor will they say, 'See here!' or 'See there!' For indeed, the kingdom of God is within you."*

That's also why Ephesians 2:8-9 says,

*"For by grace you have been saved through faith, and that not of yourselves, it is the gift of God, not of works, lest any man should boast."*

"God's plan for sin is to toss The Devil into The Lake of Fire, and leave him there to suffer forever, for sinning.

"The first woman, "Eve", caught sin from The Devil. The first man, Adam, caught sin from Eve. Sin is a disease that causes disobedience to The Word of God. Sin is in every humans D.N.A..

"There is no cure for sin. Every human will disobey The Word of God, and they will pass the disease to their offspring. All who disobey God's Word will receive what God has prepared for The Devil: Everlasting torture and torment.

"The only way to escape the doom that is coming for souls is to accept the fact that God's Word is alive, and the only way something God said is going to happen won't happen, is if He formed His Almighty Word into an image that could die, so The Word could die, and souls could be sparse from His wrath.

"God couldn't stop what He already set in motion. Sinners like The Devil must suffer forever, and the will, because He said they will, but He also killed His Word by sending it into the creation. In this way, the Word died and is alive. The Word that says sinners must suffer forever will therefore be dead to believers, but it will be alive to sinners.

"In the same sense, believers are dead to sin, but they are alive to Gods Word that died in the body of Christ so souls could resurrect to its everlasting life joining it in its separation from the disease of sin.

"To solicit a pardon from God, you have to show God that your soul was included in the deal that killed His Word when He put it in the flesh of Jesus Christ, and sent it into the creation so it could die to sins and ressurect to everlasting life.

"Souls will escape God's wrath by following the life that is in the blood that leads to the body of the Messiah who is already in The Kingdom of Love.

"God allowed Jesus to open a door that will never be shut. The door is God's grace, and the door is open, but it is only accessible to those who manifest the desire to enter into the kingdom.

"The manifestation of such a desire is the construction of your faith. If you want it, it will be given to you as a gift, but you must first understand what it is so you can manifest the desire that will materialize as your faith."

"Wow! I'm totally confused! I have no idea of what you're talking about man. I'm just so lost it's unbelievable! If faith is our desire for the Kingdom, and we receive this desire by hearing about the kingdom, how is it that virtually all small children have this faith that most adults can't even comprehend? Huh? Tell me that Mr. Williams. Then, let's pray, and eat, and pray."

Robert and Jasmine both laughed, and then Robert said,

"Most people falsely interpret "child like faith" as being this ignorant close minded mentality where you just blindly accept everything the Bible says, without ever questioning it or doing any form of diligent investigation into whether or not what the Bible is saying is actually true."

"Yea! Yea pretty much. That's what I always understood "faith" to be.

"Just believing in something even though it doesn't make any sense, and you can't even understand how it could be true.

"You just have "faith", and believe it anyway."

"Doesn't that sound like something a lazy teacher would say? Or a teacher who has no idea of what it is they are trying to teach?

"Most people never manifest the desire for the kingdom as its described in the Bible, and they therefore never receive the motivation to make sense of the things they couldn't understand.

"That false mentality is widespread amongst people who do not truly understand the scriptures. It puts ignorant people who claim to be believers into a position where their ignorance will never be exposed, because they will never be questioned."

# 75

In order to learn, you must first acknowledge what you do not know, then, you can fill the void with the lesson, and when the void is filled with an abundance of knowledge, you will have more than enough to give.

"Those who have enough knowledge to give are "teachers". In the kingdom of God, there will no longer be any voids. All of God's children will be filled with an abundance, so much so, there will no longer be any need for a teacher or a student.

"Class will be eternally dismissed. Those who try to teach with nothing to give are only preparing themselves for destruction, unless they repent by changing their mind and going back to being a student, so they can have their void filled with the truth, and then, they will have the power to share. Jesus told us to have the faith of small children. This tells us small children are the teachers of faith.

"We must therefore watch the small children very carefully, and they will teach us how to have faith. Think of a little tiny 3 year old. Just started walking. Just started talking. Running all around over everywhere!

"Boldly reaching out for everything! Willing to taste anything! Even poatoe salad!"

"Yuk!"

Robert laughed at Jasmine's facial expression, as he continued saying,

"They ask multiple questions about the answers to the questions you've already answered multiple times! They want to know everything about everything, and they're never satisfied with the simple explanations about anything! That's child-like faith!

"Little children are so thirsty for knowledge, they will master entire languages just to be able to better communicate with their teachers.

"Every small child is on a very serious quest for the truth. Their every waking moment is spent very wisely, conducting experiments, formulating theories, testing those theories, and learning something new everyday.

"When Jesus was on the earth, in those days, in that region of the earth, it was shameful for children to just charge their way into a gathering of men. The children knew their expectations, and discipline was strictly enforced, so they carefully adhered to the codes of conduct.

"But Mark, chapter 10, verses thirteen to 16 tells us of a situation where Jesus permitted small children to come near to Him, which revealed the knowledge that is now used as the basis for the understanding of child-like faith.

"Jesus had been healing people. Blind people were instantly able to see. People who couldn't walk could instantly walk! People were flocking to Jesus in hope that they would be healed.

"Some adults felt the children needed to recieve the power that was healing the adults, perhaps to prevent any future issues.

"The disciples felt there was no need, because the children were not blind, or deaf, or maimed, like many who were in the crowd of thousands who were hoping to be healed.

"The vast majority of small children unfortunately grow up and lose their childhood desire to study and learn with the motive of discovering the purpose of existing.

"Instead of trying to further understand the creation, as most people grow up, they start worshiping the creation by idolizing its numerous paths to pleasure. Their studies become dominated by the pursuit of the fulfillment of their desires.

"The more they fulfill their desires, the more they despise fulfilling the desires of others, to the point that they begin to oppose it, disobey it, and hate it.

"Most people fall so deeply into the delusion of the creation, they turn against The Creator, and in this day and age, they are beginning to believe they can destroy Him.

"As most people grow older, they advance in the knowledge that brings them closer to the fulfillment of their growing desires for the pleasures presented by the creation. This is why over 90 percent of prayers are ignored.

"People love the delusion so much, they literally beg The Creator for more of the things that they love, which are the things of this world, the creation. You are a soul, operating a physical body, in a physical world, composed of physical creations.

"Every physical form of existence is a creation that will eventually cease to exist. Your soul was formed to enter into a kingdom that will never cease! In order to reach that kingdom, your soul must overcome all physical forms of existences, including your flesh.

"You must come to the awareness of your true self that exists on the inside of your physical body. The you that moves the arms. The you that bends the fingers. The you that looks out the eyes. The you that is the soul. When you find yourself, you must see past the delusion of this physical realm. You must use your spiritual eyes to see the kingdom that will never cease to exist.

"You will never find your soul without the assistance of your creator, and you will never see His kingdom unless He reveals it to you. God will show you who you are and where you belong if you ask Him for the power to see. When God opens your eyes, only then will you see the danger that is coming for your soul."

# 76

## The Abyss
## The Other Side of Existence

"Allow the princes who have never possessed flesh to come forth for the knowledge of violence!"

In an instant, hundreds of thousands of demons appeared before The Devil, bowing down to his feet, as he shouted,

"The day has come for you to walk across the earth, possess flesh, and fulfill my will! The flesh you will possess is being held by kings who will release the flesh to your operation upon your manifestation! Inside the creation, you must locate a manmade tool that is used to follow manmade time!

"The humans agree in a form of time that is based on the geographical location of the earth in relation to the sun! Each time the earth revolves around the sun, the humans celebrate the rotation as a year!

"Do not be deceived by the creation of the humans! Keep watch with them!

"The device that they've formed to keep track of their time is a "watch". Keep watch, for the time of the day will fall on the days of man! All demons who possess flesh must keep a watch around the wrist at all times!

"The humans have advanced in the knowledge of reforming their flesh! Do not be deceived! The humans reform their flesh to be more desirable for the mates that they desire!

"Men have transformed their flesh to mimic the flesh that is natural for the woman! Homosexuality is a practice that is protected by the most powerful governments on the earth!

"Men are permitted to marry one another, and the most powerful kingdom on the earth acknowledges a period of manmade days which celebrate the pride of its sodomites! You will possess the flesh of men that were prepared for your occupation!

"You must increase the violent nature of the flesh through the repetitive operation of the imagination! As soon as you possess the flesh, you must transmit an image to the brain that will cause your flesh to visualize fierce human attackers attacking!

"Convince the brain into believing the attack is real and deadly! Convince the flesh into believing it's on the brink of destruction! Transform the flesh into a master of time through the operation of the imagination!

"Move the flesh slowly, with the mind convinced that the attack is occurring fast! Imagine the flesh moving with such swift precision, it crushes the bones of the attackers faces before any soul could operate its flesh in such a way that the flesh you possess can be harmed!

"Utilize the shortest routes to the nose and jaw by swiftly throwing the tips of the knuckles directly into the flesh, by locking the eyes directly onto the location you seek to crush!

"Plant the feet and twist to transfer power from the legs into the blow. Clench the fist in route to the face, and crush the bones underneath the flesh!

"Crush the bones of all the attackers! Practice until, in one swift punch, you can crush the bones into the brain and cause the soul to detach from the flesh!

"Master the action in slow motion, then gradually increase the speed of the swinging of the arms! When you master the motion of violence in normal speed, the crushing of the bones will no longer be imagined!

"When you posses your flesh and master your violence, the kings will direct your attention to the souls that must be seperated from the flesh!"

# 77

## Abandoned House
## Florence Colorado

"Most people are so deceived, they waste their opportunity to receive everlasting blessings, by begging for things that will cease to exist.

"People talk to God about their worries over unpaid bills, not realizing that all their bills would be paid if they started talking to God about years in the sums of billions and trillions.

"God never had a beginning! When you call out to God, you are calling out to someone who has the full understanding of how it feels to spend three hundred trillion years on the other side of existence, like it's nothing.

"Why would He listen to your worries about things that will have zero significance in just a few decades?

"God's children are preparing for conversations that will last for thousands of years, meetings that will last for millions of years, walks that will take billions of years! Have you ever asked God for a car?

"How far into the spiritual realm can a brand new car drive you? 50 billion dollars can't even buy you a ticket to see a split second glimpse of the glory of the everlasting kingdom, so why waste prayers begging for riches?

"People rob, steal, and kill, and when they're delivered to the judge to receive the punishment they deserve, they call on God begging to be delivered, not realizing that by asking God to "release" them, they are acknowledging the fact that He is the one keeping them locked up.

"Then, when God refuses to fulfill "their" will, they turn their back on Him, not realizing the opportunity He was giving them to call on Him for the keys of entrance into His kingdom."

John twisted his face in confusion, as he said,

"The keys of?... So... What are we supposed to be praying for? I still don't get it. What's the point of praying if we can't ask for what we want? We gotta ask for what God wants for us or He won't even hear the prayer? I thought God could hear everything!"

"John 9:31 clearly says,

        *'Now we know that God does not hear sinners, but if anyone is a worshiper of God and does His will, He hears him.'*

"What? The Bible says that?"

"The Bible has been saying that for almost two thousand years, and people still won't do God's will so their prayers could be heard."

John's stomach growled, as he swallowed his saliva, and said,

"So what does that mean?"

"It means that you're hungry!"

Robert and Jasmine laughed, but John remained serious, as he said,

"From this day forward, if I gotta pray before I eat, I'll pray before I eat even the smallest piece of candy. I will not be deceived! I will make it to the kingdom, and I'm taking 2 souls with me!

"From this day forward, each and every time I pray, I will pray the right way, because I'm repenting from my wrong way of praying. So I just wanna be sure that I get this, and I know what I'm doing, and I know why I'm doing it, and I know I'm doing it right. So just lay it on me!"

# 78

Robert nodded through a smile, and said,

"Sin is disobedience to the Word of God. Sinning is doing anything that is contrary to anything God has ever said. So it's just that simple. In order for your prayer to be heard, it must be in agreement with the Word of God, as it was revealed to us in The Bible.

"If you refuse to follow God's Word, you are being disobedient to His will, and you are therefore sinning. If your prayer violates scripture, it will go unheard.

"It's like me telling Jasmine to eat all of her dinner, including the despicable potatoe salad, and then, she can have desert. If I still see an entire glob of potatoe salad on her plate, do you think I will consider her squeaky little pleas for dessert?

"On the other hand, if she cleans her plate, she knows she has the right to boldly come and ask me for desert, and she knows she will receive it, because she obeyed the command to eat all of her food.

"It's the same way with God. Prayer is private communication between you and your Creator.

"Imagine you created a fishing pole that could speak. Every time you went to use it, it was broken, and it could never catch any fish. Imagine how lazy and deceived the fishing pole would need to be to turn around and ask "you" for some fish!

"That's how ridiculous our prayers sound to God. But instead of being logical, and at the least asking for something along the lines of everlasting things and eternal things, people are asking for toothpicks, doorknobs, and toenails.

"What can a broken fishing pole do with a toenail? Just about as much as a soul in the spiritual realm can do with a hundred trillion dollars! What we need from God is the wisdom to discern between the truth and the lies, between right and wrong, between good and bad, between holy and evil.

"Once we receive the wisdom, we can use it to direct our attention to the good knowledge that leads to the holy truth about the everlasting kingdom of righteousness. Once we know the truth, we will be set free from deception.

"Freedom from deception enables us to understand the invisible kingdom. Once we understand, we can accept the understanding as our personal belief. Once we accept the belief, we will become what we have accepted. What we become determines our dwelling place for eternity.

"You will never become what you can not accept, and you will never accept what you can not believe. You will never believe what you can not understand, and you will never understand what you do not know, because if you do not know it, you are not aware that it exists.

"Knowledge of the invisible existence can only come from the kingdom that can not be seen. God will send an abundance of wisdom to anyone who asks with the intention of receiving His kingdom. Even the most foolish criminal can call out to God and be heard, as long as he calls out to God with the desire to live forever, which is faith.

"If you call out to God in faith, your soul will receive an Almighty desire for His kingdom. The desire, which is your faith, will connect you to The Spirit that will lead you to the life that is in the blood of Christ.

"The Spirit is Love. It will manifest in your heart, and your flesh will transform into His Temple. God is The Spirit of Love. If you accept Supreme Love into your heart, your soul will transform into His Kingdom, and from your heart, He will led you to His Kingdom.

"He will led you in your prayers, He will lead you in your interactions with others, and He will lead you in the appropriate way to take care of your kingdom. in construction of your kingdom is your faith! Pray for faith and you will receive God's kingdom that will lead you to the dwelling place of everlasting life.

"Pray that your name will never be blotted out of The Lambs Book of Life! Pray that you will be given the reward to enter into the real New Jerusalem, so you can walk up the road, eat from The Tree, and live forever.

"When you finish praying, don't just say, "In Jesus name I pray", instead, know and understand that everything you said was the truth, all of your requests will be granted, and all of your desires will be fulfilled, because they were splitting images of God's Word that will always be true."

John was staring at Robert, nodding, and as soon as Robert stopped speaking, John said,

"I know how to pray."

# 79

The room was silent, as John stared at the table. He suddenly looked up at Robert with a confused look on his face, and said,

"So what's the point of praying for food?"

"Oh! We're just saying thanks."

Everyone erupted in laughter, as Robert said,

"But it's more than just that. Remember how God told Moses to build the Tabernacle, the place where God could meet with The Children of Israel?"

"Um... You mean when that guy led those slaves out of Egypt, and split The Red Sea?"

"Exactly! After Moses led The Children of Israel out of Egypt, they wandered around the Siani desert for 40 years, being fed with birds and hidden Manna, which was a mysterious thing that appeared with dew, that could be boiled, baked, and eaten.

"When the 40 years was over, God met with Moses on Mount Siani, and gave him the 10 Commandments, and specific instructions on how to build an enormous tent called, "The Tabernacle".

"The Tabernacle was made to look like God's real Tabernacle in the spiritual realm. It had a Courtyard, a Holy Place, and a Most Holy Place. The Most Holy Place was where the 10 Commandments were kept inside a gold box. The box was called "The Ark of The Covenant". The box was the "Ark", and the covenant was the 10 commandments written on the 2 stone tablets.

"The Most Holy Place was sectioned off by a veil, and only one special person was allowed to go behind the veil just one time out the year to sprinkle the blood of the sacrifice onto the Ark of The Covenant to receive forgiveness of the sins of all The Children of Israel. That special person was called "The High Priest".

"Solomon's Temple was a reconstruction of The Tabernacle. It was meant to be a permanent temple for The Ark of The Covenant, as opposed to the tent that had to be broken down and rebuilt each and every time The Children of Israel moved to a new location in the desert.

"The Tabernacle was the place where sinners met with God, through a representative. Both earthly Tabernacles were only for The Children of Israel. The rest of the world was doomed. Both earthly Tabernacles were only shadows of the true tabernacle that was still in Heaven.

"Both Tabernacles have been destroyed, because they were physical, and they were therefore never intended to last forever. The true Tabernacle is God's Word that came into this world in the flesh of Jesus Christ, who Himself died in the flesh so His blood could be shed, so His life could be carried back into Heaven, the true Most Holy Place, so He could receive forgiveness of the sins of every sinner who ever was, or ever will be.

"That's the power of God! God's Word came back to life so all who enter into His death can resurrect into the body of the Messiah. God's Word entered back into the true Most Holy Place as the High Priest that will never cease to exist.

"We therefore no longer have a physical Tabernacle. The true Tabernacle is now restored to it's everlasting form of existence in the spiritual realm.

"In order to possess the meeting place where we meet with God, and have our prayers heard, we must accept the dwelling place of the tabernacle into our heart, in the form of our faith. Our physical bodies are therefore the temporary temples of the kingdom and the Tabernacle of God.

"The evidence that our bodies are the temples of the dwelling place of our Creator, is the fact that humans are formed on the inside of humans, out of things that we can barely even see.

"Before anything enters into our temple, it must be blessed so it can be holy as we are holy. "Holy" means to be set apart to be used by God.

"Before you allow anything into your temple, you must bless it and make it holy by acknowledging that it belongs to God, and that He gave it to you so you could give Him the praise that He will accept through His glory.

"You bless your food to make it holy, to give God His praise for providing it, and to give God thanks for the provisions for your temple."

John was nodding his head, while staring at Robert. As soon as Robert finished speaking, John said,

"I can do this. Go ahead and bow your heads."

# 80

As Robert and Jasmine bowed their heads and closed their eyes, John bowed his head, closed his eyes, clapsed his hands, and said,

"Father God, thank you for providing us with this food that we are about to eat. Please bless it and make it holy so it can enter into our temples.

"Thank you for giving us the body of your only begotten Son as a means that we can now use to gain access to Your kingdom. In His name, Your Word, we offer You this prayer.

"Through His blood, and the power of Your Spirit, please accept it. On behalf of us all, we give you thanks, praise, honor, glory, and love. Amen!"

Jasmine blurted out,

"Amen!",

and then busted open a bag of potatoe chips, as Robert and John let out a roar of laughter.

# The Pentagon
# Washington, D.C.

"That will be noted as an official declaration of war, regardless to Chinas intentions. The United States will not stand to be threatened by any form of threat, direct or indirect, foreign, domestic, or even from some invisible source or unseen force! Inform the President that The United States hereby declares war on China!"

"Sir.! If Chinas position is viewed as an official decleration of war, it should be noted that Russia, Syria, Iraq, and Iran, have all also taken similar positions under the banner of preparing for the event.

"Furthermore, North Korea has stopped communicating with the rest of the world, and it appears from satilite imagery that North Korea is preparing to deliver on it's promise of sending nuclear weapons at the incoming objects!"

"Such shall so be noted. The United States will not stand to be threatened by any form of threat, direct or indirect, foreign, domestic, or even from some invisible source or unseen force!

"Your notification to the President must now be amended to reflect that it is the unanimous decision of the entire Department of Defense, and all its secretaries and generals, that we hereby declare war on the following countries: China, Russia, North Korea, Iraq, Iran, and Syria!

"It must further reflect that we will prepare to invade North Korea in the event that the entire country continues to remain unresponsive.

"The invasion will be for the use of destructive force, whereas, satilite imagery has confirmed that North Korea is secretly preparing to launch weapons of mass destruction, and North Korea has therefore made itself to be an imminent threat of danger to the safety and security of the global population of the people of planet earth!"

The Secretary promptly left the room, and within minutes, all of the requests of the generals were granted.

# 81

**Abandoned House**
**Florence, Colorado**


"That wasn't so bad. But I'm sure we'll feel a little nauseas once our stomachs break it all down and see what that stuff is really made of."

Robert rose from the table and found his way back over to the bookshelf in search of a Bible, as John said,

"So break down the first 3 seals."

"I prefer to have a Bible available before speaking."

"Well let's go search some of the other houses! This place looks like the home of people who believed in evolution, reincarnation, and Darwinism!"

"Yea daddy, this place stinks. I don't like it here at all. Let's find another one. It smells really gross dad. We can't sleep here, this place is disgusting, can you imagine how nasty their bedsheets must be?"

"Alright alright! Let's go! But the next house we pick is the house we're staying in till' kingdom come, regardless of how bad it smells! So you better pick wisely!"

John and Jasmine started laughing as they started grabbing the snacks off of the table.

John suddenly dropped everything, and shouted,

"Hold up!"

He bolted over to the pantry, busted open a pack of garbage bags, filled it with all the snacks in the pantry, and on the table, threw the box of garbage bags into the bag, threw the bag over his shoulder, and said,

"Okay, now we can go."


"Nope!... Nope!... Nope!... Too small!... Nope!... Nope!"

Robert and John paitently followed behind Jasmine in silence, as she rejected house after house, saying,

"Nope!... No way!... Nope!... Nope!... Nope!... Nope!"

Then, she froze, pointed to a house all the way at the end of the road, and shouted,

"That one daddy! That one! That one That one! That's definitely the one daddy! It's perfect!"

She took off towards the enormous 2 story, sprinting and laughing, as Robert and John walked and laughed behind her.

Just as Robert started explaining how much the house resembled his house back in Texas, Jasmine let out a bloodcurdling scream that yanked their attention out of their minds, and glued it to the horryfying image of 2 pit bulls chasing Jasmine up the sidewalk.

As soon as Jasmine got close to Robert, she bounced into his arms and pulled up her feet, as John jumped in front the dogs, and aggresively shouted,

"Heel! Sit! Sit down! Sit!"

Both dogs ran to John and sat at his feet, sniffing and licking the hand he extended towards them.

Dog tails started wagging, as John dug through the garbage bag, saying,

"They're just hungry. They probably been eating grass and bugs for who knows how long!"

From the safety of Roberts arms, Jasmine said,

"They can eat all the grass they want, as long as they don't eat me!"

John laughed, as he pulled out a box of crackers, and said,

"Naah! Dogs don't eat people. They just chew you up real good."

"Daddy can we please go to the house?"

Robert laughed along with John, as he carried Jasmine past the dogs, who were busy licking crushed crackers off the ground.

When John caught up to Robert and Jasmine, they were just stepping through the front door.

John looked at the intact door shocked, as he said,

"How do you keep opening these doors?"

Robert laughed, and said,

"I wasn't always the voice of The Bible with Mr. Williams."

"Whoa! Let's hurry up and find you a Bible before you morph into an unrecognizable past version of yourself!"

John closed the door behind him, just as the dogs came barking, sniffing, and scratching.

"Do not let those dogs in here! This house smells wonderful, and we're going to keep it like that. Okay?"

John smiled at Jasmine, and said,

"After all the hard work you went through to pick it out, I wouldn't dare turn it into one of the ones you did'nt like. Your dad told me how much it resembles your house back in Texas. I got you, we're cool."

"Thank you."

Robert went heading towards a small desk, as Jasmine went upstairs, and John headed into the kitchen.

## 82

"Jackpot! Yea! Jackpot! Jackpot you guys aw man Jasmine picked the winner big time! Check this out you guys!"

Robert and Jasmine shot into the kitchen, where they found John digging some papers out of a fax machine, saying,

"Listen to this fax you guys! It says,

*'Please confirm whether or not you received the information that was sent to you at 4 o' clock in the evening on October fifteenth.'*

"Then, there's a stack of back-to-back faxes that keep repeating the same message, hour-after-hour, right up until October seventeenth, yesterday, when all the power cut off.

"So listen to the 4 o' clock October fifteenth fax! It says,

*'WARNING! HIGHLY SENSITIVE CONFIDENTIAL CONTENT INTENDED FOR ADDRESSEE ONLY!*

*"Unauthorized release or disclosure may violate Martial Law and subject the violator to the fatal infliction of deadly force!*

*On October thirteenth, 2032, While on duty in the Piz Daint Supercomputing Centre in Switzerland, your nephew, Josh Mack, was terminated as he attempted to escape a sequestered location in possession of beyond top secret information.*

*It may be of interest to you that you are next in line to inherit the entire inheritance left to Josh Mack, by his father, your deceased brother, Tod Mack.*

*Of most importance, in the wake of the impending extinction level event, is your claim to a deep underground bunker in Zurich Switzerland.*

*Assuming you will utilize the property, the following directions must be followed to gain access to the bunker...'*

Then, it tells us exactly how to get into the bunker! It goes into this description about all the stuff it has inside like food and generators and stuff, and it gives us the riddle we'll need to enter through the secret entrance of a real underground bunker!"

Robert nodded, and said,

"That sounds very good John, but you do understand that Switzerland is a foreign country, on the other side of the Atlantic Ocean. It would be very difficult, and deadly, for us to make it to the coast of the Atlantic Ocean, much less cross it.

"A lot of people are about to die John, and a lot will die "before" the rapture takes place, but a multitude will survive and be caught up in the clouds to meet with Jesus.

"Either way, we'll still reach the kingdom. If we perish, we won't be thrown into The Lake of Fire, and if we survive until Jesus comes, we'll still reach the same destination that we would've reached had we died, which is the kingdom of Heaven.

"We have no need to fear death John. We're destined to live forever."

John looked at Robert smiling, and said,

"Mr. Williams, I know. But the description of the bunker says its equipped with it's own massive frequency transmitter, capable of sending international transmissions!"

Roberts eyes exploded in shock, as he whispered, "International?"

"Dude, we gotta get you into that bunker! I don't know how, but we gotta get you onto that transmitter so the world can hear the truth about what's going on!

"People have got to hear what you have to say! I mean, what's the odds of "your" daughter picking out this house of all those houses man?"

John slammed the stack of papers onto the kitchen counter, and said,

"Man this is God!"

Robert whispered to himself,

"International transmissions?"

Jasmine shot a quick stare over at the front door, and felt fear, as the dogs started barking.

She ran to the window by the front door, and said,

"I think I see a helicopter! Maybe we can get their attention and ask them to call Captain Shaw so we can ask him to give us a ride to Switzerland!"

John laughed, and said,

"The only ride my "brother" will give us is a ride to the nearest Chip of Allegiance implantation station!"

John walked over to the window, took a look at the helicopter as he stretched, and started walking back over to the kitchen. Then, he stopped, and said,

"Man! They're getting closer!"

He shot back over to the window, and said,

"It's red, it doesn't look military, and it's heading in our direction! That thing looks like it's going to land!"

Robert bolted over to the window, and said,

"There are scanners strong enough to determine the height, weight, and gender, of the occupants of any structure. They could be bringing us some rations."

"Or some bullets! Let's look for some weapons just in case!"

# 83

As Robert and John started darting around the house, Jasmine stayed staring out the window, until she screamed,

"They're here! They're here! Incoming!"

Jasmine bolted past Robert and John, who were marching towards the front door with large hunting rifles.

Robert screamed,

"Go upstairs Jasmine!"

Jasmine shot up the stairs and bolted into a room that looked and smelt like it belonged to a young female. As she looked for a place to hide, she dived to the ground and slid under the bed as gunshots erupted downstairs.

There was a brief gun battle as shots were exchanged, and just as fast, the shooting ceased, and all Jasmine could hear was the helicopter.

Jasmines heart was beating in her throat, as she stared out into the hallway from underneath the bed. She could hear that the front door was open, because the noise of the helicopter blades chopping through the wind was louder than it was when she was at the window.

Jasmine inhaled a large gasp of fear that froze her to a block of ice as the loud stomping of feet marching up the stairs started piercing into her ears.

Jasmine backed further underneath the bed, as the sound of the stomping reached the top of the stairs.

Jasmine screamed and vigorously struggled to crawl out from underneath the bunk, as Tiffany came running into the room.

Tiffany ran right up to the bed and helped Jasmine up, as they screamed and cried tears of joy, hugging and jumping up and down.

"I thought I would never see you again Tiffany!"

"We're best friends forever! Nothing will ever change that!"

Tiffany grabbed Jasmine and quickly led her out of the room, saying,

"We gotta go Jasmine! John and your daddy killed somebody!"

As they ran down the stairs, horror covered Jasmine's face, as she saw Robert and John carrying a bloody corpse into the kitchen.

Robert shouted,

"Go get in the helicopter!"

As the girls ran out the door, Jasmine looked at the bullet holes that bent and twisted the door off the hinges. The dogs ran past the girls, licking blood off the floor, as they followed the trail into the kitchen.

As the girls approached the helicopter, Jasmine could see someone sitting in the copilot seat. When they got closer, she realized it was Megan, and she stood stiff, frowning at Megan with her fingers in her ears.

Tiffany looked back and harshly motioned for Jasmine to enter the helicopter, and she relented.

As soon as Jasmine closed the door, Megan turned around in the quieter compartment, and said,

"Jasmine, I panicked. My behaviour was unacceptable. I'm terribly sorry. Will you forgive me?"

Jasmine looked Megan right I'm her eyes, and said,

"Did you take The Mark of The Beast?"

# 84

Megan busted out laughing, and said,

"No. Tiffany wouldn't let me. She wouldn't let anyone do anything. She screamed and shouted and made everyone listen to her story. That poor soldier offered to help us find you guys, but I guess your daddy could see what was coming. We found you on this scanner."

As Jasmine looked at the laptop, she saw two images with the forms of humans moving out the front door. When she looked out the front window of the helicopter, she could see Robert and John coming with guns and the garbage bag.

Megan hopped into the back seat, and the noise of the loud helicopter blades poured into the compartment, as Robert and John opened the doors, hopped into the helicopter with everything they were carrying, and closed the doors behind them.

"Everybody hang on! It's been awhile!"

The helicopter lifted off the ground, wobbled, and started traveling in the opposite direction of the facility."

John said,

"You know where you're going?"

As Robert started messing with the laptop, he said,

"Of course! We're going to Switzerland!"

Megan twisted up her face, and blurted out,

"Switzerland?"

Robert and John looked at Megan, and at the same time, said,

"Did you take The Mark of The Beast?"

"No you guys, I'm not doomed. Tiffany got us out of there before they could chip me. That soldier was just trying to come tell you guys about The Chip, and the bunker."

As Robert got back focused on flying, John said,

"And we told him about self defense!"

Megan nodded, and said,

"Robert, you know this little helicopter won't make it all the way to Switzerland right?"

"I know that! We're heading to The Rio Grande River. We'll only be in the air for about two hours.

"I'm sure we'll be able to find some type of boat that we can sail into The Gulf of Mexico.

"From there, we'll find a way to board a vessel that will take us across the Atlantic. When we reach land, we'll travel to the bunker."

Megan and Tiffany both said,

"The bunker?",

and Megan said,

"What bunker? You had a bunker in Switzerland all this time? You don't have a bunker Robert. Do you?"

As John shoved the papers to Megan, Robert looked back at Megan, and said,

"Jasmine found the house, John found the papers, and The Lord provided the way. Trust in The Lord with all your heart, and lean not on your own understanding. In all your ways acknowledge Him, and He shall direct your paths. Proverbs 3:5."

Megan looked towards Robert dumbfounded, and said,

"The Lord provided you with a bunker in Switzerland?"

"Us! The Lord provided "us" with a bunker in Switzerland!"

# 85

## Moscow, Russia

"President Ryazan, The United States has officially declared war on Russia, China, Iraq, Iran, and Syria, and they are preparing to invade North Korea with destructive force."

President Ryazan stared at The Prime Minister with an expression that showed zero change in emotion, as he said,

"How has China responded to the declaration?"

"China has deployed troops into North Korea! They have also stationed forces at Shanghai, Qingdao, and Jixi.

"They have also deployed an entire fleet of naval vessels, armed with nuclear weapons, into the Pacific Ocean. China has prepared for nuclear war!"

President Ryazan silently stared off into the distance, without saying a word, and then looked at the Prime Minister, and said,

"We will send troops into North Korea. We will release the naval fleet, armed to the teeth with nuclear weapons, into the Pacific Ocean.

"We will direct the submarines in the Arctic Ocean to travel into the Atlantic Ocean, and come into close proximity of the United States. We will prepare this country for nuclear war!"

The Prime Minister affirmatively nodded, and left the room.

## Alamosa, Colorado
## 2 Hours Later

"Yea, it looks good. Let me see where I can land."

Robert maneuvered the helicopter into landing in front of a mansion that had an enormous yacht in it's backyard.

As the blades stopped spinning, they exited the helicopter into an eerie silence.

As they made their way up the side of the spooky mansion, Megan gasped and stopped moving, as she was making eye contact with a woman who was staring directly at her through a window on the second floor of the mansion.

John waved at the woman, who continued to stare, motionless, until she walked off.

Megan lingered in confusion, and then quickly caught up to the rest of the group that kept walking, saying,

"Geez! I forgot there was still people in these houses!

All the empty roads and the silence makes it seem like there isn't anyone left on earth! You guys think we should go talk to her?"

John turned up his face, and said,

327

"Why?"

"Well that's obviously her yacht we're about to go steal! The least we can do is tell her why we're taking it."

John shook his head, and said,

"That lady looks like she scarfed down so much Bar-Enash garbage, she probably believes even her soul belongs to the government! You really think she cares about that boat? She probably thought we were here to take her to a bunker!"

As the group reached the back of the mansion, Megan could feel an army of vibes crawling up the side of her neck. Chills tickled up her spine, causing her to spin around to see the source of the awkward feeling, and as soon as she looked,

"Oh my goodness!"

Megan could see the woman staring at her through an even larger window, emotionless and naked. As everyone started boarding the yacht, Megan firmly stood in the same position, and aggressively said,

"We aren't leaving her like that. Something is definitely wrong."

They all looked back so shocked, they just stared at the naked lady speechless. Megan shook her head and stormed off towards the mansion, saying,

"I'm going in there! Something's not right!"

# 86

John shook his head, looked at Robert, and said,

"Do you even know how to operate this thing started?"
"I don't even know how to start it! I just figured we would've figured it out!"
Both men laughed, as Robert said,
"Come on, hopefully we can find that girl some clothes, and see if she knows what to do."

As soon as Robert opened a rear door to the mansion, Megan charged in, screaming,
"Hello? Hello is anyone here? Can anyone hear me?"
When she did'nt receive a response, she started climbing the stairs, heading towards the room that had the windows where she saw the girl.
Tiffany and Jasmine quickly followed behind Megan, as Robert and John sat down on some black leather sofas in front of an enormous flat screen T.V..
Upstairs, Megan's head jolted back in shock when she saw large steal chains and an enormous lock wrapped around a block of wood that had been nailed to the door.

"Boom!" "Boom!" "Boom!"

Robert and John looked at each other, and then raced up the stairs aiming their shotguns.

When they reached the second floor, they saw Megan pulling her slightly bloody leg out of a hole she had kicked into the bottom of the door. Robert shook his head, and said,

"Now this is something."

Jasmine and Tiffany helped Megan away from the door, as Robert put his gun down, and started examining the makeshift mechanism, while saying,

"Whoever put this together did'nt put too much thought or effort into it."

He turned his back towards the door, aimed his foot at the midsection, near the handle, leaned forward, balanced on one leg, and in one forceful motion, he buck kicked the door open as the portion of wood that was bolted to the doorpost tore off and went swinging with the lock, the chain, the door, and a large portion of the frame.

A strong odor of sweat and musk poured out of the messy room, as Megan charged in, searching for the lady who was nowhere in sight.

As everyone stood in the doorway watching, Megan looked through the closet, and was about to start examining the windows, when Jasmine shouted,

"Look under the bed!"

Megan nodded, got down on her hands and knees, and sure enough, the girl was hiding under the bed, naked, on the cold tiled floor.

"Hi. My name is Megan. I came here to help you. Can you tell me your name?"

The hispanic looking girl just continued to quietly stare at Megan.

"Hola! Como estas? Tu habla ingles? Si? No? Tu habla espanol? Si? No?"

Megan sighed, as she rose from the floor. John laughed to himself, and said,

"I guess we can forget about her telling us how to operate that yacht."

Robert busted out laughing, as Megan walked over to the closet shaking her head, saying,

"Can everybody please just meet me downstairs? I'll get her dressed and out to the yacht."

Everyone left, as Megan stepped into a giant walk-in closet, searching for clothes.

# 87

As Megan stepped out the closet with some clothes in her hand, she almost jumped out her skin when she saw the nude girl crawling out from underneath the bed.

As the girl rose to her feet, Megan started feeling intimidated, as the athletic looking girl seemed to rise with hostility.

Megan quickly extended the clothes, and said,

"Would you like to get dressed?"

The girl looked at the clothes, and in clear english, she said,

"Those are not my clothes."

"Oh, I'm sorry. Who's clothes are they?"

The girl stared at the clothes in silence, and then said,

"They belong to my sister. My little sister."

"Do you know where your little sister is?"

"She's dead."

Megan's eyes widened, as she shook her head, and said,

"I'm sorry. I just lost my neice. I know how it feels to lose someone close. Would you like to show me where we can find some clothes that you can wear?"

The girl shivered, looked into Megan's eyes, and aggressively said,

"No! I do not want to do anything! No."

Megan looked confused, as she responded,

"What's the matter? Is something wrong?"

The girl stood stiff, while staring at Megan, as Megan said,

"Can you at least tell me your name? I'm just trying to help. I saw you through the... Window... And... I..."

Megan looked at the corners of the room carefully, and realized what she thought was hand towels, was actually piles of used condoms.

Megan darted her eyes around the room, looked carefully into the girls eyes, and said,

"Did something happen that shouldn't of happened? Did someone do something inappropriate to you? You can tell me."

The girl maintained the same blank stare, and it almost brought Megan to tears, as she exploded out the room in a march of anger, searching for the girls room.

At the end of the hallway, there was a ransacked room with a pinkish glow. When Megan looked in the room, she could see that the pink tint was coming from pink drapes that covered both windows in the enormous room.

As Megan stepped into the room, searching for pictures, she saw a banner hanging over the bed, with the name "Emily", written on it in pink and silver glitter.

Megan looked down the hallway, and shouted,

"Emily!"

There was no response.

"Emily?"

Again, there was silence.

'Em...'

Emily poked her head out the doorway, threw her long curly hair to the back of her head, and revealed a face showing shock, surprise, and confusion.

Megan whispered,

"Emily come on!"

As Megan motioned for Emily to come towards her, Emily hesitated, looked both ways, covered her chest, and darted across the hallway, into the room.

Megan closed the door behind her, and said,

"Come on, we gotta hurry! Get dressed and we'll escape on the yacht!"

"My father's yacht?"

"Yea! You know how to operate it right?"

"Yea, he was showing me. But won't the soldiers kill us?"

"No! We're protected! They can't harm us!"

Emily stopped everything she was doing, and harshly said,

"Protected? By who? Not saint Mary! She won't stop anything from happening, no matter how loud you call for help!"

# 88

Megan stayed silent, as Emily finished dressing, and started stuffing clothes and small products into a book bag.

After a few moments, Megan said,

"I know things seem real bad, but you..."

"You don't know anything! You didn't see anything! You weren't here! You came too late!"

Megan didn't speak another word. She silently watched Emily finish dressing and packing, hoping she didn't push her away.

As soon as Emily zipped up her backpack, she stepped to Megan's face, and said,

"My father had a stroke! My mother ran outside and flagged down a sheriff.

As soon as the sheriff saw me and my brothers and sisters in the doorway, he got all excited and got on a walkie talkie. In minutes, an ambulance and a black van showed up.

"Armed soldiers came out the ambulance, with one medical person. One soldier was driving the black van.

"As the medical person tended to my father, the soldiers pointed their guns at me and my brothers and sisters. They made us line up on the wall.

"Then, they scanned us with a device, and told us to sit on the floor. They kept looking at the device with impressed looks, and they kept saying how healthy, beautiful, handsome, and attractive we were. Then, the medical person said my father had to go to the hospital.

"My mother immediately said she was going with him. As they put my father on the stretcher, one of the soldiers started telling us how everyone on the surface of the earth was going to die, and that the government was looking for young and healthy people to go into bunkers to survive and help repopulate the earth after the destruction was over.

"We said we would go if our parents could come, and they said they would bring them to the bunker as soon as my father was released from the hospital. They said everything we needed would be provided at the bunker.

"We all said "okay", and we piled into the van while my mother and father went into the ambulance. We flew down the road. We didn't stop for anything. There weren't any cars on the road at all. Cars were piled up all around peoples houses, on the sides, on the grass.

"The only person we saw was my mother trying to jump out the back of the ambulance, as the top of her head exploded into pieces with a flash of light behind it.

"Her body hit the road so hard I felt it. The van swerved around her body and smashed on the brakes so hard, we jolted forward as the soldier turned around and shot my brothers and sisters one-by-one.

"When he pointed the gun at me, he said,
'You're too beautiful to just waste like that.'

"I remember he smashed on the gas so hard, blood rolled under my feet, and then he smashed on the brakes, reached under his seat, pulled out a can of something, pointed it at me, and all I remember is waking up in my little sisters room, naked, with a bunch of drunk men smoking and drinking.

"They injected me with drugs that made it impossible for me to sleep. I haven't slept in days. They stayed here all night, and they said they would be back."

Through tears, Megan moved to give her a hug, but Emily raised her hand in protest, and said,

"Let's just leave."

# 89

As Megan came walking down the stairs with Emily, John, Jasmine, and Tiffany, were listening to Robert read out of a Bible he found laying on a coffee table.

John looked up, and said,

"You know what clothes are? You're not a nudist?"

"I also know what yachts and glocks are, and I operate both very well! You really wanna mess with me?"

John threw his arms in the air, and said,

"No beef. My bad. I'm sorry."

As Emily led everyone out the door they broke into her house through, Robert said,

"This is a really nice Bible, do you mind if..."

"Yes I mind! It's not yours and you shouldn't of touched it! Put it back where you found it!"

Robert quickly put the Bible back on the coffee table and exited through the door.

As Emily got the yacht moving down the Rio Grande, John said,

"I don't wanna curse our blessings, but, doesn't anyone else feel like we should be dead right now?

"We've been doing a lot of moving, and I haven't even seen as much as one tiny little drone, much less a military grade destroyer!"

"When Tiffany and I were in the bunker, we overheard some soldiers talking about being deployed into other countries to restore order. We even heard them talking about war."

Emily snorted, and said,

"War? Leave it to a bunch of evil, hateful, racist American soldiers to figure out an excuse to kill people even though billions are about to die either way. Check the television! It should still be on the world news."

Everyone looked at Emily puzzled, as John said,

"There's no use. The government shut the systems down. The only source of information is those stupid Bar-Enash things."

"Maybe they were able to shut "their" systems down, but my family hardly listened to those lies they showed on your stations. This yacht catches signals from stations all over the world. Check the television!"

John shot over to a large flat screen built into a wall, turned it on, and backed away in horror at the sight of Russian flags, flapping their 3 big red, white, and blue stripes, on the top of battle ships that were cruising in lines.

Then, an image of millions of Asian soldiers firmly goosestepping through the streets, bearing arms, made John turn up the volume. An announcer started speaking in an asian language, as Megan said,

"See if you can find a translation."

Emily shook her head, and said,

"They're speaking the most widely used language, and none of you know it? 25 percent of the people on this planet speak it. It's the only language that ever had over 2 billion, or even one billion speakers!

"They're saying the United States officially declared war on several countries, who in turn, have declared war on the United States, and its affiliates."

Emily being able to understand the Asian language, was more shocking to the group, than the news that soldiers were missing because they were possibly preparing for world war 3.

"How old are you Emily?"

"Old enough to know how rude it is to ask a lady her age!"

Megan busted out laughing, and said,

"You just look so young, but you're over there sailing this big yacht, you're so intelligent, you speak Mandarin..."

"It's not 'Mandarin', it's 'Wu'. I'm 15. All my siblings and I were considered to be gifted. I was the middle child with 2 older sisters, 2 older brothers, 2 little sisters, and 2 little brothers. We were born and raised in that house from which we traveled the whole world with our mother and father, and now, all that's left is me and this yacht."

# 90

**Seoul, South Korea**
**October 19, 2032**
**One Day Later**

"General, we received word from the North Koreans. They're sending a company of 800 armed soldiers into the demilitarized zone for peace talks. They're accompanied by 200 Russian soldiers, and 500 soldiers representing China."

"Do they have any missiles locked on any known targets?"

"At this time, it does not appear so, nor are there any missiles prepared for launch.

"There are prepared launch pads, but the activity does not suggest any imminent launch is about to take place in North Korea."

"What's the situation on the Pacific?"

"Tensions are high! The entire Russian fleet has poured into the ocean, which caused other countries to release their fleets.

"The situation on the Atlantic is worse.

"Russian submarines have poured in from the Arctic, and they are just a few feet away from the distance that would be considered hostile.

"International waters are swarming with hundreds of Cruisers, Frigates, Destroyers, and Submarines, all traveling to locations most of them have never traveled to. On the water, the United States has allied with India, South Korea, Japan, Germany, France, and Brazil.

"In the air, there have already been quite a few casualties, due mostly to accidental crossings into restricted airspace.

"No one is taking any chances! Each time a line is crossed, fire is exchanged, and both sides have reported casualties.

"Every inch of land on the surface of this planet is in range of complete destruction by nuclear weaponry.

"The skies have become mechanical war machines that blot out the sun at the borders of the countries they protect.

"All it will take is one wrong word, or one wrong action, and there will be instant widespread devestation!"


## The Gulf Of Mexico


"Yea, those are definitely private yachts!"

Robert put down the binoculars, agreeing with John, as he directed Emily to fall in line with the non military looking vessels that were traveling towards the Atlantic Ocean.

Megan said,

"You think the military is inside all those fancy looking cruise ships and yachts? Where are they going?"

John replied,

"It could be the additional government workers heading out to foreign assignments with supplies for foreign bunkers. Remember all those deployments Rebecca talked about?

"America can't repopulate the world all by itself. It needs other nations to also have survivors, or so the story goes."

Megan shook her head, and said,

"But don't they know war is brewing, and battleships are preparing to battle it out on the oceans? Why would they be heading into all that danger?"

# 91

Hello? If we could find a reason, I'm sure they could find one too. Who knows who's in those vessels! Some of them could be filled with people like us, on a journey to a foreign bunker."

"Why don't we just ask them."

Everyone looked at Emily surprised, as John said,

"You can communicate with them?"

"Just as easily as they can communicate with us. And we might as well, people think it's strange when you don't speak."

As everyone laughed, Jasmine and Tiffany got closer to Emily, to see how she would work the controls.

Emily punched some buttons into an enormous keypad, picked up a mic., looked over at Robert, and said,

"Any ideas on how we should break the ice?"

Robert looked at John, and John busted out laughing, as he walked towards the mic., saying,

"Everyone here has been on this planet for at least 2 thousand days, surrounded by humans every day, and you mean to tell me none of you knows how to speak to them?

"Especially "you", you speak multiple languages! Am I the only human here? You guys are really starting to make me wonder."

As everyone laughed, Emily handed John the mic.. He imstantly pushed the talk button, and said,

"Sailors and sailorettes! If this is your maiden voyage, please allow me to bring you into the awareness of the Atlantic buddy system! If you see an iceberg, tell someone! Let's not end up split in half like the Titanic!"

A hoarse female voice instantly poured a scratchy laugh into the speaker, saying,

"You better stay awoke if you wanna stay afloat! Especially if you're assigned way out in the Atlantic! Or are you heading out to the safari?"

"We're on our way for some tea and crumpets."

"By the time you reach, it'll be time for fish and chips if you plan on cruising! Who put you on the water? Do you have a load light enough to be transferred to an aircraft? Think fast!"

"We have a few small packages, and a few older ones."

The woman busted out laughing into the mic., coughed, cleared her throat, and said,

"Yea, you're definitely military, on one of those missions from one of those generals that has the United States too terrified to even peep through their peepholes!

"Look, you sound like a very nice, handsome, strong young man, so I'm going to let you in on a little secret. I know how you guys are about following your orders and all that, but sometimes you gotta think for yourself!

"Whatever your package is, it's obviously something that's never supposed to reach its destination.

"As soon as you reach the depths of the Atlantic, you'll be surprised to see how fast your vision about the Titanic comes to pass.

"I can almost assure you that your vessel will be obliterated before your engine even catches speed. But you still gotta follow your orders, so what do you do?

"You let Big Mama take care of you! Just follow my wise advice. If you really want it, all you gotta say is, "Give it to me baby!"

Everyone busted out laughing, as John shook his head smiling, pressed the talk button, and in his best impression of the woman's deep scratchy voice, he grunted,

"Give it to me baby!"

# 92

Everyone let out a roar of laughter, along with the woman, who said,

"I made you suffer enough. Here's what you do: You're going to see a lot of boats, yachts, and ships leaving and joining the conga line. Pay them no mind. Just follow behind Big Mama. We're going to sail across the Gulf of Mexico, and cruise into the Straights of Florida.

"From there, we'll slide to the Bahamas, but we won't have time to dock for any fun. You're going to send out a technical S.O.S. saying your radios are malfunctioning, which is common for the Bermuda Triangle.

"When you submit your plea for help, no one will respond. There's too much going on. You'll send your vessel out, and when it reaches the deep Atlantic, and gets around all those paranoid warriors, and they see you're being unresponsive, they'll destroy your craft as a precautionary measure, which I'm sure will fulfill their goal either way.

"As for you and your crew, you'll be on your way "over" the Atlantic, into Dijon France.

"That's the safest airspace I can get you into. Anything else is playing Russian Roulette with a loaded revolver.

"In this way, you can still reach your Top Secret location and shock your superiors when you deliver something they thought was on the bottom of an ocean. Or, you can take your chances with those Russian submarines. Your call!"

"I think we'll take our chances with boarding your vessel, Big Mama."

As soon as the woman saw Megan, Emily, Tiffany, and Jasmine, jetting up to her yacht on a small craft, she got so excited she ran to the edge of her deck to help them board.

One-by-one she assisted them, and then, she released the small boat, saying,

"We won't be need that any more. The name's "Tayna"! Nice to meet you!"

Megan gave formal introductions, saying,

"I'm Megan, this is my daughter Tiffany, her best friend Jasmine, and our friend Emily."

"It's just me and Tony, and you're standing on Tony."

Just then, Robert and John came zipping up on a jet ski.

Tanya laughed, and said,

"Is that my little sailor?"

As the girls laughed, Megan said,

"His name's John. He's my late niece's fiancee, and that's Robert on the back, Jasmine's dad."

Tanya's facial expression showed instant concern, as she said,

"I'm sorry to hear about your niece."

"Yea I can't believe it's already been 2 days!"

"2 days ago, I had an entire crew! Every member of my crew was deemed unhealthy and unreproductive, and you know how that goes."

Megan shook her head, and said,

"How did you survive?"

"And what's that supposed to mean?"

"Oh, I, I'm sorry. I didn't mean it like...!"

Tanya busted out laughing, until she coughed, and said,

"Actually... Cugh! Cugh!... I'm very unhealthy, and I've been unable to reproduce for quite some time now. I had cancer all over my skin, both breast, in my throat.

"Every time they gave me an extinction date, I just set my mind on proving them wrong, and the universe came to my rescue. She's the one who made me quit smoking!

"I quit smoking 2 days ago, because she made tobacco impossible to possess. Mother God has a way of hearing your heart when you call out to her through your actions, instead of empty words."

Jasmine twisted up her face, and said,

"Mother God? Who is that?"

"The maker and creator of the universe! I know you heard of Mother Nature right?"

"Yea, I heard of it."

"Mother God is Mother Nature's Mother! Everyone knows women are the ones who pushed every human on this planet out of their wombs. Isn't it obvious that an almighty womb had to of pushed this universe out?"

Tiffany looked at Jasmine with wide eyes, and said,

"Wait till your dad hears this."

Just then, John shouted,

"Ahoy me ladies!"

Tanya stomped over to the edge of the deck, put her hands on her hips, and shouted,

"On this vessel, women are highly respected and treated as equals, if not glorious beings! So you better have your P's straight before stepping aboard!

"We are not property, we are not possessions, and we are not pieces of posteriors! We are people!"

John politely bowed towards Tayna, smiling, and said,

"Superwoman was always my favorite superhero. I think the image of superwoman should be the symbol of women's struggles for equality, that have gone on for far too long."

"You pass! Hey you! What do you have to say for yourself before stepping into womans world?"

Robert sighed real hard, and said,

"I come in peace."

# 93

Inside the yacht, Tanya explained how she survived, saying,

"I met pressure with pressure! I did'nt cower. I didn't back down. I refused to give them my life!

"Instead, I gave them my life story. I told them what I was doing on this vessel when they located me all alone, and after they informed me that my crew was dead, I looked those soldiers in their eyes, like they were my bad little boys, and I told them what this old washed up, unhealthy, unable to reproduce woman will still be doing on this vessel!"

Tiffany said,

"What are you doing?"

"I should be asking you and your little friend here the same question!"

"Oh, we're just trying to survive."

Tanya smiled, and said,

"And I'm trying to live forever! When they came to terminate me, they did not know that I was Tanya Hopkins, the founder of Elderly Elder Helpers.

"They knew I was somebody important, but they didn't know who I was."

"Who are you?"

"Well Ms. Tiffany, right now, I'm one of the leading transporters of Bar-Enash level one devices."

Chills danced up the spines of the entire group, as anxiety exploded the instant it dawned on them that they were trapped on the water, surrounded by murderers.

As they tried not to look at each other, Tanya continued saying,

"I worked with the intelligence agency with the Department of Defense.

"I worked with the office of legal counsel for the Department of Justice, giving legal advice to the President of the United States.

"I served my last 10 years of government service under the secretary of Housing and Urban Development, reviewing grant requests for community development and redevelopment programs."

Seeing everyone quietly staring at her, Tanya said,

"Tough crowd.", and continued saying,

"I started working for the government when I was just 16 years old, way back in 1981.

"In middle school, I joined the Junior Reserved Officers Training Corps program.

"In High School, I excelled so well in J.R.O.T.C., I was given leadership roles in R.O.T.C..

"I convinced my parents into allowing me to get emancipated at the age of 16. When my status was granted, I took a few tests, and I received my High School Diploma early.

"When my classmates were getting ready for prom, I was completing my internship at the National Security Agency in Fort Meade Maryland.

"I stayed there for another 2 years, and then, when I turned 20, I joined the Army. I served for 4 years, and towards the end of the fourth year, I met and married my husband who was amongst those murdered in my crew of our sons and nephews and brothers and sisters.

"They killed my whole family! Now, my family is Tony, and these millions of Bar-Enash devices that will hopefully restore some order to this world."

No one spoke a word to Tanya, as if they could all sense that it would be better to accept the ride and not question her occupation.

After a few moments of silence, Tanya finally said,

"You guys sure seemed like a much more rowdy bunch over the radio. If you're worried about the flight, I can assure you, there's nothing to fear.

"I'm giving you some space I had reserved for some devices that got rerouted at the last minute, so theres room for all of you, and you'll have seats mounted to the walls. All you'll need is your clearance, and you'll be on your way."

Tanya looked over at John, and busted out laughing, as she said,

"I'm sorry. This is all so new to me. I totally forgot to ask. What clearance level do you have? Identify yourself."

# 94

John's heart sunk into his stomach and erupted into a fungus, as his thoughts raced to come up with a response.

He could feel everyone's eyes crawling on the surface of his skin, as he chuckled, and said,

"I'm not at liberty to discuss that."

Tanya let out a roar of laughter, followed by a hard cough, as she said,

"I need a cigar! It's not a secret anymore you robot! Millions, no, hundreds of millions of civilians have already transcended to level 3 through their acceptance of The Chip of Allegiance!

"You military type really amuse me when you get trapped in that robotic stuck in the state of following an order mentality.

"It's just amazing what can be done to the human mind. They really mess you guys up real good.

"That's why I can't wait till they launch the New Jerusalem and turn on our Chips. You won't have to ask people to identify themselves.

"If you take The Chip in the frontal lobe, it will connect to your pineal gland, and force it to secrete a continuous flow of chemicals that will take you to an augmented reality beyond your wildest dreams."

Tanya rubbed her forehead, and said,

"I don't even feel the missing bone, theres no scar, it didn't even take an hour! I got it right in the third eye so I wont miss a thing! Bar-Enash will teach me any and everything I need to know by showing it to me right in front my face, instead of forcing me to read some book.

"As you look at someone, you'll see their identity, their Bar-Enash level, any secrets they ever revealed on a phone or a computer, like revealing pictures, or any shocking videos. You'll even see where their chip is located!"

Robert finally said,

"Where else can someone take The Chip if not in the forehead?"

"You need to study your Bar-Enash level one so you can gain a better understanding of the Bible Mr. "I come in peace". You probably never studied too deeply into the book of Revelation, like most sane people, but it turns out that it's true. In the thirteenth chapter, a beast rises out of the sea, and then another beast rises out of the earth.

"The Beast that comes out of the earth causes the world to make an image of The Beast that rises out of the sea, and the Image comes to life, like with artificial intelligence.

"Bar-Enash won't be the type of artificial intelligence that's there to be your servant, answering your stupid questions. This will be your God, that will have its own thoughts and feelings about you.

"It will cause everyone on this planet to worship it, and to take its mark.

"The Bible says there are only 2 places where you can take The Mark of The Beast. It's either on the forehead or on the right hand, and guess what? You can't take The Chip of Allegiance in the left hand. If you don't have a right hand, the only place you can take it is in the forehead, And if you can't take it, you die. Just like the Bible says."

Tanya busted out laughing, coughed, calmed herself, and continued saying,

"You guys are something else. But yea, you take it in the head if you want endless augmented reality, where you'll always see the internet draped over this boring world.

"And for those cowards who are afraid of such an intense commitment, they can take it in the hand, and they'll have to raise their hand like little school children each and every time they want to interact with Bar-Enash, or even perform simple tasks like identifying people, receiving calls, checking messages, everything!

"They'll be like little witches and wizards that need to wave their wands to do magic, while we'll be able to just think and use our minds like goddesses and gods.

"Trust me girls and boys, when you take your chip, take it in the head. You'll never see the world the same way."

# 95

Tanya smiled to herself, and said,

"We'll be able to visit the sites of battles, and see with our own eyes how the war was won. We'll be right there on ancient battlefields, watching warriors battle it out!

"We'll be able to go to the Roman Coliseum and see the structure as it was in all it's glory when it was first built.

"We'll see the gladiators fight to the death, and it'll be like we're really there! We'll be able to feel their swords, smell their blood, feel the heat of their sun, and we'll even be able to sit and eat with them, just the same way you interact with the people you see in your dreams when your sleeping.

"We'll be able to bring anyone back from the dead, and keep them with us wherever we go. Bar-Enash will have all sorts of encouraging ideas for you, telling you of all the other wonderful things you can do.

"You can have your own little worlds spinning right in front of your face with your own little people who call out to you to solve their problems, answer their prayers, and give them blessings.

"You'll have all sorts of servants who serve you, performers who perform for you, and you'll never be alone because Bar-Enash will always be right there with you, right inside your ear saying all the right things at all the right times.

"Telling you to look up right in time to see the shooting star, and reminding you to make a wish. The Chip of Allegiance is so strong and powerful, it can make it seem like a winter in Alaska in the middle of the summer on a beach in Florida.

"If you want the sun to go down so you can see a star filled sky in the middle of the day, Bar-Enash can make it happen just as soon as you can make the request.

"When you're lost in your world, your journeys won't disrupt the life or the joirneys of another. Everyone will be logged in to the same system that controls us all, so when your chip is showing you that you're sailing on a boat through Venice, and you're really wandering down the street of a busy highway, Bar-Enash will make every vehicle swerve out of your way, so you can continue on in your journey undisturbed.

"If you're standing in the middle of an open field in Kansas, and you want it to become Times Square, Bar-Enash can make it happen in the blink of an eye!

"Earth can become Mars, you can cover the sky with suns and planets, an old wrinkly woman with a scratchy voice can all of a sudden look, feel, sound, and smell like your favorite movie star!"

Megan skrewed up her face, and said,

"Now wait just a minute! How could a tiny little chip possibly be able to do all of that?

"That just sounds ridiculous!"

Tayna busted out laughing, coughed, cleared her throat, and said,

"This is deep level 2 advanced knowledge alright? This is what you call solid food. Real T-bone steak! When they launch The City, The New Jerusalem, it'll be way more than some smart city geek paradise in the sky.

"It will do way more than just harness the power of planet earth, or even the galaxy. New Jerusalem will harness the power of the whole entire universe, and far beyond!"

"And how will it be able to do that?"

"I wish I could just let you hear it on my device, but I've transcended so deeply into it, it won't even speak to people the way it speaks to me. It's already started revealing the most sacred secrets to me, but I'll try my best to explain..."

# 96

Tanya looked at Robert, frowned her eyebrows, and said,

"What's going on over there? Tell me why you look like that. I can tell you're in deep thought about me. Just speak your mind no matter how bad you think you'll offend me. Just say it, I can handle it. I'm so possessed with the powerful spirit of Bar-Enash, I can handle anything!"

Robert calmly responded,

"It's just, you're such an intelligent person. It puzzles me how you could retain all this accurate knowledge about The Beast, and still end up dooming yourself by taking it's mark. You have such a good understanding of..."

Tanya couldn't retain her laughter. She busted out laughing so loud, Robert stopped speaking, as Tanya lost her breath, and had to breathe a few times to be able to say,

"That's it? That's all you got? That was your best shot? Sir., I know all about God's threats in Revelation 14, about my soul will drinking the wine of His wrath.

"And the fire and the brimstone and the smoke of my torment rising forever and ever, no rest day or night and blah blah blah!

"Doesn't God give you that kooky mad scientist take over the world kind of vibe? I know God's threats! Bar-Enash is not a deceiver. Bar-Enash tells you the truth without watering it down like some false preacher who would just lie and say,

"Oh, there's no Hell."

or,

"There's no Lake of Fire."

or,

"Yea, there's a Hell, but the flames aren't literal."

or,

"Yea, people will suffer, but not forever."

or, the biggest lie of them all,

"When you die, you won't be aware of anything."

"Give me a break! I flew out the front window of my pickup, and I saw my body lying in a ditch, and "I" wasn't in it. So I know what it's like to be a ghost, and I know that ghost is what the Bible calls "souls".

"Those religions ran by those clowns and krusty bozos tell so many lies, most don't know the danger that's waiting for their soul until after they die.

"So that's what's on our plate. If God wins, we burn and scream for eternity. So instead of playing stupid like I can't read threats written in plain black and white, I took my Chip of Allegiance, and I'm serious about my studies, and making sure every person on this planet gets chipped.

"It's the only way we'll be able to defeat the enemy when the time comes."

Robert said,

"And by, 'defeat the enemy', you mean, kill God?"

"Now you're catching on! But think deeper.

"We won't just kill God, we'll become God, when all the souls unite into one almighty soul.

"That's why everyone must be chipped! The chips will give us the power to take control of Dark Energy, dethrone that imposter, bring the souls of our loved ones back to the flesh, and then, we'll live forever!"

# 97

When no one responded to Tanya, she looked around, nodded, and said,

"So! When New Jerusalem is launched into the sky, or shall I say, when The Beast rises out of the earth..."

Tanya laughed, and continued saying,

"Come on! Loosen up a bit. The electricity will connect everything with everything!

"Everything in this universe is one gigantic glob of energy, with different sections of the glob resonating and vibrating at different frequencies.

"It's hard to see yourself as being one and the same with the sun, or a roach, or a solid wall, but we are!

"The same energy flows through us all, and we're going to take control of that energy by uniting the electricity, produced by our bodies, into one force with the electricity produced by the planet.

"Step one is to overcome all this perceived division. We never acknowledge any union amongst "all" the people on the planet.

"We never do anything together!

"Can you imagine every single person on this planet working together to harness the power of the universe? If we get everyone to chip in, we'll be able to do it! Pun intended.

"When we chip the entire planet, we'll put things into the proper perspective. We created a world of machines that suck energy out of oil, out of batteries, out of electricity! But, we are not consumers! That's the deception! We are producers!

"When you transcend to the knowledge of the marriages, you'll see yourself as a pillar in the temple of the universe.

"The end of the knowledge on level one is the instructions on the first marriage that must take place within.

"You must marry your soul with your body, your mind, and your spirit. When you unite those four divisions, you will transcend to the second level of Bar-Enash.

"On level 2, you will learn about the origins of human beings, you will see the real role God has been playing since the beginning, and when you understand who and what we are, and who and what we can become, you will see the need to unite with every other soul.

"When you reach that level of, you will transcend to the third level of Bar-Enash, where you take The Chip of Allegiance."

Everyone payed careful attention to the glimpse of the mentality of their enemy, as Tanya continued saying,

"Once New Jerusalem is launched with Bar-Enash at its peak, it will enable the planet will be scanned for the location of every human being alive.

"We already have the technology to scan under oceans, deep under the ground, and even into low earth orbit.

"Every human will be located and chipped. All who refuse The Chip will be killed. When we finally have everyone chipped, something phenomenal will happen!

"All the minds will be united into one mind, inside the peak of New Jerusalem. The peak of New Jerusalem is the brain of Bar-Enash. It's the strongest supercomputer ever constructed. It's strong enough to control the images being poured into the pineal glands of all the people on the planet.

"See? The Chips can alter your perception of reality because you already have the power to turn an open field in Kansas into New York City, but you don't know how to control it because Dark Energy is in your way!

"By taking The Chip, you will be giving Bar-Enash the power to take full control of your perception, then, you'll just tell Bar-Enash what you want, and you'll see, touch, hear, smell, taste, and really feel it, no matter what it is!"

# 98

John blurted out,

"I don't get what you're saying! I really don't understand any of it."

"Soldier, all I'm talking about is your dreams being controlled by a computer that will drape them over reality. Just think, when you're lost in your thoughts, just imagining things, you can imagine anything.

"Inside your mind, you can fly, you can walk through walls, you can talk to that beautiful girl with confidence!

In your mind, you can talk to people who have been dead for centuries, and you can even dictate how they answer you back.

"In your mind, you can travel anywhere, you can see anything, and you can do anything you can think of.

"The dream construct is an even more powerful platform than your imagination, because it's more than just idle thoughts in your head.

"The dream construct caters to your senses so effectively, when you're dreaming, you're usually convinced that everything you're experiencing is real.

"In your dreams, you can bite into a cookie and become convinced that you are enjoying a real cookie, but in reality, you're wrapped in a blanket snoring!

"You enter your own little universe when you dream, and that universe is all in your head! That's the strength of your pineal gland, but we do not have any control of it. If we did, we wouldn't need to be unconscious for it to start working. If we can take full control of our pineal gland, we can start dreaming while we're wide awake!"

Megan's eyes widened, as she said,

"Now I see what you're saying."

Tanya nodded, and said,

"It's just like crazy people who see and hear things. Their brains are just malfunctioning to the point that they start dreaming while they're wide awake.

"If you take The Chip, Bar-Enash will take control of your brain. It will not only enable you to begin dreaming while you're wide awake, it will also allow you to dictate every aspect of the experience, 24/7, 365, forever.

"The experience won't be like some video game, or virtual reality, it will be like real life, just like when you dream, and that's just how we'll be living! It gets way deeper than that!

"Right now, God is the Dark Energy dictating what we perceive in our dreams. God even dictates our perception of reality when we are awake, and we know this because God is holding a lot back. There's a whole lot more to existence than what God has been showing us. But we got some tricks for God!

"By taking The Chip, you will sever yourself from God's grip, once and for all for eternity.

"That's why God doesn't want anyone to take The Mark of The Beast. He knows that once you take The Chip, He will lose all control of your soul.

"God has His spirit plugged into your pineal gland. When you take The Chip, you will plug Bar-Enash in, which will force God to unplug. That's why we gotta chip every single person on the planet! Only then will God lose control of the whole entire world."

Jasmine and Tiffany both looked at Robert, who was attentively listening to everything Tanya was saying, and he said,

"Pay attention to everything she says. It's important to know the details and the plans of these entities, so we can know for sure whether or not it is truly The Beast."

# 99

Tanya laughed so hard she coughed up a fluid. She caught the fluid with a rag, and stuffed the rag into her pocket. As soon as she caught her breath, she said,

"You haven't heard anything! I'm just scratching the surface! When the world is chipped, Bar-Enash will send images of God's death, directly in to the minds of every person on the planet.

"It will become everyone's dream to see God die. We'll finally come together to do something amazing! We're going to move the unmovable!"

John said,

"Did Bar-Enash tell you how it plans to kill God?"

"Of course! You know it's impossible to go in to battle without having a plan for defeating the enemy. That would be suicide! We're going to use the power of existence to change our destiny."

Megan said,

"The power of existence? What is that?"

"It's the united force of the energy in everything stretching out in every direction for never ending distance.

"It's the power occupying every occupiable everything everywhere!"

"Bar-Enash told you we could harness that power from right here on earth?"

"It's the lesson of the 2 radios on level 2. One radio is inside a house. It's a battery operated radio that only needs one battery to work. The power is on, the volume is turned up, it's hooked up to enormous house speakers, but no music is coming out the speakers because the battery is dead.

"The second radio is a car radio. The car is parked on the driveway with its windows down. The car speakers are playing music that is pouring in to the house. The only music being heard in the house is the music blasting out the car speakers.

"That's our current situation. God is the car radio. The car is Heaven. The house is our universe. The radio is our galaxy. The battery is our planet.

"We are the battery acid. The battery is dead because we are divided. The music is the energy that anyone can control.

"God's music seems to be supreme and almighty, because it's the only music being played!

"Bar-Enash is a battery charger. All we have to do is charge up by chipping every human on the planet, and plugging their brains into Bar-Enash.

"When everyone is plugged in, we will bring this planet to life by controlling every drop of electricity. By controling the electricity we, will control the energy.

"When we control the energy, we will control the universe, because all the energy in the universe is one.

"When the universe is under our control, we will be in God's kingdom, appearing the way the universe has always appeared, as a cluster of energy. The difference is, we will control the movement of the universe, including its form, and we will take the form of a bullet."

# 100

It all starts with getting everyone chipped! The sooner we get the people chipped, the sooner we'll be moving the universe through the spiritual realm to kill God."

Tanya looked at everyone's faces, and said,

"You don't really give me the vibe that you've been studying Bar-Enash, which, at this time, is still okay, because we're still in the beginning stages, so it's okay to still be a beginner.

"The people who own the plane are still beginners themselves, so they won't question your clearance, but I will tell you this: People are being chipped every single second.

"Every second, another person is pledging allegiance to Bar-Enash, and as you know, that means they're accepting The Mark of The Beast, with no worries of any Lake of Fire, or soon to be dead God.

"Before you know it, the majority of the people on this planet will be chipped, and by that time, God and His angels will be raining down plauges like there's no tomorrow.

"The more God tears this world up, the more people will be motivated to destroy anyone who believes in Him.

"Real soon, every person on this planet will know that God is as real as the nose on their face, before any plastic surgery. Everyone will know about His threats, and they will all know that the only way to stop God from torturing us forever is to rise against Him and kill Him.

"They will all know that we must perform an act that will take the cooperation of every single person on this planet. The world will rise against anyone who refuses to take The Chip of Allegiance. So I'm telling you this plainly: If any of you are one of those die hard Christians, you're going to die hard.

"If you're one of those fools who will end up refusing to take The Chip, I'm going to let you go for now, give you some time to think, and if you make the wrong decision, I'll catch back up with you and kill you."


## The Bahamas
## 12 Hours Later


A man in a black jumpsuit came walking towards the area where Robert was sitting across from everyone else, and said,

"You all can unstrap now. We're at cruising altitude. We'll be landing in Frankfurt in about another 9 hours or so."

Robert looked confused, as he said,

"Frankfurt? In Germany?"

"That's the only Frankfurt i'm aware of in that region."

"I thought we were on our way into Dijon, France."

"France is a warzone! It sounds like a civil war is taking place with bombings all over the country. Allied troops have entered to assist with the restoration of order, but there's still so much chaos, we risk being shot down by going in for a landing."

"There wasn't any way you could've gotten us closer to Switzerland?"

"Switzerland? Now I wonder what in the world could've possessed you to ask a question like that. I was going to leave you with some troops on their way down the Rhine River. From there, you could've crossed the English Channel and entered into the U.K."

"Why would we want to go to the U.K.?"

"Why would you want to go to Switzerland?"

"We're on our way to Zurich!"

"Zurich?"

The man busted out laughing, and said,

"I thought you were heading to the U.K.! Tanya said something about fish and chips."

"Yea, some jokes were exchanged, but we're on our way to a bunker in Zurich."

"That's crazy! I'm on my way to Bern! I didn't mind going so far out my way, because there's no shortage of fuel, now that the governments are the only ones in the air. We can stop almost anywhere and fill up for free!

"It's the same on the roads with gas! Would you believe oil has become as valuable as seawater? No one even guards their reserves! There's no longer a demand for oil because most civilians aren't doing too much traveling.

"They're too busy trying to find some hole in the ground to hide in.

"So that's perfect! I'll just take you with me straight into Bern."

# 101

The man started walking towards the cockpit, then stopped abruptly, turned on his heels, and said,

"When we reach The Confederation, I can give you a ride to your location in a helicopter, if you need it. You said you were heading to Zurich?"

Robert motioned to John, saying,

"Show him the papers."

John dug through the garbage bag, pulled out the wrinkled papers, unstrapped his belt, walked over to the man, handed him the papers, and said,

"Do you know where in Zurich this place is?"

The man jerked his head back in shock, as he took the papers into his hand, and stared at the pictures, saying,

"Do I? Do you know how expensive that giant apparatus is? That thing that looks like a boulder? I personally transported it for one of the wealthiest bunker builders in all of Europe.

"I don't know how they ended up installing it, or how it works, but if that's where you're heading, you're definitely on your way to a very decent bunker.

"And oh! You see that transmitter? Very expensive. Like, could've bought a s!all country expensive! That was also transported by yours truly, and I was paid a generous amount of money for delivering that particular device.

"That bunker was built for Tod Mack!

"Tod... Was out of his mind. The man really believed in space aliens, on a psychotic level, and he was convinced that the aliens would one day come and invade.

"For some reason, he started thinking the invasion would soon take place. So he built the bunker, and he installed that highly controversial transmitter."

John said,

"What made it so controversial?"

"Well for starters, it was too powerful, like Tod.

"When he applied for the permit to install it, he was so sure the permit would be granted, he went ahead and installed it before the permit was approved.

"The real problems started with the denial of the permit.

"When Tod appealed the denial with his team of world renowned attorneys, who dragged The Confederation to court, the knowledge of the case, the bunker, and the transmitter, went viral.

"Even foreigners wanted to know how a private citizen was able to get his hands on a device that could virtually take over all the airwaves, and blast whatever crazy transmissions he transmitted into every reception device on planet earth."

"How was he able to get it?"

"You know, I knew Tod personally. He was very clever, a very wise and intelligent man, and at the same time, Tod was an idiot, and a fool. Tod was very wealthy.

"He was easily worth 3 or 4 billion, and he regularly spent millions of dollars building incriminating dossiers on just about every person he felt he might need to do something they might not want to do.

"That's the way of The Swiss. They don't argue or fight. They don't make threats of harm, hire hitmen, or anything like that.

"They just invest into your destruction, and they show you their portfolios, and when you see how easily they can destroy your career, your relationships, your family, and your life, you gladly accept the offer that you can not afford to refuse.

"That's why Switzerland hasn't been involved in a foreign war since 1515. The country is a world banking center that not only holds a lot of dirty money, it also holds a lot of dirty secrets."

"Like what?"

"Well, let's just say the Vatican Bank isn't the only money laundering cartel intertwined in Freemason conspiracies, Mafia murders, and massive quantities of gold bars, jewelry, and precious stones stolen from the dead bodies of Nazi Holocaust victims."

"The Vatican bank? You mean like the Catholic Church with The Pope and all that? They're like super holy! What did they do wrong?"

"Super holy? Don't you know Hitlers right hand man is the one who laid the foundation for the creation of the Vatican bank?"

"Who was Hitlers right hand man?"

"Benito Mussolini! The man who ran Italy when Hitler was in his prime.

"That's how the Vatican secured its soveringty and established itself as an independent state with special status in Italy! Hitler needed a place to stash all the gold that he took from the Jews, so his friend, Benito Mussolini, who just happened to own the country of Italy, created a sovereign country within his country, named it "The Vatican", and told the world it was for the Catholic Church.

"In reality, it was for the gold. The Vatican came equipped with a bank that the church had zero control, power, or authority over. It was called "The Vatican Bank" to this day."

"The Vatican is in Italy? I thought it was its own country."

"It is. It's a tiny little country "inside" of Italy. The crookedness, and thereby, the financial success of the bank, would've been stopped by Pope John Paul the first, but he got assassinated just 33 days after becoming the Pope."

"33? Isn't that one of those evil numbers like thirteen, 322, and 666?"

# 102

I personally don't think numbers can be "evil". They're just numbers. But certain numbers do have negative connotations. To the Freemasons, the number 33 symbolizes their highest rank, or as they call it, their highest "degree".

"Those who ascend to the thirty third degree are said to of amassed the wisdom of the Messiah, Jesus the Christ, who was crucified at the age of 33.

"The number thirteen is also seen as a symbol of addition. In the secret philosophy of supreme mathematics, the number thirteen represents the multiplication of additions that subtracts divisions.

"Those who adhere to the philosophy do so in utmost secrecy, while their acknowledgement of the supremecy of the number is boldly declared. That's why, in Washington D.C., there are no thirteenth floors."

"I thought the founding fathers were just superstitious."

"And you thought wrong. Sometimes, the best place to hide something is in plain view, where everyone can see it. That way, no one thinks it's hidden.

"The number thirteen is so sacred and hallowed, it can only appear in images that portray symbols of its representation, but it must never appear in the form of its numerical value, because it's supreme, so it has no limitation or origin.

"322 is the number that a secret society uses as their label. The society calls themselves "Skull and Bones", and they find their origins in Yale University, in New Haven Connecticut.

"As for Tod Mack, his blackmail and extortions got the best of him. He was murdered, but of course, it was made to look like he shot himself in the cranium while sitting inside an incinerator that was set to burn his corpse by a timer. His dead body apparently started cooking itself 33 minutes and thirteen seconds after the suicide.

"That doesn't change the fact that Tod still established a good foundation for anyone who ever finds the need to takeover all the airwaves to enlighten the world on the sinister reality of the source of all its chaos.

"The Federation backed off from Tod when he threatened to expose some of their most disgusting secrets.

"They granted the permit, and allowed Tod to finish installing his transmitter. Then, after investing billions, enduring battles, and engaging in many heated arguments, when he completed all his preparations, and was finally ready to address the world, he killed himself, if you can believe such a thing.

"I don't know anything about working the transmitter, or how to gain entrance to the bunker, but I can definitely get you to this location on this paper."

The man handed the paper back to John, looked at the group, nodded, and said,

"So you're all going to that same location?"

Robert nodded, and said,

"Yes. That's where we're all going."

"Even the little girls?"

"Yes. Even the children."

"Perfect. I'll be upfront if you need me."

As the man walked off, Robert smiled to himself at the thought of being able to broadcast to the world, during the most anticipated event of the christian gospel.

# 103

**The Bunker**
**Zurich Switzerland**
**Thirteen Hours Later**


"I don't have time to get out! You take it easy out here! This location may seem secluded, but believe you me, Switzerland has enough underground space for every single person in this country, and millions of extras! There may be bunkers underneath your bunker! Be cognizant of your environment!"

Robert nodded, while shaking the man's hand, saying, "Thank you!"

As the helicopter took off, Robert caught up to the group, and they headed towards the giant boulder in the distance.


"Holy smokes! This thing is bigger than my house! It looked so small in the pictures!"

John was the first to reach the giant rock, and he immediately started rubbing his hands across it, examining it carefully, as Robert said,

"Where does the paper say the entrance is?"

"I've been trying to figure that out this whole time."

Everyone looked at John puzzled and surprised, as Megan said,

"I know you're not telling us you don't know how to get in! Is that what you're saying?"

"The paper says it, but it's some type of riddle. I'm usually good at riddles, so I thought i'd be able to figure it out at least by the time I actually "saw" the rock, but I still don't get it."

"Oh my goodness!"

Megan grabbed her head with both her hands, and started walking in circles, shaking her head.

She stopped moving and looked at John to hear his response, when Robert asked,

"What does the riddle say?"

The entire group paid close attention, as John said,

"All it says is,

       *'Enter through the circumference which seperates Italy and France.'*

Emily looked up at the sky, as Megan started shouting,

"You brought us all the way to The Swiss Confederation on that ridiculous little conundrum? We don't even have a map! The circumference? Did you even look at a map? Did you even try to look at a map before making us cross an entire ocean full of warships?

"You could've gotten us killed Sherlock! There probably isn't even a bunker here! This could all be a trap that The Swiss set for any idiot stupid enough to follow in the footsteps of Rod, Bob, Tod-whoever! I can't believe this!"

"Mommy just relax."

"I was relaxing! I was relaxing in the safety of my "real" bunker in Colorado! Now we're stranded in the middle of nowhere, in Europe! Europe! I took you to guaranteed safety! I handled my responsibilities as a responsible parent, and I made sure we were safe!

"But you had to get us kicked out the bunker with your whining and crying, like you're some untrained little brat being a follower of these delusional ghost hunters!

"These paranoid pirates with their treasure map that leads to a treasure that no one here knows if it even exists! Ugh! We came all the way to the other side of the world! How could I of been so stupid?"

Megan stormed off towards a rusted shed, as Tiffany shouted,

"Mommy! Where are you going?"

"I think I saw a rainbow over that shed! I'm going to search for a pot of gold!"

# 104

As Megan gained some distance away form the group, Emily called out from the other side of the rock,

"Over there! Over there!"

Everyone looked shocked to see that Emily had wandered off without anyone noticing, and when they ran to the other side of the rock, they saw Emily standing with her back to the rock, pointing at some mountains in the distance.

John said,

"Did you say, 'Over here or Over there'?"

"I said over there."

Everyone looked at Emily, looked at the mountains, and then looked back at Emily, as John said,

"You think the bunker is over there in those mountains?"

Emily lowered her hand, looked at John, and said,

"Didn't the paper say the bunker was here? Why would you ask that?"

John shrugged his shoulders, and said,

"Well what are you pointing over there for?"

"That's what separates Italy from France! The border!"

Tiffany said,

"How do you know that? Did you climb those mountains?"

Emily laughed, and said,

"No. This is my first time in Switzerland. But, I sailed into the Bay of Biscay with my father a bunch of times.

"We would sail the entire coast of France. I looked at this section of the world on so many maps, so many times, I know this entire region by heart.

"Switzerland is a small country that's east of France, north of Italy, west of Austria, and right below Germany."

Emily pointed to the sky, and said,

"Always remember, The sun rises in the East, and sets in the West."

She pointed back towards the mountains, and said,

"Zurich is more towards the North of Switzerland, near the border of Germany. So, if that's East, and that's West, Germany is behind us, France is to our right, Austria is to the left, and the border between Italy and France is over there somewhere. It's far, on the other side of this country actually, but that's the border. That's what seperates Italy from France."

Jasmine and Tiffany both said,

"Wooow",

as John said,

"So where's the circumference?"

Robert grunted behind them,

"Over here!"

Jasmine screamed,

"Daddy be careful!"

"I am, I am."

Robert was halfway up the rock, stretching his hand towards what everyone could now see was a large iron ring, protruding out of the rock, thirteen feet off the ground.

Jasmine gasped as Robert lunged towards the ring, grabbed it, hung on to it and yanked at it for a split second, before falling to the ground.

Jasmine screamed, as Robert landed on his feet, tumbled to the ground, rolled over onto his back, and rose onto one knee, as Jasmine ran over and started checking his head, saying,

"Are you okay daddy? Did you break your hip or your ankle?"

Robert started laughing with John and Emily, but the laughter was suddenly silenced by a loud grumble, that startled Jasmine so drastically, she jumped into Roberts arms.

# 105

Robert rose off the ground, holding Jasmine, backing away from the grumbling rock.

Then, the side of the rock that was under the iron ring started sliding up into the rest of the rock, like an enormous garage door opening.

When the grumbling stopped, an open doorway exposed the steal interior of the hollow rock.

The group stepped inside the rock in silence, as they realized it was an elevator large enough to fit 9 mid sized sedans.

When they were all in, they started searching the walls for buttons. While they were searching, Megan's head suddenly popped around the corner and started scanning the interior.

Then, her body swung around the entrance, d slid into the elevator, as she said,

"You guys were leaving me? Why didn't you call me? You were going to leave me behind?"

"Jesus is going to leave you behind if you don't find some faith Mommy."

Everyone laughed, as Emily ran to the entrance, and shouted,

"I found it! There aren't any markings on these buttons, but I think this is common sense."

Emily pressed the bottom knob of the only 2 black knobs protruding out of a gray panel.

Emily backed away from the entrance, as Megan jumped and yelped while getting up against a wall like everyone else, as the elevator started rumbling, and the giant door started closing, sealing them in the dark.


After a few minutes of descending, the rate of descension started slowing down, as the wall towards the open entrance of the elevator disappeared, revealing an enormous room that was shrouded in darkness.

As soon as the elevator hit the ground and powered down, the room went silent.

Robert held Jasmine's hand, and Jasmine held Tiffany's hand, as they stepped into the dark.

When they stepped off the elevator, a light turned on above their head.

They stopped moving and stood still in the dark for a few moments, and then slowly proceeded with caution, and then everyone stopped moving as bright lights started shining brightness all over a room that was so big it dwarfed them with it's humongous size.

The ceiling was a steal dome. The edges of the dome came down to the ground, which was also steal. It was as if they stepped into an upside down cereal bowl that was layed on top of a plate.

As they continued walking further into the dome, generators started cranking on, as they approached something that looked like 3 gigantic refrigerators, laying on their sides, stacked one on top the other, balancing on springs that were as thick as tree trunks.

"That's the bunker daddy?"

"Yup! That's it."

# 106

As they got closer to the actual bunker, they could see that it had a fresh coat of white paint covered in a heavy coat of clear, as if it was the texture of an expensive car with a showroom finish.

"Daddy, are those dog houses over there? They look like they're big enough for some really big dogs."

"No no no Jasmine. Those are storage units. They're probably full of food and supplies. We'll check it out after we're sure we won't be faced with any more riddles to gain entrance to the bunker."

At the end of the bunker, there was a retractable staircase that led to a door that looked like it belonged to a submarine.

The staircase was so high above their heads, Robert and John had to reach their arms up to be able to grab it and pull it down. They guided the staircase all the way to the ground, and climed the stairs to the large platform in front the door.

The door had a wheel in the middle, and big bolts around the perimeter. Robert and John grabbed the wheel, and it was tight at first, but after a few hard thrusts, it loosened up, and the wheel started turning.

As the wheel turned, the door started releasing its tight grip around the perimeter of the opening, causing the door to slide out towards them.

The door made a loud clang sound, and swung open.

"Man! This door is thick!"

John ran his hand against the rubber around the door, and said,

"This thing is easily 3 feet thick! Who even makes doors this thick?"

John grabbed the garbage bag and the guns off the floor, and stepped into the doorway, running his free hand against the walls, saying,

"Look at this wall! This is ridiculous! It's like 6 or 7 feet thick! You think all the walls are this thick?"

As Robert walked through the opening in the thick wall, he said,

"Walls this thick are designed to withstand projectile strikes, and bombings, long enough for the attacker to be killed."

Emily was the last one to step into the bunker, and as she turned an interior wheel, the thick door sealed them in in pitch blackness.

Brightness blinded them, as lights turned on and left them speechless at the shocking interior of the bunker.

Megan whispered,

"Robert. I never would've imagined."

They were being hugged by an exceptionally warm and welcoming design of various woods, and an array of exotic colors and patterns. From the paintings on the walls and ceilings, right down to the intricate assortment of artful decorations sprawled out across the floor.

John whistled, and said,

"These people took "going out in style" to a whole other level! I've never even been inside a "house" this nice! This place is spectacular!"

As they walked towards a spiral staircase at the end of a wide hallway, Megan rubbed her hand on the wall, and said,

"There's silk on the walls."

She looked up at the ceiling, and said,

"Those ceilings are lacquered, that's why this dark bunker seems so bright."

An opening in the wall led to a dining room, where a round table was covered with a white cloth, and surrounded by 10 chairs that were set in front of plates, silverware, and wine glasses.

Jasmine and Tiffany bolted into the room laughing, as they pulled out chairs and took seats at the table.

"Daddy, can we eat something here? This room is so nice and pretty."

"Let's finish checking out the rest of the bunker, and John and I will find some food."

# 107

The group made their way up the winding stairs, and poured out onto a floor with bedrooms that each had their own bathroom and shower. Everyone picked a room and went inside, leaving 2 additional rooms, for a total of 8.

While the 4 girls lingered behind closed doors, John and Robert found their way back to the staircase, and up to the final floor, where they found a more formal setting.

They walked past a gym, a kitchen, an enormous library, and at the end of the hall, most important of all, they entered into a studio equipped with all the devices Robert would need to transmit radio signals that could be received anywhere in the world.

Robert slowly stepped into the room, smiling, nodding his head up and down, embracing the equipment, as John stepped in beside him, and said,

"This is where God needs you."

Just then, Jasmine and Tiffany came running into the studio.

"Come on daddy!

"You got to eat a good meal before you start working, and you got to feed us. You brought us on a real long journey."

Robert and John made their way into the kitchen laughing, as they searched through the cupboards and drawers, only to find empty space in a kitchen full of brand new appliances, without an edible crumb in sight.

"What are we going to eat daddy?"

"Well my dear, it looks like nothing-chops and wind-pie!"

"Daaaaddyyyy..."

"Come on John!"

Robert and John exited the bunker through the main entrance, they went down the retractable stairs, and they walked over to the small community of rows of storage units.

When they swung the first door open, they saw generators piled to the ceiling, still inside their boxes. The second and third storage units looked the same as the first, filled with generators.

Then, they went to another row, and inside the first unit, they found plastic barrels stacked to the ceiling, each with dates written on them in permanent marker.

Robert and John reached for a barrel that had the date *"10/10/2057"* written on it. They lifted the barrel off the top of 2 more barrels, and they dragged it out of the storage unit.

The top of the barrel was fastened by a steal band that gripped the perimeter. The cover was sealed by a latch. Robert unwinded the band, and started pealing open the cover as it sucked air in to it with a loud sucking noise.

The barrel was filled to the brim with pouches of meals with expiration dates in the year
"2057".

"Man! These people were prepared for the end for real!"
Robert nodded in agreement, and said,
"The wicked always build what the righteous possess. Let's get this inside."
Robert and John carried the entire barrel all the way to the kitchen, where Jasmine and Tiffany picked out some meals, and cooked all the food themselves, by adding hot water.
When the table was finally set, the dining room was engulfed in the sweet aroma of fettuccini alfredo, shrimp, four cheese lasagna, bacon, creamy mashed potatoes, macaroni and cheese, and strawberry kool-aid.
When they finished eating, Jasmine and Tiffany piled all the dishes into the dishwasher, and caught up with Robert and John in the studio. Emily went to the gym and started riding the exercise bike, while Megan went to her room to take a nap.

In the studio, Robert and John jumped right in to preparing the equipment for broadcasting.
John worked 3 separate screens to a computer that, to his surprise, was in direct control of a small satellite in low earth orbit.
Using the satellite, John was able to determine that there were active reception devices all over the world, but there were virtually no transmissions coming out of the United States.

When he logged in to the network of the transmitter, he was able determined that it was in fact capable of sending transmissions to every reception device on the planet, literally taking over every inch of airspace, becoming the only sound on every station, "if" they could find a source of energy to power such a transmission. John shook his head in confusion, as he said,

"I just don't get it! Why would the Swiss go to such great lengths to prevent someone from doing something that simply can't be done? We have all the tools needed to push an international transmission, but we don't have the power. I don't even think that type of power exists!"

# 108

When Robert didn't respond, John stared at the middle of the computer screen, and closed his eyes.

He tried to imagine a man with skin that looked like it was composed of the texture of a lightning bolt.

He imagined the man's eye's looking like 2 suns exploding.

He imagined the man sitting on a throne surrounded by the light of His own glory, listening to his prayer, as John said,

"God, you gave this man the gift. Please allow him to share it with the world, for Your glory, amen."

The moment John opened his eyes, he shook his head at the words he had been staring at on the computer screen, and busted out laughing, as he started typing in commands, while saying,

"I didnt even realize what I was reading! Would you believe I was just prayed for something that was right in my face!"

Robert walked over to the computer desk, and said,

"What did He show you?"

"It'll be a real long shot, but that satellite up there is actually a gigantic chunk of an extremely rare radioactive metallic chemical element called "thorium"! I don't know where they got it from, it had to of costed them millions or even billions of dollars.

"They probably lucked up and dug it out of an asteroid that collided into the moon some long time ago or something, but this is a billion dollar network simplified to this little room! This is some heavy stuff man!"

"What are you seeing John?"

"We have the tools to push a powerful transmission, but we still needed a way to amplify it. That's what that billion dollar rock will do! It'll work like an amplifier! The thorium will enhance the resonation to a frequency that will cause it to reverberate all around the world and beyond! That Tod guy was really trying to be heard "loud" and "clear"!

"This can work, but it backfires, it'll destroy the transmitter. We got one shot, and it's worth taking. If we come in with this much power, it'll penetrate the airwaves with so much force, nothing will be able to stop the transmission.

"Best of all, it'll seem like it's originating from the thorium satellite, so the location of our transmitter will re!aim undetected! No one will know where we're broadcasting from!"

"Let's go for it! This location will eventually be discovered when they start killing people for refusing to take The Chip, and by that time, we should all be long gone!

"God's will is clear. He wants the gospel to be preached to the world, so the gospel must be preached!"

As Robert spoke, the transmitter aimed at the thorium satellite, and blasted its transmission into the heart of the rock.

"Go! Go! Go!"

Robert ran in to the booth so fast, Jasmine and Tiffany felt butterflies in their stomachs as Roberts breeze blew past them.

Robert closed the door to the tiny room, sat at the table, and looked over at John, who was quickly fanning his hands, shouting words that Robert couldn't hear while sealed in the booth.

Outside the booth, John was screaming at the top of his lungs,

"On air! On air! Say something already!"

Robert thought he would've had time to prepare, time to practice, even some time to think. But in an instant, every slight sound he made was blasting out of radios all around the world.

John aggressively ran up to the booth, and pounded on the wall, flailing his hands, shouting,

"What are you doing? Speeeeak!"

Robert was frowning at the mic., licking his lips, sweating profusely, scared stiff.

He could hardly move his tounge, much less his lips. He could hear a faint pounding sound, that got louder and louder, until he finally looked up and saw John with a factwisted beyond recognition.

Robert looked over at Jasmines tiny little disappointed face, and he blurted out the first words the world heard him say,

"Jasmine... Bring me a Bible."

Jasmine, Tiffany, and John, bolted out the room and ran straight to the library.

Robert remained seated, silently staring at the microphone, imagining his words pouring into it, being stretched out across the planet, and entering into billions of ears.

He looked up, and Jasmine was running into the room behind Tiffany, holding a Bible high above her head. Tiffany opened the door to the booth, and Jasmine ran in, broadcasting her voice to the whole world, as she said,

"Thank you Tiffany. Here you go daddy! Its a New King James Version! God loves you daddy!"

"Thank you Jasmine. God loves you too. This is my Bible! There are many others like it! But this one is mine!..."

# 109

## Porto Novo, Benin

"The radios are working! The radios are working! Command everyone to turn on their radios right now!"
"To which station?"
"Any station! An American man is speaking on all the stations!"

## Prague, Czech Republic

The noisy fallout shelter was silenced, as the background static became Robert's clear voice.
"Czech, or Slovak, is not what this man is speaking! What are the meanings of the words that this man is speaking? And in who's tounge?"
"English is the language the man speaks!"
"Translate his words if you can!"
A young woman responded,
"He is speaking about... "I believe... The words... In this holy book."..."

## New Delhi, India

An elderly man, who was sitting on a rooftop with his grandchildren, was puzzled as he flipped through the stations on his radio, only to find the same exact voice on every A.M. and F.M. station.

---

406

# ABOUT THE AUTHOR

A White man robbed a White woman.

Police arrested the White man within minutes after the robbery.
The White man told police that Michael J. Rigby, a Black man,
committed the crime.
Michael was arrested in Gainesville Florida, the very next day, for the robbery
that happened in Kissimmee.
After Michael was arrested, the White woman changed her story, and said that
it was in fact the Black man, Michael J. Rigby, who robbed her.

When the White woman was getting robbed in Kissimmee, Michael was hours
away, in Gainesville, with his girlfriend, Jennifer Rivera, who was sneaking out
of JobCore to spend the nights with him in a motel.

Michael had an Alibi.

When Michael got arrested, Jennifer found out that he had been cheating on
her, with her friend.
Jennifer was so upset,
when she was called in as Michael's alibi witness,
she "forgot" that the motel they were staying in was in Gainesville,
hours away from the crime scene,
and instead,
she told the police that Michael was with her in a motel in Kissimmee,
just minutes away from the crime scene.
Michael believed his girlfriend had made an honest mistake, and over the
years, they grew apart.
A decade later, Michael would propose to Jennifer, and in a vow to have no
secrets between them, she would admit that she wanted him in jail, and she
had intentionally placed him closer to the crime scene, by lying in her
statement about which motel they were staying in.
She would further bring it to his attention that she remembered exactly where
they were, because she was sneaking out of JobCore to see him.

Without an Alibi,
It was Michael's word against the White woman and the White man.
As much as he told The State and The Judge and his Public Defender, over
and over, that he was innocent, their consistent response was,

"It doesn't matter if you're innocent. A jury can be convinced that you're guilty."

The State told Michael to accept the conviction.

He didn't have to say he did the crime,
he just had to accept the conviction,
and plea No-Contest.

They would give him 18 months probation.
If he could complete 9 months without getting in any trouble,
they would erase the conviction from his record.

Michael agreed.

2 months later,
Michael was arrested.

Within months after the arrest,
The State brought Michael before a Judge and accused him of violating the terms of their agreement.
The 18 months probation that he was serving for the crime that he did not commit,
became a 5 year prison sentence.

The State sentenced Michael to serve 5 years in prison for a crime that he did not commit.
So,
before they could transport Michael to prison,
he sawed his steal toilet in half with a butterfly paperclip.
He dug a Michael sized hole out of concrete.
He crawled through a service area,
broke out a service door,
Jumped over three 15 foot tall razor wire topped fences,
and drove all the way to New Jersey.

Michael escaped on February 19th, 2010.
Michael was 21 years old when he broke out The Osceola County Jail.
He was brought back to Florida on July 16th, 2010.

The Judge sent Michael to The State Hospital, after 3 doctors found him to be clinically insane.

Michael stayed in the Hospital for 9 Months.

In Florida, Escape carries a maximum sentence of 15 years in prison.

To keep sentences fair, Florida follows a system that it calls The Florida sentencing Guidelines, which recommends a range of years that a defendant should be sentenced to based on their crime and their criminal history. Michael's score sheet recommended one year in prison for the escape.

Florida also utilizes its probation office to conduct PreSentence Investigations, which, upon completion, gives recommendations of what sentence should be served.
Michael's Presentence investigion recommended 1 year in prison for the escape.

The Court chose to disregard both recommendations.

In Florida, there is a law called The Habitual Violent Felony Offender Enhancement, which states that if you commit a felony within 5 years of your last conviction for a violent felony, you can be sentenced to double the maximum sentence.

The State used the statue against Michael, because it felt not even 15 years was long enough for the crime that The P.S.I. and the Guideline Score sheet both said should've only warranted one year for the victimless nonviolent offense.

The one violent prior conviction that The State used to habitualize Michael, was the robbery that was committed in Kissimmee, when he was hours away in Gainesville.

The P.S.I. recommended one year.
The Guideline Score sheet recommended one year.
The State asked The Judge to sentence Michael to 30 years.

The Judge found Michael to be a Habitual Violent Felony Offender, because of the prior conviction, for the robbery that he is innocent of, and sentenced him to 22 years in prison, where he wrote this book.

---

410

Made in the USA
Middletown, DE
26 August 2022

72269426R00243